THE

COAST

ROAD

THE

A NOVEL

COAST

ROAD

ALAN MURRIN

 HarperVia

An Imprint of HarperCollins*Publishers*

THE COAST ROAD. Copyright © 2024 by John Alan Murrin. All rights reserved. Printed in the United States of America. No part of this book may be used or reproduced in any manner whatsoever without written permission except in the case of brief quotations embodied in critical articles and reviews. For information, address HarperCollins Publishers, 195 Broadway, New York, NY 10007.

HarperCollins books may be purchased for educational, business, or sales promotional use. For information, please email the Special Markets Department at SPsales@harpercollins.com.

Originally published in the United Kingdom in 2024 by Bloomsbury Publishing.

FIRST HARPERVIA EDITION PUBLISHED IN 2024

Designed by Yvonne Chan

Library of Congress Cataloging-in-Publication Data has been applied for.

ISBN 978-0-06-333652-0
ISBN 978-0-06-341535-5 (Intl)

24 25 26 27 28 LBC 5 4 3 2 1

THE
COAST
ROAD

PROLOGUE

Ardglas, County Donegal, March 1995

When the detective asked Izzy what had woken her that night she could not say exactly. She'd been sleeping badly all winter. It was not uncommon for her to wake three or four times in the night. It was also the first time in several weeks she'd shared a bed with her husband, but she did not mention that. At some point she'd needed the toilet. Crossing the landing, she'd stopped at the window and looked out across the bay. It had become her habit in recent months to pause there and try to locate the point where on a clear day the gable of the cottage was just visible. The sky was mottled with cloud, the first of the morning light seeping through. Black smoke hung over the headland.

'And straight away, I knew something had happened,' she said. 'Even before I really knew, I *knew* – do you know what I mean?'

The two men stared back at her.

'But *how* did you know, Izzy?' Sergeant Farrelly asked her.

'Well, when I saw the smoke I—'

'No, Mrs Keaveney,' the detective said. 'How did a woman living two miles across the bay look out her window and see a bit of smoke and know the fire had been set intentionally?'

'Oh,' she said. 'That's another story altogether.'

CHAPTER 1

October 1994

There had been two masses already that morning and the air was thick with incense. The church was packed and Izzy found herself squeezed between two bodies. Each time she went from kneeling to sitting to standing, she felt their shoulders press against hers. She pulled a balled-up tissue from her sleeve and wiped the sweat from her forehead. She thought of removing her woollen jumper but wasn't sure if the top she had on underneath was decent, and besides, she'd never manage the manoeuvre without hitting the person next to her or exposing some part of her flesh. She didn't think she could suffer an embarrassment like that this morning. Raising her head, she was confronted by the sight of Stasia Toomey's broad back looming before her. Stasia stood stately and proud, tightly wrapped in a coat of royal-blue gabardine.

Kneeling again, Izzy caught the smell of sweat rising from her armpits. She bowed her head and closed her eyes.

And then the responses started. She took a long, slow breath.

'Lord have mercy.'

Lord have mercy.

She had managed to drag herself out of bed for half-eleven mass. It was one thing to have been drinking, but to stay in bed with a hangover was to admit you had been drunk. She rarely drank to excess, so she wasn't going to give James the satisfaction of using this against her. She'd slipped out of the spare room to make a cup of tea, saw the pictures lying scattered across the floor. The night before, when they'd returned from the local businesses' dinner-dance, she'd insisted to James that she was sleeping downstairs in the spare room. She went careening down the hallway, knocking every picture frame off the wall. James had grabbed her arm and she'd planted an elbow in his ribs. He'd let out a roar, and of course, Niall and Orla had woken. And that was the image she couldn't get out of her head – the two of them conjoined in horror, staring down at her from the landing.

She'd hurried back to bed with her cup of tea so as not to have to face any of them, but now as she knelt in the church, the collective responses to the prayers rising and falling in her empty stomach, she wished she'd eaten something.

'Christ, have mercy.'

Christ, have mercy.

She tried to focus on Father Brian – the solid shape of him behind the altar. He was decked out in his Sunday finery, his vestments so clean and crisp and trimmed in shades of gold and silver, the stole embroidered with tight little bunches of grapes and ears of wheat. She reminded herself to say this to him next time he visited her: *You*

4

were all decked out in your finery last Sunday, Brian. It suited you. The finest dress I've seen you in so far. Because she knew this was the part of the job he hated most, that it would forever be an embarrassment for him to present himself to people in this way. She thought of the wry smile he'd offer when she said this, the gentle putter of his laugh.

Oh Lord, it is your will that all shall be saved.

Someone near the front of the church rose. A tall woman with a mane of black hair stepped up and turned to face the lectern. Izzy felt a sharp little breath escape her. Colette Crowley, she thought – in all her glory. Such a fine-looking woman, it did you good just to rest your eyes upon her. The way she held her head so high. The length of her. The graceful tilt of her chin. And as she looked out at the congregation a smile played about her lips for a moment like there was something funny to her about all of this. Like she'd played a trick on them. Like she'd never really left at all. Izzy saw Stasia Toomey nudge her husband. A few people were overcome by fits of coughing. She cast an eye around to see if Shaun or Ann was present but couldn't spot them anywhere.

And then Colette spoke in that beautiful, soft Dublin accent of hers – a reading from the prophet Isaiah – but Izzy was not listening to the words, just the sound of her voice. She was neither a coarse jackeen nor a pretentious south-sider – she was something else altogether and Izzy could have listened to her all day. And people stared up at her, like the vision she was, and when Izzy's eyes drifted across the altar to where Father Brian was seated in his big marble chair, she saw the soft, sympathetic look he offered to Colette Crowley.

Give the Lord glory and power – that was the response Colette demanded of them, and Izzy thought that a bit bombastic: Hadn't he power and glory enough?

And then Colette descended from the lectern, stepping carefully, minding the hem of her long skirt. A shuffling of bodies filled the silence that had fallen over the church. Izzy watched Stasia Toomey's gaze track Colette all the way down the aisle, the hard set of her jaw easing only when Colette had knelt in her pew. But Father Brian did not move from where he was seated. He looked so still, so poised, his hands resting delicately on his knees like he was meditating over every word Colette had said. Izzy brought the tissue to her brow but there was nothing in her hand. She looked down and saw the tissue scattered across the hassock like snow.

*

He was purposely avoiding the main street of the town; this was what she'd thought to herself as they drove along the Coast Road the previous night. James was avoiding the main street, so they wouldn't have to pass the shop. The papers had needed to be signed and returned to the agent that afternoon but James had arrived home late from work, unknotting his tie as he came through the door and complaining about how they'd never make it to the dinner on time. She'd left the contract on the kitchen table where, she knew, he'd seen it every time he passed. It had lain there for a week with only her signature filled in. And now they were taking the Coast Road to get around a conversation about how he had reneged on his side of the deal.

The road rose steeply and narrowed as they drew away from the town. It followed the coastline more closely – hills rose up on one side and tumbled down into the Atlantic on the other. The moon hanging low over the bay looked like someone had pared a sliver off it with a knife. She lifted her handbag from the footwell, snapped it open, took out a mint, and snapped the clasp shut again. She unwrapped the mint and popped it in her mouth, clacked it against her teeth. She turned on the radio, heard the beat of dance music, turned it off.

'It must be great not to want things,' she said, at last.

She watched his arms stiffen against the wheel. A muscle flickered in his cheek.

'It must be great to be so satisfied with your life, to have all your needs met,' she said. 'I wish I could say the same.'

'You know it wasn't the right time,' he said.

'And when will the right time be?'

'I don't know . . . maybe it's not the right property.'

'It's going for a song.'

'Exactly. Why do you think that is?'

'Because it's been allowed to go derelict – a lick of paint and bit of money spent on it is all it needs.'

'It failed when it was a gift shop, it failed when it was a bakery, it failed when it was a music shop—'

'Well, it worked when it was a flower shop and I ran it.'

'You never made that much money at it.'

'I made enough and we were damn glad of it at the time.'

'Look, it's throwing good money after bad. Maybe if the price drops again, we can—'

'Don't!' she shouted. 'You never had any intention of buying that property. You just thought you could placate me with it, dangling it in front of me.'

'It doesn't look good for an elected member of government to be going around buying up half the town.'

'Half the town? Half the town? One shitty-assed shopfront on the main street and you call that half the town? I'm sick of having nothing just so that we don't look too flash in front of your constituents.' She folded her arms and turned her face to the window. 'Anyway, it doesn't work,' she said. 'People still think we have money.'

'Which is not the case.'

'And don't I know it – you've made everyone else in this town rich except us.' They rounded a corner and the waning moon swung back into view. 'We can afford that property,' she said. 'You just don't want me to have it.'

The car pulled up in front of the hotel.

'Are you going to spoil another night?' he asked.

She watched couples gliding up and down the steps of the Paradise Lodge. Brass railings and polished handles glinted beyond the glass-fronted doors of the hotel.

'Oh, don't worry,' she said. 'I won't embarrass you.'

All through dinner she allowed Tom Heffernan to refill her wineglass and stare at her chest while she glowered across the table at James. She smoked one cigarette after another, the butts piling up in the ashtray in front of her. She'd worn a black satin culottes-suit with a low-cut top and a little bolero jacket she'd thrown off as soon as she sat down. Neat on her top half, and wide at the hip, she'd chosen the outfit to accentuate above and disguise below. James was usually quick to offer her compliments on her appearance but that evening he was barely fit to look her in the eye. And everyone so far at the event had admired the outfit, except her husband, who sat nursing the same whiskey he'd bought when he'd arrived. He had his hand over the mouth of the glass tumbler, rocking it back and forth in that uneasy way of his, as though he lived in dread of someone topping it up.

She'd pushed her loin of beef around the plate, and when the profiteroles arrived, she ignored them and withdrew another cig-

arette from her pack. While James gave his speech on the importance of business in the local community she looked up at the light
fixture, a long cylinder dripping with strings of glass beads. As she
stared at the lights shrouded in cigarette smoke, they melted into
one and for minutes at a time she could distract herself from her
husband's voice. She listened to the applause and kept her arms
folded on the table. There was a great deal of backslapping when
James sat down again.

'Fair play to you,' Manus Sweeney said. 'You're damn right. It's
hard work that saves communities. You can't be relying on government funding all the time.'

'Well, Manus, I didn't want to spell it out up there, but that's
just it. There are people nowadays who want everything for nothing and they're not willing to work for it.'

There was a lot of nodding and agreement to that and Izzy
turned her face away. Seated at the table opposite were Shaun
Crowley and Ann Diver. Ann was the only woman and the men
were mostly bachelors who had no one to bring to an event like
this. Shaun was leaning a conspiratorial ear to the man next to him,
and to his right sat Ann, looking like she'd been squeezed onto the
end at the last minute. She wore oversized silver earrings, ornate
things that dangled almost to her shoulders, and as if she regretted
the decision now, she gripped one earlobe, hiding the earring. A
waitress at the Harbour View Hotel for years, she was probably
more used to serving at these events than attending them, and
Izzy told herself to go and chat with her before the night was over.
Poor Ann was unlikely to get much in the way of conversation out
of Shaun, who was not in the habit of small talk. He was polite
enough if you tried to engage him, but he always looked bored out
of his mind at these things, sitting there in his shirtsleeves like it

would have been too much bother for him to have worn a jacket and tie like every other man.

'God, he's an eccentric, that fella, isn't he?' Teresa Heffernan whispered to her. 'All the money he has, you'd think he'd make a bit of an effort, iron his shirt at least.'

Izzy considered this. 'Well, he has Ann to do it for him now,' she said.

'Yeah, but she's back on the scene.'

'Who?'

'Colette.'

'Is she, indeed.' Izzy took a drag on her cigarette. 'Well, she's never ironed a shirt in her life. Poets don't iron shirts.'

'Apparently she showed up at the front desk of the factory today, brazen as anything, and asked to speak to Shaun. She was all of two minutes in his office, and when she come out again, she wasn't looking too happy.'

'Maybe she got wind of his new woman.' And Izzy had struggled to get her head around this recent news, that Ann and Shaun were an item – quiet, homely Ann, who'd been a widow most of her life. Ann and Shaun were closer in age, which made a kind of sense, but otherwise she was as different from Colette as it was possible to be.

'Word is he won't let Colette see the kids,' Teresa said.

'Ah, now,' Izzy said. 'That seems a bit much. Imagine if someone wouldn't let you see your children?'

Teresa settled back into her chair and tapped the head of ash off her cigarette. 'Well,' she said, 'doesn't he have his reasons.'

Izzy was about to argue this point when she was distracted by James jabbing his finger onto the surface of the table.

'My parents were never given a single thing,' he said. 'They had to work for every penny.'

'And were your parents from the town?' Manus Sweeney asked.

'They were not,' Izzy said. 'They were from some boreen up north of the county. They were probably third cousins.'

There was a silence.

'Second cousins,' James said, and everybody laughed, but Izzy recognised the cold glimmer that had entered his eyes.

'Testing, testing, one two,' someone said into a microphone. A bass guitar thrummed. There was a clash of cymbals.

'And I don't know how you can say that your parents were given nothing,' Izzy said. 'Didn't the council give them the house you grew up in?'

James looked away from her. 'Well, that's just it,' he said. 'Back then you were given what you were given and you had to just get on with it.'

'Jesus Christ, when's the music going to start,' Izzy said under her breath.

'People led simple, ordinary lives,' James went on, 'and those are the people who I want to help, the people who are willing to go out and work and help themselves.'

She looked at her husband – simple and ordinary. She thought about getting the wine bottle and going to the end of the table and bringing it down over his simple, ordinary head.

A sound tore through the speakers so loud that the room gave a collective swoon.

'Sorry about that, folks,' said the man on the stage. 'But sure, that woke yous up!' He gave a cackle and the band launched into the opening bars of 'Your Cheatin' Heart'.

'Oh, I love this one,' Izzy said. 'Come on, who'll dance with me? Tom.' She grabbed him by the arm and stood up and her chair fell backwards onto the floor. Tom rose and she felt his hand on the small of her back and hoped to God James was watching.

*

Father Brian was back at the pulpit to deliver the gospel, and afterwards told them he'd not prepared a sermon because he'd been down the country attending a funeral, which she knew to be a lie because he'd spent all afternoon on Thursday in her kitchen, smoking and drinking tea, and had mentioned nothing about a funeral. Still, she was relieved the sermon was to be left out. It happened only a handful of times a year, and given her current condition it was a stroke of luck. It would shave a good ten minutes off proceedings. But then the responses began again, the lurching cadence of them, and she knew she wasn't going to make it to the end.

Lamb of God, you take away the sins of the world.

Oh, the sweat was dripping down her back.

Lord, I am not worthy to receive you, but only say the word and I shall be healed.

And the taste of bile snaking up her throat.

'Excuse me,' she said to the person next to her, and pushed her way past the seated congregants without lifting her head or looking one of them in the eye. She scurried down the side aisle, her eyes fixed on the floor. Near the church door she jostled her way through the men who, either too late or too drunk to be seen going into the church, had gathered in the porch. A speaker hung above the door echoing what the priest was saying at the altar. She rushed towards the church gates with Father Brian's voice calling after her.

CHAPTER 2

Dolores Mullen had just reprimanded her three-year-old daughter for slapping her one-year-old son across the face, had lifted him off the floor screaming and placed him in his playpen, and was just about to put a fitness video in the cassette player when an ad came on the TV. A woman lifted a glass, a tiny champagne flute filled with blue dye, and poured it over a sanitary towel. The women in these ads were always flinging blue dye around, she thought as she watched the liquid being absorbed by the white pad and disappearing, and a thought surfaced in her mind – she had missed her period. She was certain of it. She was late by at least ten days. It was not uncommon for her to be late, especially when she was dieting, but *nearly two weeks?* she thought, and then, 'Fuck,' she said, out loud. Her last period had been at the end of August when they'd had the whole family over for a barbecue for Madeleine's birthday, and that was six weeks ago. Four kids – a teenager, a toddler, a baby, and another on the way. Donal had been on at her to lose weight and she'd only just gotten her figure back after having Eric.

She dropped down on the enormous sofa, ran her hand over the smooth grey suede where, despite having tried everything to remove the stain, she could still make out a pair of tiny palm prints. She looked over at Jessica sitting on the floor on the other side of the room, scraping at the hair of a doll with a little brush.

'Don't you be giving me that eye, madame.' Her voice echoed, bouncing off the pure white walls, and the tiled floors, and the expanses of glass that covered one complete corner of the house so that the entire length of the beach was always visible to them. It was like the house had been designed to keep her forever polishing glass. They had light and space in abundance, that was for sure. There were four bedrooms upstairs and two on the ground floor, and they were going a good way towards filling them. How had they managed to go ten years without having a second child and then she'd gotten pregnant three times in such quick succession? But she pushed that thought away. There had been miscarriages too, there might be again. Was there any point in telling Donal about this until she was a bit further along? There were only so many times she could blame his carelessness. He'd lost interest in her over the summer, which was usually a sign he had another woman on the go, and when his attention returned to her, she hadn't the heart to refuse him.

She heard a car coming up the drive. She sometimes got a visit from one of her sisters in the morning, or else it was the postman, but now a sleek black BMW was pulling up in front of the house. The door opened and a leg emerged, clad in a black high-heeled boot. A woman stepped out, and when she rose to her full height, Dolores saw that it was Shaun Crowley's wife. Dolores couldn't understand why she didn't tie up her mop of thick black hair. How had she been able to see the road in front of her with such a mess tumbling down over her face? She wore the strap of her leather saddlebag across her body, adjusting it so the bag rested on her hip. She was all covered up in a polo-neck jumper and a long plaid skirt. Dolores pulled on a zip-up hoody over her little tank top and went to open the door.

'Hello, Dolores,' the woman said, and right away Dolores could see that she was not as dowdy as she'd first appeared. She had pale, even skin and sharp blue eyes.

'Hello,' Dolores said.

'Do you remember me? I'm Colette.'

The woman smiled and Dolores watched faint lines appear in the fine skin around her eyes and mouth. She had seen her down the town before, knew she was married to Shaun Crowley, but why in particular she was supposed to have remembered her she couldn't say.

'Hello, Colette,' she said.

'I was wondering if I could have a quick word with you – about the cottage.'

She smiled again, and it was extraordinary to Dolores how it transformed her face so her cheekbones became even more pronounced, her jaw two clean lines meeting at the neat point of her chin. And Dolores with not a stitch of make-up on. She pulled up the zip on her top, folded her arms across her chest.

'The cottage?' Dolores asked.

The woman threw a look over her shoulder at the white stone cottage perched on top of the hill flanking their land. 'You own that cottage – am I right?' she asked.

'Yes.'

'And you rent it out sometimes?'

'Aye, but not this time of year.'

'So it's empty?'

Dolores's daughter laced herself between her legs and Dolores reached down to pick her up. 'I suppose you better come in for a minute,' she said and opened the door wider to allow Colette to step into the hall. The heels of her boots clacked against the tiles.

'You have a beautiful home, Dolores. I always admire it when I'm walking the beach. The view you must have!' She was pivoting, staring around her at the hallway, the wide staircase leading up from it. She looked through the door of the sitting room to the view of the beach. 'And how many children do you have now?' She poked Jessica's soft round calf, and the child smiled and turned her face into Dolores's neck.

'This is number two,' she said, 'and Eric's number three. He's in there in the playpen. The two of them had to be separated because they were acting up.' Dolores scrunched up her face and rubbed her nose against her daughter's. 'Isn't that right?' she asked, and her daughter rubbed her forehead vigorously against hers and threw her arms around her neck.

'Madeleine's the only one I know,' Colette said. 'She was in one of the plays we did at the Community Centre a few years back.'

'That's right,' Dolores said. 'She's thirteen now. In first year at St Joseph's.'

The child had gripped the chain that hung around Dolores's neck. It read 'Dolly' in gold script. She began to stab at her mother's throat with the pointed end of the *y*.

'Stop that, Jessica,' Dolores said, trying to pick the child's fingers from the chain.

'Look, Dolores, I won't keep you, but I wanted to let you know that I'm interested in renting the cottage.'

'Where are you stopping at the moment?'

'I've been staying at a B and B for the past two weeks but that's not much of an existence for anyone. I'd like to try and get a bit more settled.'

Why she couldn't go home and settle with her husband was unknown to Dolores but she did know they'd been separated for some time.

'Well, we've never rented it out during the winter. I'm not sure we've had the place properly cleaned since the last lot moved out in August. They might have left it a complete tip.'

'But maybe I could go up and have a look at it, see if it would be suitable for me? Sure it might not be right at all. Does it have heat and electricity and—'

'Oh, it has everything,' she said. 'Donal's an electrician, he did the place up himself. You should have seen it when we first got our hands on it – it was falling down. We had to put on a new roof, new plumbing, new everything. It cost a fortune.'

'Who owned it before you?'

'Some fellow from the North who only used it one week of the year and wouldn't sell it to us when we were building our own house. We would have tossed it and built on that site. It has an even better view of the beach than we have. We were five years in our own house before he finally agreed to sell.'

Dolores saw how keenly the woman was observing her. Her smile never wavered but her eyes were scanning every inch of her face.

'And would it be OK to go up and have a look at it?' Colette asked.

'I can't go heading up there now. Who's going to look after these two? Anyway, it would be better to come back another time when Donal's here. I couldn't decide without asking him first. It might not be practical to be renting that place out this time of year.' But she knew they might need the money. 'And if you were still in it by next June, we'd have to charge you three times the price.'

'I won't be here by next June,' Colette said. 'Maybe you could give me the keys and I could go up and have a quick look now. I'll be five minutes. At least that way I'd know whether or not I want it. You wouldn't even have to bother Donal about it then.'

A scream came from the living room.

Dolores walked to the hallstand and pulled out a drawer. She threw her hand around inside and it rattled. She pulled out a bunch of keys with an anchor key ring and held them out to Colette. 'The gold one is the one for the front door,' she said. 'It might be a bit stiff so pull it towards you when you're opening it. It has its own driveway from the main road but you don't need to go back up there. There's a path up the hill at the bottom of the garden. It might be a bit damp, so mind yourself.'

She watched a smile spread across Colette's face as she looked Dolores directly in the eye and withdrew the key from the end of her finger.

'Thank you, Dolores,' Colette said. 'I'll drop them back to you shortly.'

And with that she was out the door and right away Dolores wanted to call after her, to ask for the keys back, but the shout that rose from her stomach caught in her throat, and all that emerged was a small, tired sigh.

*

Colette began to make her way down through the Mullens' front garden, the heels of her boots softly puncturing the earth. She thought about turning back and following the road up to the cottage, but plodded on. At the foot of the hill she looked around and saw Dolores still watching from the doorway, the child slung across her hip.

The hill up to the cottage was so steep she could see only the slate roof from the bottom. She could recall a time when the cottage had been thatched but she guessed the Mullens didn't want to pay for the upkeep on that. There were footholds worn in the side of the hill and she took each one carefully, grabbing fistfuls of grass to steady herself as she climbed. At the top she passed through a gap in the drystone wall that divided the properties. Up close she could see where the whitewash was fading on the façade of the cottage and the old stone showed through. The blue paint on the door had almost entirely flaked away to reveal the grey undercoat. She held the little brass handle and pulled the door towards her as she turned the key. The cottage released a stale breath.

She flicked the switch by the door and an exposed bulb cast a cold light over the room. The furniture was a mixture of cheap-looking, self-assembled pieces and older items that looked like they'd been salvaged from some estate sale. And it was pokey, the room, with a low ceiling that made everything look like a miniature version of itself or too oversized and bulky for the space. But there were homely touches too; you could see that some effort had been made. There was a polished flagstone floor and the fireplace was a neat little square cut from the wall. There was a pine dresser with bits of old crockery displayed on each shelf.

Green-and-pink tieback curtains framed the window that looked out onto the beach. In the bathroom she slid back the plastic door on the shower cubicle and tried to imagine how she would ever fit herself inside. The only bedroom was almost as big as the living room, so it was like the house had been divided in two by one wall, probably the only structural change that had been made in however many hundred years. The bedroom had a chest of drawers, a wrought iron bedstead, and a few wire hangers dangling from a rope hung between two walls. And tucked at the foot of the bed was a child's cot with sides of slim white railings, just big enough to sleep the smallest of infants.

The cot would have to be gotten rid of. And wire hangers could be thrown away, light bulbs replaced, she thought, as she walked slowly back to the little banquette that had been built into the wall beneath the window, with cushions upholstered in the same pink-and-green fabric as the curtains. She took a seat there and looked out at the beach. She had walked the length of it every single day since her return. She had looked up at this cottage and wondered who owned it and made enquiries around the town. People from the North owned most of the holiday homes, but when she'd learned that the Mullens had bought the house a few years ago and done it up to rent out, she'd begun to imagine herself into it. She could wake each morning to the sound of the sea dissolving in her ears, and watch the weather change over the bay as she sat at this window, writing. She could bide her time there.

She looked around her again and 'cosy' was the kindest word she could think to describe the room, 'quaint' at a stretch, and while it was not quite the traditional Irish cottage she'd envisaged, it would do well enough. Turning back to the window, her eye settled on a little pine chest resting on the floor beside her. She lifted the lid. It was filled with bed linens. She ran her hand over the rough, starched sheet that lay on top and her finger brushed against something smooth. She pulled back the sheet and there was a magazine. On the cover a woman with an enormous perm, wearing nothing but white stockings, high heels, and a lace choker, leaned forward with her breasts squeezed between her arms. Her face was frozen in a look of mock horror, mouth hanging open, like some invisible assailant had surprised her and the camera had caught her mid exclamation. Colette smiled as she looked through the magazine. It was readers' wives stuff: women who were either slightly overweight or bone-thin decked out like Christmas baubles in cheap, colourful lingerie. They wore knickers with an open crotch that exposed lengths of untrimmed pubic hair, pointed at the camera with their fingers peeling back their labia. There were no men to be seen anywhere, and in the back of the magazine, pages and pages of adverts for chat lines and escorts.

Was this why Dolores had looked so frightened when she'd mentioned going up to the cottage – was she worried she would find this flimsy rag? But the woman had looked tense from the moment she'd arrived, brittle and fearful. Then Dolores had taken her daughter in her arms and Colette had watched all the tension leave her body. But so thin, so cold-looking. Her hands, Colette had noticed, red-raw like she'd just pulled them from a bucket of water. Those gleaming tiled floors, slick as an ice rink. Was that what she did all day, scrubbed floors until her husband came home and gave her permission to do something else? She'd never met the man but she knew him to see, and when she'd spotted him in that picture in their hallway, she'd been reminded of his handsomeness. He was hard to miss – it was the only family photo on the wall. Dolores looked drawn, smiling wearily, the child on her lap festooned in a white lace christening dress and pointed awkwardly at the camera. Front and centre sat Donal, composed but absent, not a hair on his dark head out of place.

She stared down at the magazine in her hands. It could be Donal's or have been left behind by some man staying in the cottage and hidden away at the last minute – or a teenager, Colette thought. She wondered if her own teenager, Barry, was at that stage now, procuring magazines and keeping them under his mattress and getting into a panic when Sheila, who had worked for them since he was a baby, came upstairs to clean his room. Even if he would speak to her, it was not something they would ever discuss, her angry son who had been butting his head against the world since the day he was born. Ronan was in his first year in Trinity now and had never had an angry phase, and Carl was still too young. But Barry, he blamed her for everything.

The last time she'd phoned the house he'd answered, and she'd asked him how he was. She could hear how foolish she sounded, the forced joviality in her voice because she feared so much her son's response. 'Fuck off,' he'd said. 'Just, fuck off,' and he'd hung up the phone. She realised later that she should have kept phoning back until Shaun answered so they could discuss how to deal with their son's behaviour. But when Barry had said this, it had stopped up the breath in her. The receiver was frozen in her hand, the dial tone ringing off. She was sitting in the hallway of the B&B, staring at the little wooden box where she'd just placed the 20p for the phone call. To have been dismissed by her son so violently, and for that to simply be the shape of things – she felt more foolish for being surprised. And she had tried to collect this incident in her head, to carry these thoughts back up to her room, moving slowly and carefully, like the ideas might spill out of her. And she'd sat down at the little fold-out table and written as plainly as she could of the hurt her son's words had delivered to her. Like colliding with a glass wall, it was – the shock and pain and embarrassment of it – to see your life on the other side and not be able to touch it. And when she'd written the lines, when she thought she had said exactly enough, she left them. The flourishes, if the poem called for them, could come later. What was required in this first stage was accuracy, and honesty.

What is required is honesty – and as she thought this a wind rolled in off the bay, and it was like the eaves of the cottage heaved in air and the entire structure expanded just a little and settled back on itself again. Her sons would never visit her in this house – that was the truth of it. Ronan would come but he would be mortified for her and she wouldn't be able to stand it. Barry would not deign to spend a single second here, nor should he or Carl be asked to. They had a home, a fortress that their parents had built for them where they'd all been happy together for the most part, and why should they be made to visit a two-room cottage where the roof lifted when the wind blew and the windows rattled in their frames?

She slipped the magazine back beneath the sheet and closed the lid of the chest. No, this would have to be her sanctuary, and hers alone. She could make a home of it, she was sure of that. And she would not hide away; she would simply retreat. There was work to be done.

CHAPTER 3

Niall could not find his school uniform. His mother had washed it for him the day before and he'd checked in the utility room. He couldn't ask his father because he was doing a radio interview on the telephone in the hallway, and anyway, his father always got cross with him for losing things. Niall always seemed to be losing something. He knew that his father had to go to Dublin that morning and was dropping him off at school on his way, and he could already imagine his father shouting at him for making him late.

'There's a reason why Donegal is called the "forgotten county",' his father blared into the phone. Niall crept past him down the hallway to the spare room. He pushed open the door and smelled the warm fug of sleep; saw the rustling pile of her beneath the quilt. His mother always slept here when she'd had a fight with his father, and when things were this way between them, she usually didn't get out of bed in the mornings. She became like this a few times a year – sometimes it was after they'd had a row and sometimes it just happened. When he got home from school, she'd have managed to get herself to the sofa in the living room. She'd be wrapped in a blanket with the applause of an afternoon chat show washing over her. He'd try to give her a hug or ask if she was OK and she'd butt into him gently, the way a cat turns its head against the back of a hand. She'd never really say what was wrong, and when she spoke, her voice would have this phlegmy rasp to it like it didn't really belong to her. When things were normal, he looked forward to getting home from school to joke and laugh with his mother about what had happened that day, because really his mother was the funniest person he knew. But often, there'd be someone else there with her and this made him mad because he wanted his mother to himself. Sometimes it was her friend Margaret Brennan. His mother said that Margaret had time to be sitting around chatting all day because she was separated from her husband. But lately Father Brian's car would be parked at the house and they'd be in the kitchen smoking and laughing and drinking tea.

He leaned over her in the bed and whispered in her ear, 'Mammy, do you know where my school uniform is?'

She stirred but did not open her eyes. 'In the hot press,' she said, in a voice soft and sticky with sleep. Her dry lips sort of peeled apart each time she opened her mouth.

He retreated quietly back down the hallway.

'There has been zero investment in infrastructure for the past twenty years and that situation has to be rectified,' his father shouted into the receiver.

In the kitchen, Niall reached for the door of the hot press to open it slowly because the door was made of heavy wood and if it banged shut it made a loud noise. Opening the door, he saw the black hairy arse of a rat bounce back up through the hole in the wall where the pipes went out.

His father appeared in the doorway. 'What the fuck are you screaming about?' But then a worried look came over him. 'Niall?' he asked. 'What's happened?'

'I saw a rat in the hot press.'

His father stared at the wooden door. 'Shite,' he said. His shoulders dropped. 'Well, listen, don't worry.'

'But I can't get my school uniform out because it's in there.'

'That rat'll be more scared of you than you are of him.' But his father didn't seem convinced of that as he edged open the door and tugged on Niall's school tie so that his jumper and shirt and trousers fell into a pile on the floor.

He gave Niall a brief hug. 'Calm down – go upstairs and put your uniform on. We need to be on the road in the next ten minutes.'

Niall tied his tie in the car, his hands still shaking. All he could think about was the way his father had looked at him when he'd screamed, like he suspected Niall of having done something.

At school, Mrs Mallon tacked a map of Ireland to the wall. She pointed to areas on the map and they had to name the county, first in English and then in Irish. Then she pointed to rivers, lakes, and mountains, and they shouted the names in unison. She moved around the map clockwise, and then counterclockwise, and then she just swatted the long wooden pointer against the map at random and they had to think of the name as quickly as they could. She moved faster and faster until they were roused into a collective giddiness, and they were rocking back and forth in their seats and laughing.

Niall glanced to his right and saw that Carl was not laughing and so he stopped laughing too. He wanted to tell Carl about the rat but these days when Niall spoke to Carl he barely responded. Niall felt that if he could just say the right thing Carl would like him again and so Niall got in trouble a lot for talking. Mrs Mallon had seated them beside each other because they were friends, telling them that if they started messing, they'd be moved. Niall was hoping now that they might be moved because something had happened over the summer and Carl was off with him.

Niall knew that Mrs Crowley had left Mr Crowley and gone to live with a man in Dublin. He'd overheard his parents talking about it. And when he'd gone to Carl's house to play over the summer, things were different. Carl only wanted to stay inside and play computer games. When Mrs Crowley had been there, she used to make them go outside or, if it was raining, she would set up games for them. She had once placed two easels beneath the covered porch at the back of their house, put newspaper over the concrete floor, and given them smocks to wear so they could cover each other in paint if they wanted to. Colette was always coming up with nice things for them to do. Part of the reason Niall had liked going to Carl's house was because of Colette. She was usually upstairs in her study, working, which meant she was writing poems, and when she was doing that, she couldn't be disturbed. But sometimes she would come out of the room to get something, and she always smiled at Niall and asked him how school was, and once Niall had read her one of his poems that he'd won a prize for. She sat down to listen to him and Niall could tell by the way she looked at him that she was really paying attention. And when he'd finished, she smiled and stood up and placed her hand on top of his head. She'd walked to the shelf, taken down a book of poems, and said, 'That's for you, love – to bring home with you.' But Carl had looked at him funny when this had happened.

It had felt important to Niall for Carl to know that his mammy and daddy fought too. He hadn't been able to stop thinking about his parents' fight – his father chasing his mother down the hallway, the shout he'd let out when she elbowed him in the ribs. The next day his father had been shaving with the bathroom door open, and Niall saw on the right side of his body a deep purple bruise, like one of the inkblot paintings they did at school.

And so Niall had told Carl about the fight one break time when the weather was bad and they weren't allowed to go outside. When Niall finished the story Carl said nothing for a while, just carried on eating his ham sandwich, and after he'd finished chewing all he said was, 'We went to see *The Mask* in Letterkenny cinema on Friday night.'

Mrs Mallon whacked the map with the wooden pointer.

'*Lough Neagh*,' they all shouted, and Niall noticed that Carl was roaring the answers louder than anyone else.

Niall nudged him. 'Hey,' he whispered, 'guess what happened this morning?'

But Carl just kept his arms folded on the desk and stared ahead of him.

'Hey,' Niall said, and nudged him again, but this time Carl drew his elbow away.

'Niall Keaveney,' Mrs Mallon shouted. 'Are we going to have a repeat of yesterday's performance?'

At lunchtime he played football with the other boys in his class. He wasn't much good so he ran around a lot but tried to stay as far away from the ball as possible. When the bell rang, they all lined up at the main door to the school and waited for Mrs

Mallon to call them in. Carl was standing with his back to Niall. He was talking to Luke Hanley, a boy he'd started hanging around with recently who sometimes went to his house after school. Niall had heard them talking about the computer games they played and now he could hear them discussing their plans for the weekend. Niall decided then to tell Carl about the rat and he tapped him on the shoulder but Carl didn't turn around – he just kept on talking to Luke.

'Hey, Carl,' Niall said, trying to sound relaxed, but Carl did not respond. He prodded the back of Carl's shoe with his foot, and still nothing. Then he poked him on the shoulder.

'Hey,' Carl said, turning around. 'Don't punch me.' He pushed Niall.

Niall tried to smile, to make it seem like there had been some misunderstanding, but it felt like the more he tried, the more he might start to cry.

'What kind of a punch was that anyway?' Carl said. 'You fight like your mammy. You wee poof.'

Niall pushed Carl hard. 'Aye, well, at least my mammy's at home and didn't go off with some man up in Dublin.'

And then he felt the full weight of Carl's body rush against him and they were tangled up in each other and he wrapped his arms around Carl's neck and wrenched at his head. And everyone in the lines surrounded them and shouted 'fight, fight, fight'. They were both trying to lift their knees and jab them into the other's side but they were holding on too tightly and toppled into a pile on the wet ground.

'Get up out of that,' came the voice of Mrs Mallon, and he was hauled off the ground by the hood of his anorak. The crowd backed away.

He watched Carl stumble to his feet. His sallow skin was blotchy and tears streaked his cheeks.

'What did you do that for?' Carl asked.

Tiny black stones stuck to Carl's jawline where Niall had pressed his face to the ground.

CHAPTER 4

The blinds were drawn in the middle of the day, which Brian thought odd. He rang the bell and tried the handle of the front door but it was locked. He looked over to where her little red Nissan was parked in its usual spot in front of the house and wondered if she'd gone for a walk. But he hadn't anticipated this, how disappointed he'd feel at the prospect of not seeing her. Ever since he'd watched her run out of the chapel on Sunday he'd meant to call and visit but it had taken him a few days to get around to it. He decided to drive back to his house and phone her, and if there were no response, he'd call James at his office. He remembered then that the back door was usually left on the latch, but just as he stepped away the lock rattled and the door opened a few inches.

'Is it yourself?' Izzy said in a flat tone, peering out at him. Such a short distance between them and yet her voice sounded like it was coming from somewhere very far away. Before he could say anything, she'd turned and was walking down the hall. She closed the door of the sitting room and looked back at him. 'Come on into the kitchen,' she said.

'I was just bringing back a few of your books,' he said, following her. 'But I left them in the car. I'll try and remember to give them to you when I'm leaving.'

'Sure, don't worry – give them to me any time.'

She was filling the kettle at the sink, her back to him. How slight she looked, her shoulders drawn so tightly together. He imagined laying his hands there, how they would cover the entire span of her back. She had her hair tied in a neat little ponytail, the mousy-brown wisps at her nape exposed. The cheap elastic tie was like something a child would use. She usually wore her straw-coloured hair held back by an Alice band, and tucked behind her ears.

'How did you get on with them?' she asked.

'What?'

'The books.'

'Oh, not so bad. I enjoyed the Roddy Doyle. It was sad – so, so desperately sad, but I liked it. It's the child's perspective, isn't it? It just makes you feel it more. But I couldn't get on with the Doris Lessing – the darkness, so relentless.'

'Oh God, Roddy Doyle is dark too in his way.'

'Yes, but at least there's some levity, some humour. And there's a familiarity to it too, I suppose.'

She placed a teapot on the table between them.

'But anyway, listen to me going on. You'd swear I knew what I was talking about,' he said.

She sat down, dropping onto the seat like she could not have supported the weight of her body for a second longer.

'Are you all right?' he asked.

She looked off into the corner of the room and for a moment he thought she had not heard him.

'You saw?' she said.

'I just saw you leave the church.'

'Oh, I'm embarrassed,' she said, closing her eyes. 'I thought I was going to faint and so I extricated myself before I toppled over on someone. I was grand as soon as I got a bit of fresh air. It's just something that comes over me from time to time. I'll survive.'

Her face was so slack and expressionless. He'd hardly been in the parish six months and several times already he'd witnessed these depressions she fell into, but never had he seen her quite so at a distance from herself. She reached for her cigarettes and drew one from the packet, and he took his lighter from the inside pocket of his blazer and lit it for her.

'Is James around?' he asked. It always had something to do with James.

'Dublin,' she said, blowing out a train of smoke as though she were deflated by the very word.

She placed her cigarette on the lip of the ashtray and poured the tea.

'I have four christenings and a wedding this weekend,' he said. 'Imagine.'

'God love them,' Izzy said, taking up her cigarette. She took a drag and rested her chin on the heel of her hand, her eyes cast down at the table. But then some hint of divilment seemed to stir in her. She smiled, looking up at him. '*And* you had that funeral to go to down the country.'

He laughed, flicked the ash of his cigarette. 'You have me there.'

'Imagine having the gall to get up in front of your flock and tell them a barefaced lie like that.'

'Ah now, settle down, it was only a kind of a lie. I *was* occupied with church business, as it happens. I'm working on something, or working up to it rather, but it's not fit for human consumption yet. We've been given a directive – from on high.'

'Oh?'

'It appears likely the government will call another referendum on divorce before too long. James might have mentioned something about it.'

'He never tells me anything.'

'Well, we've been asked to get out in front of it, to head it off at the pass, to deliver a stirring sermon on the sanctity of marriage that'll terrify the wits out of anyone who has ever considered leaving their spouse.'

'Jesus – is that what they think is going to happen? That people will be leaving their marriages in droves as soon as they legalise it?'

'Oh, absolutely – there'll be no one married within a year.'

'And what do you make of the whole thing?'

'Well – and now don't go saying this to anyone or I'll be shot – but I don't think you have to be married to be a good Catholic. However, it is one of the seven sacraments, and . . . well, I think if you bother to go through with it, you should try and stick with it.'

'And if it's too easy to get out of, who'd bother trying?' she said. 'In my day the worst thing you could imagine was being unmarried – you just went with the first fellow who asked you.'

It was something he'd heard her say before.

'Is there something you'd like to tell me about?' he asked.

Pastoral care – that was what they called it – attending to the spiritual and emotional needs of the meek and downtrodden, and while he could never describe Izzy as such, she was the person in the parish he visited most often.

'No,' she said, with a little shake of her head.

'How was the dinner-dance?'

'I had dinner and I danced.' She flicked some ash from her sleeve. 'Those things are the same every year – a load of men telling each other how great they are while their wives pretend to enjoy themselves. I wouldn't care if I never went to another one for as long as I lived.'

'I heard James gave a great speech.'

'Did you indeed. Same things as usual – grassroots investment, less reliance on EU funding . . . or sometimes it's that we need more EU funding, it depends on what way the wind's blowing.'

He smiled. 'He must be doing something right – he's held his seat for long enough.'

She threw her eyes to the ceiling.

'Has he done something to upset you?' Brian asked.

He watched her narrow her eyes at him, the curious way she looked into him like she was trying to tell if this question was a joke. She leaned towards him a little then rested back into her seat.

'Did I ever tell you that I used to own a business, Father?'

He winced at the word 'Father' – she never called him that. 'You did not. When was this?'

'When I first got married. I had a business on the main street of the town – a flower shop. Up by where the chemist is now. The building's been empty and up for sale for so long you probably wouldn't notice it.'

'I know the place you're on about.'

'But when I came to the town first there was no flower shop and I thought it seemed like a sensible idea for a business. As you know yourself, there's no end to births, deaths, and marriages.'

'It's a thriving industry,' he said.

'And there was nothing really for me to do after we got married. I wanted to be pregnant straight away but it just didn't happen and anyway—' She dismissed this strand of the story with a wave of her hand. 'I was bored out of my head, and not being from the town I didn't know a lot of people and everyone I did know seemed to have a child. James was working at the co-op and he had a good enough wage but there's always the need of more money. So I sorted out taking on the lease. I went to the bank and filled out the paperwork and paid the first three months up front. And James just sort of let me get on with it, but took no interest in it whatsoever, like maybe if he just said nothing I'd give up. He didn't like the idea of me going out to work in case I wasn't there to iron his shirts or cook spuds for him. And he was getting busier – more involved politically, and he was out and about at after-work meetings and that sort of thing.' She stubbed her cigarette out in the ashtray. 'And I never made a fortune at it but what little I did make bought the site this house was built on.'

'And what happened?' he asked.

'James had just been elected to the local council so there was a few extra bob coming in. He decided we didn't need the shop anymore. I remember the morning he came up the stairs and I was lying in the bed and he lifted Orla up out of the cot and hugged her, and told me the news that he'd handed over the lease to Mark Carr like he'd done me a big favour. All I was thinking about was how quickly I could get back to work. You spend five years building a business and then someone gives it away on you just like that. Mark turned it into a gift shop, local crafts for tourists and so on. Ran the place into the ground within a year.'

'And do you regret that?'

'Oh, I could have fought a bit harder I suppose, but I was worn out. I'd just given birth.'

'No, I don't mean that – I mean . . . you stayed at home to look after your children, that's the most important work you can do.'

She sighed. 'I would not have been the first mother who went out to work. I was just so in love with my new daughter. I wanted her to have everything.'

'But what you gave her was more valuable – your time and your presence and your attention. You made a full, unadulterated commitment to the role of being a mother and you didn't—'

'Like Colette Crowley?'

He withdrew a cigarette and pushed it back into the pack. 'Sometimes people come to me looking for spiritual guidance and—'

'She'd need a bit of that, all right. Was that the first time you'd met her?'

'Yes. She'd left the parish by the time I arrived.'

'God, she's a good-looking woman,' Izzy said.

There was bitterness in her tone, he thought.

'Sometimes all people need to hear is that they're forgiven, and that they need to forgive themselves.'

'It's that easy, is it? So if you leave your children and husband to go off with a married man, your penance is to read at mass – that's a good one. I should try that myself.'

'I do not know the particulars of what she did and did not do. Anything I know of the woman is—'

'Oh, give me a break. It seems to me that some people are able to behave however they want and still go around like they haven't a care in the world.'

'Do you really believe that?' he asked.

She slumped forward and crossed her arms on the table as though the last of her energy had left her all at once.

'That woman lost a child,' he said. 'I don't think that's something you ever really get over.'

'I don't doubt that she's suffered,' Izzy said.

'I think it's a good thing she's back. Someone artistic and musical like her is an asset to a community. From what I've heard she used to be involved in everything – the choral society, the drama society. And she came to me with this.' He reached into the inside pocket of his blazer. He unfolded a piece of paper and handed it to her. 'She wants me to put that in the parish newsletter.'

He watched her eyes widen as they read down the page. 'Writing workshop,' she read aloud. 'Have you always wanted to unlock your creative potential through the power of words? Work with professional writer Colette Crowley to achieve your ambition. Whether you feel you have a novel inside you or a book of poems, work with other writers to achieve your goal through constructive criticism and a focus on the craft of writing. Classes are ninety minutes and cost £8 and will start on Wednesday, October 10, at 7:30 p.m. in the Community Centre.' Izzy looked up at him. 'But what's the "workshop" bit?'

'Oh, I think it's just a fancy word for a class. But it's good for the town, especially with the winter coming in. Something for people to do.'

'And you think people will go to this?'

'Apparently she's very talented. She's published books all over.'

'Oh, I'm sure she's talented but . . .'

'But what?' he said. 'Maybe you should give it a chance.'

'Oh really? And are you going?'

'Ah no – a priest can't be showing up to that sort of thing. It'd put people off. They wouldn't be able to be open or honest. They'd feel like they were at confession but without the grille.'

He heard the crunch of tyres on gravel and turned to look out the window.

'Who's that coming?' Izzy said, thrusting the piece of paper back at him.

He recognised Mrs Mallon's ancient silver Ford Escort as it slowed to a stop in front of the house.

'Oh, for feck's sake, what's going on now?' she said, heading out to the hallway.

Mrs Mallon got out of the car and a few seconds later someone stepped out of the passenger side, a school bag on their back, wearing an anorak with the hood up. Voices carried to him from the doorstep but he couldn't make out what they were saying. The door slammed and then Izzy appeared in the hall, prodding her son in the back until he stepped into the kitchen. Niall looked up at him from under the brim of his hood, his eyes filled with shame, his face swollen from crying. A bruise blossomed in the corner of his eye.

CHAPTER 5

Izzy sat in her car staring at the county coat of arms painted on the side of the Community Centre. At least she felt fairly certain that's what it was; the shield striped with green and gold, the Donegal county colours. But she'd never really looked at it closely before, at the mangy-looking bird perched on top and the red cross in the middle, and had no idea about the meaning of the Latin emblazoned on the banner beneath. When first she'd reached the Centre, she thought she might just keep driving, follow this road back onto the main road and head straight home. She could take the spiral-bound notebook and pen she'd bought that afternoon in the newsagent's, and place them in the cupboard with the sketchpads and brushes and half-full tubes of paint from the art class she'd attended last winter. But she did not want to go home and there was nowhere else for her to be.

When James had returned from Dublin, she'd continued to ig-

nore him. She stayed in bed in the morning and waited until he'd
left for his office. Most evenings she put Niall's dinner in the oven,
and was gone from the house before James got home from work.
If they happened to be fighting during the summer months it was
easy enough to avoid him. The days were so long then that she
could leave the house in the evening and play a full round of golf
before it got dark. She could drive to Lough Eske and spend hours
walking the forests, mithered by midges. Mostly, she parked at the
strand in Mountcharles and listened to the radio while she read.
And always on those nights, as she observed the failing light and
watched sea and sky bleed together, she would will herself to wait
just a bit longer – an hour, two hours. James was a worrier, and it
gave her some satisfaction to imagine the conclusions he'd reach –
that she'd crashed the car, that she'd driven off and left him, that
she'd parked at the beach and walked into the tide. But always,
before it got too late to cause him any real concern, she'd start the
engine and begin the drive home.

In the winter months, however, it was necessary to be indoors
in the evenings, and if she were to stand any chance of avoiding her
husband, she often had to take up classes that she had little interest
in. She had once joined a knitting circle with women twenty years
her senior, and had spent her time making garments that no one
would ever wear. Her jumpers were posted to her sister Majella,
in Galway, to finish the sleeves and the hem. And while a creative
writing class held some attraction for her, the most appealing thing
about it was how much her attendance would bother James. An
art class was one thing, painting landscapes and bowls of fruit, but
words were harder to hide behind – he would be anxious about
what she might reveal to their neighbours.

She reached to turn the key in the ignition and drew her hand away. She looked around the car park – there were only a few cars, not so many that there would be a crowd inside but enough to suggest she wouldn't be alone, and she reasoned that if she felt uncomfortable, she could make up some excuse to leave.

She pushed open the door to the Centre and the wooden frame juddered. The building largely consisted of a low-ceilinged concert hall with a stage at the far end, and from this direction she heard hushed, reverential voices fall silent. The group seated there was lit only by a floor lamp so all but the corner they occupied was in darkness. Izzy was conscious of the noise of her heels against the wooden boards as she crossed the room. There were maybe ten seats in a circle but only a handful were occupied. Colette's smile widened as Izzy drew closer.

'Hello, Izzy, how are you?' she said.

'Hello, Colette,' she said.

'Sit wherever you want, you have your choice of places this evening.'

Izzy sat down on one of the red plastic chairs and took her notebook and pen from her little white canvas bag.

'I was just telling the group, Izzy, that we've been instructed by the caretaker to tidy up after ourselves and leave the place as we found it – they'll be hosting bingo in the hall tomorrow night. Anyway, you may have noticed that we're not very well set up this week. I do hope that next time you come we'll have a table, and that we'll get the heating sorted before the winter really sets in.'

Izzy looked around her at the group – Eithne Lynch, Fionnuala Dunleavy, Thomas Patterson, and the only person who was not from the town, Sarah Connolly. She didn't know the Connolly woman but she'd been pointed out to her on a number of occasions as the wife of Tony Connolly, a hotelier who owned businesses all over the northwest. Izzy had never failed to be surprised by the dour countenance of the woman. Izzy knew there were those whose disapproval of Colette was so great it would forbid them from coming. But she had wondered if pure nosiness would make it impossible for some not to attend, to get a good look at her, to see what was going on so they could report back to others on the sordidness of the whole thing.

'Tonight,' Colette said, 'is just an opportunity for us to get to know each other and to have a little chat about what we write, the ways we want to improve our writing, and the kinds of things that we might do together over the next few months – and maybe we'll try a few exercises to get us started.'

Izzy watched Colette cross her legs and clasp her hands at her knee. She wore a long skirt and the sleeves of her jumper were pushed up past her elbows so that they ballooned at her shoulders. Her slender arms flashed white in the darkness. She held herself so proudly; her face so expressive – Izzy thought she was the most confident person she had ever seen.

Thomas Patterson cleared his throat. 'That's a very interesting word you've just used, Colette – "exercises". Would you mind telling us a bit more about what you mean?'

A retired doctor who had lived in the town his entire life, Thomas was known to be of an artistic bent. He was an amateur photographer who'd documented the town's development over the decades and displayed his work at various self-mounted exhibitions that locals then felt obliged to attend. He had been her family doctor and Izzy had always thought him to be pleasant enough, although as an educated man who was used to being listened to, he was also prone to delivering every statement with a certain weight and bombast.

'Well, Thomas—'

'Because when I hear the word "exercise", I think of aerobics or calisthenics or some kind of activity that gets the heart rate going.'

'Well, Thomas, the kind of exercise I'm talking about is not entirely—'

'Surely you're not comparing writing to a brisk walk?'

'Will you let the woman speak. She can't answer your question if you keep talking over her all the time.' Fionnuala Dunleavy had buckteeth and every word sounded like it was spat out of her mouth. She sat with her hands crossed on her stomach; her breasts perched on top of her round belly like a coconut shy.

'Thank you, Fionnuala,' Colette said, and Izzy saw how the corners of Colette's mouth flickered like she was trying not to laugh, and she had to suppress a laugh herself. She imagined retelling all of this to James, then remembered she was not speaking to him.

'I'm sorry, Colette,' Thomas said. 'Please continue.'

'Well, to answer your question, Thomas—'

'I'm sorry to interrupt you, Colette,' Eithne said. 'But you mentioned that there was a problem with the heating and I was wondering when that might be fixed?'

Fionnuala tutted.

'I'm going to mention that to the caretaker, along with the tables and a bit of extra lighting. Hopefully it'll all be sorted out by next week.'

'But could you ask that he doesn't turn the heating up too much – it's even worse when it's too hot. The heat from those radiators would suck the air dry. You'd be parched by the time you're leaving.'

'I can mention that, Eithne.'

Eithne Lynch was an ageing hippie who lived in a thatched cot-

44

tage on the outskirts of the town that made Izzy shiver every time she drove past it. Izzy thought she would have been happy with whatever residual heat she could get.

'But to get back to your question, Thomas, about this idea of "exercises" – I like to think of writing as a skill or a craft. Maybe the exercises are not ways of raising our heartbeat but they are ways of limbering up for a difficult task. Stretches, if you will.' She smiled at Thomas when she said this. 'People often feel that they have an idea or something to say but they don't quite know how to put pen to paper, and I hope that some of the exercises we'll do together will get us over that particular hurdle – the fear of the blank page.'

'Well now, that's the bit I struggle with, Colette,' Eithne said. She was holding both hands in the air, rubbing her fingertips together like she was summoning spirits. 'Because I feel all the time like I'm inhabited by ideas and voices that I need to find a way to channel but when I actually come to articulate those ideas, they evade me.' She was clenching her fist then, shaking it at the air.

'Well, hopefully these workshops will help with that,' Colette said. 'And this is another term you might not be familiar with. I was first introduced to the idea of a creative writing "workshop" when I did a residency in Sacramento. Americans are more into the idea of writing as a craft, a skill you can develop. I want us to get rid of the idea that writing is a God-given talent and start to think of it as something we can all learn to do. I hope that by working together on something that is dear to us, and sharing our work, and offering each other constructive criticism – that is, criticism that's helpful and respectful – we'll all become better writers. And I hope I'll learn something from you as well.'

It was extraordinary, Izzy thought – she seemed to mean every word she said, and yet there was no conviction to it. They were never what she would have called close friends, but Izzy always made a point of speaking to Colette whenever she saw her. Just chatting to Colette for a few minutes was like sliding into a current of warmth and charm and good humour. Colette's eyes held a keenness and intelligence that had a way of taking you in and absorbing you entirely, and Izzy would leave her company feeling heartened. But today Colette's words sounded rehearsed, like she was reading from a script. And every smile that passed across her face did nothing to lift the dull gleam from her eyes.

'And don't think that just because I'm a poet you have to write poetry.' She threw her hands apart and brought them together. 'If you feel compelled to write prose, then write a short story or start a novel. It's about finding the correct vehicle to convey whatever story you want to tell. And the only stipulation is that you have to do a little bit of work at home every week and present it in class. Going off and writing by yourself and making time for it in your day is also part of what it means to become a good writer.'

'But Colette—'

'Ah-ah-ah,' Colette said, raising her hand to Thomas. 'Before we have any further questions, I'm going to get you to do your first exercise. Now I want you to try some stream of consciousness writing.'

'Stream of what?' Sarah Connolly asked in a pained voice.

Whenever Izzy had seen Sarah before, she was never with her husband, and when she'd seen her husband, he was usually with another woman.

'Stream of consciousness – I would like you to write for five minutes without thinking, without stopping, without having to make sense or—'

46

Sarah let out a little moan.

'There's nothing to worry about, Sarah. You can't fail at this exercise. Well actually, you can, you can fail if you stop writing. But you don't have to bother about grammar or spelling or punctuation, just concentrate on keeping the pen going.'

'But what are we supposed to write about?' Sarah asked.

'That's what I'm telling you. It doesn't have to be "about" anything. I am freeing you from the obligation of aboutness,' Colette said, spreading her arms wide and smiling openly at them.

Izzy glanced at Fionnuala Dunleavy, who was eyeing Colette suspiciously, chewing on a piece of gum that seemed to be welded to her back teeth.

'And what would we hope to achieve by doing an exercise like this?' Thomas asked.

'We'll discuss that in detail afterwards, Thomas, but let's just say for now that we're trying to unlock something within us, to make ourselves think about something that we might not otherwise think of. Now take out a piece of paper and a pen.'

Everyone placed their notebooks in their laps, pens pointed at the page.

'Go!' Colette said.

Izzy wrote in a sort of secret script in case Colette would ask to see the work or for her to show it to her classmates. Her husband and son she was careful to represent with only 'he' and 'they'. Still, the exercise encouraged such speed and lack of concentration that things were appearing on the page that she had not anticipated. At one point she wrote, 'the ghost of a thought', and that surprised her. Twice she put 'and God forbid', but she had no idea what she wanted God to forbid. She was only faintly aware of the noise of scribbling. She looked up from time to time and met the eye of one of her classmates momentarily lifting their head. But there was an atmosphere of seriousness and dedication, and even Colette was partaking in the exercise.

Izzy's hand was just beginning to hurt when Colette shouted, 'Stop!'

They each slowly raised their heads, eyes wide, entreating, like children disturbed from sleep. But Sarah kept writing.

It was in a bar, in fact, where Izzy had seen Tony Connolly – a bar in one of his own hotels, sitting there drinking with another woman in the middle of the day.

'Now, how did everybody find that?' Colette asked. 'Izzy?'

'Oh,' she said, looking down at the page. 'Nonsense really, I would say, most of it.'

'But you kept going and that's all that matters,' Colette said, her eyes flitting back to Sarah, who was still scribbling away. 'Does anyone think they've written something that could potentially be the beginning of a story or a poem? Sarah?'

But Sarah did not answer, she just kept focusing on the page, writing frantically.

'Well, Colette,' Eithne said. 'It's interesting you should ask that because I'm so surprised by what that exercise brought up in me.' She held her piece of paper out in front of her like she was about to reveal whatever was written there and then placed her hand to her throat as if to stymie herself.

But Izzy saw that all of Colette's attention was on Sarah. She reached across and Izzy recognised a tremor in her hand that settled only when her fingertips lighted gently on Sarah's arm. Sarah stopped and looked up and Colette smiled at her. 'It's OK, Sarah, you can stop now,' Colette said.

It was plain for everyone to see that she was crying, but more than this – that these tears were a great shock to her. Something had been cleaved open inside her and poured onto the page, and she was mortified.

'I'm very sorry,' Sarah said, and clapped her book shut and pulled her handbag onto her shoulder. She weaved away from them into the darkness of the hall.

'Don't worry,' Colette said, quietly, 'it happens more often than you might think. She'll be back next week.'

The hall door echoed shut.

No, she won't, Izzy thought.

*

When she woke the next morning, she could hear the hollow noise of the radio in the kitchen and Niall bounding up and down the stairs, more out of breath each time he descended, his father barking directions after him. She lay there with her eyes open listening to these sounds, separating one from the other, with James's gruff demands underpinning it all. The difference was that this morning she did not feel full of hurt and resentment at the fact of his presence.

She got out of bed and pulled on the trousers and blouse she had worn the night before. She slipped into her house shoes and went downstairs.

Niall was sitting at the kitchen table, eating a bowl of cereal. He looked up at her from under his brow in exactly the way his father did – that look that always made her feel like some problem to be negotiated.

'Hello, pet,' she said.

'Hello,' he said.

'You'd better hurry up now and get a lift with your father or else you'll have to thumb to school.'

He smiled at that and ran upstairs.

She lowered the sound on the radio and sat at the table and poured herself a cup of tea from the pot. James walked into the room, tying his tie. He stopped dead when he saw her, the knot of his tie still halfway down his chest.

'Well?' she said, taking a sip from her tea.

'Well,' he said. 'Niall!' he shouted. 'Come on now, we're going.'

'How did you get on in Dublin?' she asked.

'Oh, business as usual,' he said.

She had confounded him once again, she could see that; fighting for over twenty years and still he was never able to guess when she would cease hostilities. She was never sure either, but even by her own standards this thaw felt particularly sudden.

He slid the knot of his tie up to his throat. 'Where were you last night?' he asked, picking up his cup of tea.

'Well, would you believe this – I was at a poetry workshop!' She laid her hands delicately on the table and gave a little shake of her head.

'A poetry workshop?'

'A poetry workshop.'

He seemed to consider this carefully while he took a slug of his tea. 'And who was at that?'

'Oh, the usual crowd – the ones who go to everything. Fionnuala Dunleavy, Eithne Lynch, Thomas Patterson, and Tony Connolly's wife was down from Donegal Town.'

'Oh, she's the most miserable-looking yoke.'

'Anyway, she couldn't hack it. She ran off in tears.'

'She did not?'

'She did.'

'Crying?'

'Bawling.'

'And who organised the workshop?'

'Who do you think? Colette Crowley.'

James's eyes widened. 'And what did you write about?'

'I wrote a poem about what a bastard you are.'

He laughed. 'I'd say you did, all right. And was it any good?'

'Oh, it was brilliant – everyone loved when I read it out loud.'

'But tell me this – did it rhyme?'

'Of course,' she said.

'I can't wait to hear it.'

'Oh, I'll read it to you this evening in bed.'

He swilled the remains of his tea around in the cup. 'I heard she's living up the Coast Road.'

'What are you talking about?'

'She's renting the cottage from Donal Mullen.'

'Colette? Are you sure?'

'That's what Tom Heffernan told me anyway.'

'This time of year? Jesus, you'd freeze to death up there. Does that place even have running water?'

'It does not,' James said. 'Sure she washes out of a barrel.'

'What!'

'She collects rainwater in a barrel and she washes out of it.'

'She does not, James.'

'I'm telling you. Tom Heffernan said she collects rainwater in a barrel and she uses it to wash.'

'Ah, she's probably recycling the water, using it for something else, you know what those artistic types are like.'

'Yes. Well, *that's what poets do*,' he said, in an arch tone that made both of them laugh.

Niall came into the room, hauling his school bag onto his back.

'Will we go to the hotel for our tea tomorrow evening, Niall?' Izzy asked. 'Would you like that?'

Niall looked from her to James. The poor child, she thought, waking up every morning not knowing whether his mother and father would even be speaking to each other.

'And Orla will be home from school tomorrow so I'll book a table for the four of us,' she said. 'Something to look forward to.'

And with that, Niall and James departed and Izzy was alone at the kitchen table and she became aware of the low mumble of the radio, the hum of the fridge, the ticking of the clock on the wall. But separate to all of this was a silence so complete it was like another room she could step into. Her notebook lay in front of her on the table. She placed her palm against the cover, felt the coolness of its surface, the smoothness of the paper. She opened it and reread the lines she had written the night before, in that scrawl discernible to no one but herself, and closed the book again.

CHAPTER 6

Donal was taken aback by Colette's friendliness when she answered the door – the broad smile on her face, the openness in her expression.

'Donal? How are you? Come in,' she said, pulling the door wide open.

He hesitated before crossing the threshold, wary of being welcomed into his own property like a guest.

'I just wanted to say hello,' he said. 'And to give you this – it was dropped off at ours by mistake.' He handed her an envelope – grey, marbled, and with a Dublin postmark. She took it in both hands. The smile vanished from her face.

'I thought maybe you'd come up to get rid of this,' she said, showing him behind the door where the four slatted sides of a child's cot leant against the wall. 'I've asked Dolores a few times about having it moved.'

He stared down at the dismantled cot. She'd even gone to the trouble of placing all the screws in a little plastic bag and taping it to one of the sides.

'There was no need to take it apart,' he said. 'I could have just carried it down to the garage as it was.'

'It was no bother,' she said. 'It was taking up space in the bedroom and it's small enough in there.'

But it would be a bother for him to put back together and more awkward now to carry, and he was cross with Dolores for not having said something before Colette had had time to take the thing apart. But Dolores had been almost entirely silent on the subject of their tenant. Even when he'd said to her that he'd bring the letter up to the cottage and introduce himself, she'd turned to the sink and said nothing, picked up the grill and started scrubbing furiously at it.

Two weeks since Colette had moved in and he'd been putting off this visit. He knew when she was around because her car was parked at the front of the cottage, and if they happened to spot each other leaving the house she'd raise a hand to him. But he had only a vague awareness of who she was – an artist of some kind, married to a rich man, but a rich man who wouldn't say boo to a goose. They were separated – that much he knew – but what exactly she was doing living in his cottage was unclear to him. Still, the place would have lain empty until the summer, and with another child on the way the money would come in handy.

'I'll go and get the van,' he said. 'Bring all of this down to the garage in one go.'

But he could tell she wasn't listening to him. She'd seated herself at the table and opened the letter and was already engaged by whatever was written on those pages. The torn envelope lay discarded on the table and he noticed she'd put a new oilcloth on it, with a pattern of yellow pears. The place was hers now. Photos stuck to the fridge and books stacked everywhere, on chairs and on the sideboard. He thought she might air the place a bit to get rid of the smell of cigarettes. The floor too could have done with a good sweep, and there were a fair few empty wine bottles standing beside the bin.

A cold draught passed through the room and the envelope skittered across the table.

'How's the heating?' he asked. He stepped towards the radiator and touched the cool metal. It hung on the wall just beside the window looking out across the bay. The tide was high, almost up to the sand dunes, straining to draw the coastline in, then falling back on itself, exhausted.

'You'd never get bored of that, would you?' he said.

'What?' she asked, laying the letter down. She placed her feet upon the chair in front of her and her long woollen skirt slid up her shins. She flexed her toes. He watched her touch her fingertips to her bottom lip like something very tender was held there.

'The view – you'd never get bored of looking at it.'

'No, Donal, you certainly wouldn't,' she said.

'Bad news?' he asked, and right away he was sorry he'd said it. He lowered himself onto his knees and began turning the knob on the radiator.

'Will you have tea, Donal?' she asked, rising from her chair and walking to the sideboard. He watched the dirty soles of her otherwise white feet flashing at him as she crossed the floor. And he remembered where he had seen her before – at a play at the Community Centre, one of the silly things they did at Christmas and everyone had to go and you had to pay £10 for a video of it. And his daughter had danced with a flurry of snowflakes and afterwards Colette had ushered them back onto the stage – and she was barefoot. And he had thought maybe that was to bring herself down to the height of the children, but still she'd looked so tall beside them. And he'd kept thinking what an eccentric thing that was to do. And Dolores had said on the way home in the car, 'With all the money Shaun Crowley has he should buy his wife a pair of shoes.'

'I won't stay for tea, Colette,' he said. 'I'll just bleed this for you and I'll hit the road.'

'Excuse me?'

'The radiator – it's not coming up to temperature,' he said. 'It needs to be bled.'

'Oh, right,' she said.

'Had you not noticed they weren't giving out much heat?'

'I hadn't, I suppose. I've barely had them on.'

'Well, you'll need them soon,' he said. 'Have you got an old rag lying around?'

She brought him a tea towel. He wrapped it around the base of the pipe. As he turned the little key in the knob, he saw the oily liquid pour down the pipe and soak into the cloth. 'I'll just do the one in the bedroom for you and I'll be on my way,' he said.

'Thanks, Donal.'

He walked towards the bedroom door. 'Do you mind?' he said, placing his fingers on the handle.

'Not at all. Go ahead,' she said.

Her sheets were so tangled they made one long braid that ran the length of the bed. The fitted sheet had come loose, exposing the yellowing mattress beneath. On the floor was another stack of books so high that it acted as a kind of bedside table where an ashtray rested, with two white cigarette butts curled up beside each other like maggots. The room was not so different from Madeleine's, with garments spilling from drawers and the top of the dresser covered in sprays and bottles. There was a jewellery tree with necklaces and bracelets hanging there, and he touched a silver bangle and watched it rock gently. The window looked directly at the front of his own home and he was struck by how empty it looked, the windows glaring back at him, giving nothing of the interior away, and really you could think that there was no one at all living there. And he felt her eyes on him then but when he turned around, she was reading that letter.

He bled the radiator and walked back to the kitchen. She was at the table again, her black hair falling down the back of the chair. She reached her hand around and drew her hair aside, just an inch, so that he could see where her jumper hung loose and the soft curve of her shoulder was exposed to him. It was a strange gesture, the way you might move a curtain aside to peer out. She held her hand there, pressing her hair to the back of her neck, head bowed.

'How are your children, Donal?'

There was something so direct about the way she asked the question that he wondered if she knew Dolores was pregnant. But Dolores was barely showing yet. Had she guessed somehow? Did she expect him to make some proud announcement about it?

'They're grand,' he said.

'Madeleine's the only one I know. She was in a play we did at the Community Centre, when she was very small. She had a sweet little voice.'

'Snowflakes,' he said.

'That's right,' she said.

'Oh well,' he said, wiping his hands on the tea towel, 'she's thirteen now and there's not much sweet about her.'

'Oh!' Colette said. She was taking a drink from her cup. Her eyes widened. 'Is she a rebel, Donal?'

'That might be what you'd call her, all right.'

'Ah well, Donal, we must look after our rebels, because they're the ones who'll protect us in the end. I hope so at least. That's what I'm holding out for,' she said. 'I have a rebel. My middle fellow – Barry. We sent him away to boarding school in Dublin and he was kicked out. He's back at St Joseph's now because it's the only place that'll have him.'

'Well, St Joseph's was good enough for me.'

'Of course, Donal, I'm not saying anything about St Joseph's. It's a grand school and they're great to have him. But we wanted Barry to go away and learn some independence . . . discipline. He won't listen to me, that's for sure. You should see how much he hates me. God, it's extraordinary – to have all of that anger pointed towards you.'

An ecstatic smile spread across her face. He watched her eyes close slowly and as she opened them her expression had composed itself again.

'That's what I mean,' she continued. 'He won't always hate me, it's a phase he's going through, and then imagine having all of that energy directed in your favour.'

He did not know what to say to that, but he could see she wasn't waiting for a response. She was staring at a book lying open face-down on the table. Her fingertips were back to her lips again but this time they covered her whole mouth like she was trying to stop herself from saying something.

'I remember we did him in school,' he said.

'Who?'

'Yeats,' he said, nodding at the book. 'It wasn't all woodwork and metalwork at St Joseph's, you know.'

'I'm sorry if I insulted you, Donal – I didn't mean—'

'"The Lake Isle of Innisfree" – that was one of his, wasn't it?'

'It was indeed,' she said, and picked up the book. 'Yeats is someone I have a lot of time for, poor lost soul that he was.'

'And he was the one who was in love with Maud Gonne?'

'Besotted,' she said. 'And when she rejected him, he tried it on with her daughter.'

'Jesus,' he said. 'Those bloody Protestants – you couldn't trust them.'

He had made her smile and the pleasure of that was a slow heat spreading through him. He turned his face to the floor, his cheeks burning.

'I'll go and get the van now so I can get rid of this cot for you,' he said.

'I'm very grateful to you, Donal.'

He let himself out, and as he passed the window, he could see she had picked up that letter again and was reading it more carefully, her eyes scanning every line, her lips moving as if she were whispering the words to herself. She had been thinking about that letter the entire time he was there, and while he had been so alert to every movement her body made, she had not looked at him once. And he wanted to turn around, to be back in that kitchen with her – to walk up behind her and gather her hair into his hand, to turn it around his fist. He wanted her attention.

CHAPTER 7

Colette checked the flowers in the rearview mirror. An extravagant arrangement of yellow roses and eucalyptus and baby's breath, it rocked back and forth with the motion of the car. She'd driven to Donegal Town to purchase them that morning, and to visit the off-licence there. Her not infrequent trips to restock on wine at the supermarket in Ardglas had been registered by Mrs Doherty. Often dour and reserved, on her previous visit, Mrs Doherty had taken her money with such slow and studied seriousness that Colette thought the great weight of her conscience might forbid her from completing the transaction. But of course she had, and Colette had decided there were better places to spend what little money she still possessed.

She refocused her attention on the road ahead as she approached the main street of Ardglas. Up on her left, a group of lads in the navy St Joseph's uniform sauntered along the pavement.

They moved with such synchronicity – shoulders rounded, hands stuffed in pockets, sliding along like a shoal of fish. It was only when she drew closer that she could distinguish her son as the centre of the group. She checked the clock on the dashboard – lunchtime wasn't for at least half an hour. They were probably headed for the lane near the chip shop where lads from the school went to smoke. She drove past them and pulled up at the curb and almost didn't recognise her son's face in the mirror. A smile slung ear to ear, but so taut, so sly.

The group passed her and she rolled down her window. 'Barry,' she called, but not loudly enough. She started to move the car so that it hovered alongside them. She shouted again. 'Barry Crowley, I know you saw me.' One of the boys elbowed him and nodded in her direction and Barry careened off towards the car.

'What do you want?' he said.

He had a new haircut – grown out and choppy and the fringe almost down over his eyes. He looked like one of those Gallagher brothers from that band everyone was listening to.

She pulled the handbrake. 'Barry, what are you doing out here at this time?'

'What's it to you?'

'Barry – get back to school now or I'll ring your father and tell him where you are.'

'As if he'd listen to you.'

'Barry, what did you do to your hair?'

He leaned in very close then, almost poking his head through the window, spittle collected in the corners of his mouth. He laid his hands on the window frame and she could see that each of his fingernails was rimmed with a little crescent of dirt. 'Fuck off, you old slapper,' he said, and walked away.

'Barry, don't think that you can talk to me like that and get away with it.' She edged the car along the pavement. 'Come back here now!' But just as she said that, Charlie McGeehan stepped out of Doherty's with a bag of shopping hanging from each arm and almost collided with the gang. Reeling, he swung in one direction then the other before raising his eyebrows at the departing group, and then at Colette. She put her foot to the accelerator and was on the far side of the town before she remembered where she was going. Checking the flowers again, she saw their little yellow heads peeping out above the fringe of brown paper.

She nosed the car over a narrow bridge and the road opened up before her onto a view of the bay, the lighthouse sitting squarely at its centre. Pulling up at Izzy's house, she admired her view, which took in the entire length of the coastline to where it dropped off at the horizon. Across the bay she thought she could make out the chimney of the cottage, just visible beyond the brow of a hill. She took a moment to collect herself, determined to put this incident with Barry behind her. As a politician's wife, Izzy would be used to people looking for favours, and it would require the full force of her charm to gloss over the strangeness of just showing up unannounced.

When Izzy opened the door, she took the flowers into her arms and admired them but Colette recognised the confusion in Izzy's eyes, smiling and trying to pretend she wasn't surprised by her arrival.

'Come in, Colette,' she said. 'Go in there to the good sitting room and I'll make the tea.'

Izzy went off down the hall and Colette walked into a long room that ran from the front to the back of the house. The room had a window at either end but it didn't seem to get much light.

There were two sofas and she seated herself on the one facing the door. The other was flanked by floor lamps with long tassels trimming the shades. An enormous glass-fronted cabinet took up a whole wall, one side filled with crystal vases and bowls and the other with colourful figurines – little boys in lederhosen and cherubic girls in headscarves. The side tables were covered with lace doilies where porcelain ballerinas jetéd and pliéd. On the table next to her a tall, slender girl in a pink skirt reached up as though to pluck a leaf from an invisible tree.

'Ah, you're admiring my Lladró,' said Izzy.

Colette looked up and watched Izzy carrying a tea tray into the room. She knew the Spanish word was pronounced with a *y* but she thought better than to correct her. 'I'm admiring this woman anyway,' Colette said.

'She's my pride and joy.' Izzy laid the tray on the coffee table. 'God, it's nearly dark already,' she said, and went to turn on the main light. 'There aren't many hours in the day this time of year, Colette.'

'Oh no, blink and you'd miss it,' Colette said, and after so many hours alone in the cottage not speaking to anyone the shapes of the words felt strange in her mouth.

Izzy sat on the sofa opposite. 'Thank you so much for the beautiful flowers. Such a treat. It does your heart good to have a bit of colour on a day like today. I don't suppose you remember the flower shop I used to have up on the main street.'

'Indeed I do. It was a great thing to have in the town.'

'Oh, it was a lot of work too. And when kids come along, they change everything.' Izzy lifted the teapot. 'Do you like a strong or a weak cup?'

So much energy, Colette thought. 'I'm not fussy.'

Izzy poured a pale stream into a cup and handed it to her on a saucer covered in colourful little petals.

'You have so many lovely things, Izzy.'

'Oh, I won a lot of them at golf. The Waterford Crystal, those are all golfing prizes. James won a few as well. Then the rest are gifts, but you know James can't accept gifts over a certain amount and he's fierce honest about that sort of thing. So people try to say thank you in different ways. We have more china than I know what to do with – we're coming down with all the Belleek. And people know that I collect Hummels so they keep arriving.' She stood and Colette watched her cross the room. Such a petite woman on top, it was like the two halves of her body moved independently, her wide hips swayed and her arse wagged as she walked to the cabinet. She flicked a switch so that the figurines lit up. 'That's *Little Boy with Flute*, and that's *Little Girl in Tree*, and that's my favourite, *Little Boy with Sheep*.' She was pointing in an exaggerated way so that Colette could not help but smile, and despite the gaudiness of the figurines she was charmed by Izzy's fondness for them. 'I won't even tell you how much they cost,' Izzy said. 'It's a sin.' She sat down on the sofa again and smoothed her hands over her knees. 'Are you settling back in?' she asked.

'Oh, well enough. I've made a little home for myself up in the cottage. It's starting to get cold but sure I'll manage.'

'Well, stay warm anyway, there's nothing more miserable than the cold. Have you plenty of blankets and that sort of thing?'

'Oh. I'm made of strong stuff.'

Izzy nodded and smiled. 'And what about your job at the university?'

'That was just a fellowship, a six-month thing. I had to apply for it and all of that, but the funding only lasts six months. It's grand anyway, it means I can get on with my own work now.'

'And how's that going?'

'Oh, as well as can be expected. Work is work. People think that when you're a writer you love writing so much you skip to the desk every morning, but there can be days when it's a struggle, when you'd rather do anything else.'

'Oh God! It's hard for you too? And you're a professional. There are days I sit down at that table to try and do my homework and I feel completely blank.'

'Well, it happens to the best of us.'

'I don't suppose much has changed around the town since you left. You always think when you go away you won't recognise a place when you come back and then it's the same as ever.' Izzy was staring down into her cup. 'But we have a new priest. Who I know you've met. Father Brian. He's a breath of fresh air. A great addition to the town. Just what we needed really. The last fellow was too sweet to be wholesome.' Izzy gave Colette a knowing look. 'He used to be a Guard.'

'Who?'

'Father Brian. He was a Guard up in Dublin for years and then one day he got the Call and that was it.'

'He must have some stories.'

'Yeah – but he doesn't talk that much about it.'

Colette watched Izzy's gaze wander off around the room.

'What part of Dublin are you from again?' Izzy asked.

'Terenure.'

'Oh no,' Izzy said, 'he's from somewhere over on the Northside – Drumcondra, I think.'

'Well, he seems to be kind anyway, easy going.'

'Ah yeah, he's a bit of craic. Even James likes him. And that's saying something.'

'How is he?'

'He's fine. Finding it difficult to settle in to a new parish, I think, but he says the people in the town are welcoming and try to—'

'No. I meant James – how is he?'

'Oh, he's grand. Same as ever – busy, busy, busy. On the road the whole time. But he never seems to switch off – he's obsessed with it.'

'With politics?'

'With the town, the community, the area. You'd swear he was running the country, he puts that much into it. And there's always something.' Izzy tapped her fingernails against her cup. 'You might be able to get a divorce soon,' she said.

'What?'

'I heard there's going to be another referendum next year. Depending on what way it goes – you could get divorced.'

'Who said I want a divorce?'

'Ah yeah, I know, but if you did want to you could.'

'It seems an odd thing to me that a load of strangers can get together and make a collective decision about my marriage.'

'Oh God, I'm sorry, Colette. Don't mind me. I have a terrible habit of saying the first thing that comes into my head.'

Colette looked down at her wedding ring and began to turn it on her finger. She knew that Izzy smoked but she couldn't see an ashtray anywhere or smell cigarettes. She thought about taking her tobacco from her handbag and placing it on the table to prompt her, but there would have been something almost shameful about smoking in this fussy little room.

'How are your boys?' Izzy asked.

It was like someone had walked up behind her and laid two heavy hands on her shoulders. She lifted her head and tried to focus on Izzy. The light coming through the window behind her had already begun to fade. It had reached that time of day when she started to bargain with herself, and she knew that as soon as she was done with this conversation she'd drive straight back to the cottage and pour herself a drink.

She placed her cup and saucer on the table. 'Ronan is fine. He's at Trinity now. Studying business. We've told him a thousand times he can go off and do whatever the hell he wants but I suppose Shaun would like him to take an interest in the factory so that one day he might at least consider taking it on. And he's compliant, Ronan. That's one thing about him; he's never given us one bit of bother. It was nice when I was in Dublin because I got to see a bit more of him. We'd meet up for lunch in town. And he never blamed me for anything that happened. Unlike Barry, who hates me with every fibre of his being.'

'Oh, teenagers!' Izzy said. 'They're the worst! Our Orla only comes home from boarding school at the weekends to fight with me.'

Colette felt defeated by Izzy's performance, this attempt to make it seem like their situations were one and the same.

'But Carl,' Colette said, 'I've barely spoken to Carl for the past six months and for the past six weeks I've been living less than three miles from him. I've tried reasoning with his father. I've phoned, I've written letters. I've tried everything bar going out to the house and lying down in the driveway. I need to see my son. And I'm not going to start hanging around the school gates like a mad woman. He's been through enough.'

'Have you seen a solicitor?'

'I don't want to go down that road yet.'

'But if Shaun is stopping you from seeing your sons, then—'

'I need your help.'

Izzy stared back at her in silence.

'Carl and Niall are friends,' Colette said. 'I thought that maybe—'

'Not like they used to be.'

'What?'

'Honestly, that's why I thought you were here. When I saw the flowers, I thought they were some kind of peace offering.'

'Did Carl do something?'

'They've been fighting. They had an unmerciful scrap in the schoolyard. Niall was brought home by Una Mallon with a cut eye.'

'And Carl started it?'

'No, there was a pair of them in it, but it's very unlike Niall.'

'Well, it's not like Carl.'

'Niall said that Carl has been off with him for the past few months, and when I asked him what they were fighting about, he said you.'

'Me?'

'Well, Carl teased Niall and Niall said something about you and the whole thing kicked off.'

'But how would Niall know anything about me?' Colette asked.

'Oh, he must have heard something from one of the other kids.'

'But kids . . . what would they know about . . .'

She watched something change in Izzy's expression then, like she was really seeing her for the first time.

'Well, Colette, aren't you a naïve woman if you think you haven't been discussed in every house in the parish.'

An old slapper – that's what Barry had called her.

'I have been naïve about a lot of things. But I'm ready to put them right. I need an hour with my son, to talk to him and explain my side of the story. You could take the boys away for a drive, somewhere there's less chance of bumping into anyone we know. Tell me what time to meet you and I'll just appear as if by coincidence. I'll go off with Carl and talk to him and bring him back within the hour. Izzy, you don't know what it's been like up in that cottage night after night, knowing that your family are so close by.'

'Then why did you leave in the first place?'

'I have got so many things wrong. I cannot even begin to tell you the number of mistakes I've made. For a start, I took up with a man who turned out to be the most useless, cowardly eejit I've ever met. And I thought I was going to go off and take Carl with me and start a new life with that man and Shaun would just step aside and allow that to happen, and it would make us both happier. And when that all fell apart, I spent two months sleeping in my mother's spare room when the very first thing I should have done was get in the car and drive home to my sons – and I misjudged everything.'

'Colette, do you really think that I can go driving around the country facilitating clandestine meetings for you? And what do you think is going to happen afterwards? A child can't keep a secret – he's going to go straight home and tell his father that he saw you and then where will you be?'

'You don't know Carl like I do. And anyway, even if he does say something then at least Shaun might communicate with me, something will have happened. But the way things are at the moment, I feel like I might never see him again. And you would not be facilitating "clandestine meetings", as you put it. You would be facilitating a meeting between a mother and her son. Do you think I'm going to run off with him or something?'

'No, I don't think you'd touch a hair on his head.'

'What if James tried to stop you from seeing Niall?'

'And what if James got wind of this? Yours wouldn't be the only marriage in trouble.'

'Ah, I see – that's it.' She rose from the sofa. 'You're trying to keep the peace.'

Izzy clasped her hands at her knee and stared down at the coffee table.

'Right,' Colette said, taking her car keys from the pocket of her cardigan, 'if you're not going to help me, that's fine, but I had to ask. I won't mention it again. And I don't want things to be strange between us at the workshop or for you to feel like you can't come anymore. I enjoy having you there. I mean that. I can forget about this if you can.'

Izzy nodded but she kept staring at the tea tray, and Colette felt herself to be very tall, looming over her on the sofa. She glanced at the figurines in the cabinet – their fat little faces, the weird pastoral scene they made, laid out on the shelves. She turned her gaze back on Izzy, sitting there so primly, with her legs crossed and her back straight. And Colette had to bite her tongue not to say that she knew someone who wanted a divorce, but it wasn't her.

CHAPTER 8

That Friday the fleet came in laden down with fish and by midnight every pub in the town was full. When closing time came at the Reel Inn the landlord locked the doors and extinguished the neon sign outside to allow a contingent of heavy drinkers to carry on without arousing the suspicions of the Guards. Among them was Michael Breslin, the local butcher. At forty-five years old Michael still lived at home with his mother and joked that he was unlikely now to give up his bachelor ways. Most days, as soon as he got out of his blood-stained smock, he went home to give himself a rudimentary wash at the bathroom sink, changed into a shirt and blazer, and headed for the pub.

Michael was putting on a bit of a show and a group had gathered around him. They observed him carefully to be able to imitate him later. Michael was a big man who took up all the space around him and had a thick drawling Donegal accent. He was easy to impersonate. He told stories about the time the bus broke down on the way to the All-Ireland final and he ended up watching the match in a pub in Kells. He rehashed his tale about getting heat-stroke when he went to Italy for the World Cup. Laughter rang out, backs were slapped, whiskeys slid down easily. Around four in the morning, Donal Mullen said his goodbyes and the men lifted their glasses to him. No sooner was he out the door than they were saying what a cute hoor he was, getting Colette Crowley ensconced in the holiday home. And he could go home now and throw the leg over Colette if he wanted to and leave that skinny bitch of a wife alone. Or indeed he could have them both. He had options now, did Donal Mullen, because that's what it meant when you had a c-c-c-c-c – no man was sober enough to think of the word 'concubine'. They all raised a glass to the fair Colette.

Michael was a kind of drunk he seldom was and told himself it would be best to leave. But he remained rooted at the bar. A thought had entered his mind, the thought of Colette Crowley alone in that cottage, and that thought made Michael lonely. He felt like he had run dry of chat, that he might never open his mouth again. He tried to laugh in the right places and find a way to re-enter the conversation but it was all he could do to stay steady and the thought that steadied him was Colette. When the time finally came that they were all thrown out Michael did not walk in the direction of his own house where his mother lay sleeping, but turned right out the door and began to walk along the Shore Road. It was a cloudy night, not too cold for that time of year, and Michael did not even think to pull on his coat until he was walking uphill towards the Coast Road.

The lights from the pier fell away behind him. The fields spreading out in every direction were one unbroken swathe of darkness, like a vast ocean surrounding him. But anyone watching Michael would certainly have said that he looked like a man who knew where he was going. Weaving somewhat, yes, as he made his way up the drive to the cottage, but there was no doubt he had purpose. And when finally he came to the door, he stopped so abruptly that he looked as though he might have gone right through it had he not steadied himself against the frame.

Now that he'd reached his destination he felt more sober than he cared to be. A little bit sick, as was often the case after a rake of drink, even with all that he drank. But usually at these times he was turning and turning in his bed until the drink settled in him, not standing at a woman's door in the middle of the night. And he didn't really know why he'd come. He tried to think of a reason, an excuse for why he might have walked the three miles from the town to the cottage in the early hours of the morning, but nothing came to him. He rapped his knuckles on the door three times.

Nothing. He coughed, rapped on the door three times again. There was a noise from inside.

'Who is it?' The voice was pitched somewhere between fear and annoyance.

He tried to speak but the words came out garbled. He tried again. 'It's me, Colette,' he said.

'Who?'

'It's me, Michael Breslin,' he said, and that answer seemed ridiculous even to him. 'Can I talk to you?'

'Michael, what the hell are you doing up here at this hour of the night?'

He heard the latch click. She opened the door a couple of inches but kept the chain in place. Even in the dark the pale blue of her eyes shone.

ALAN MURRIN

'Can I come in?' he said.

'What for, Michael? What the hell do you want?'

And when he failed to come up with an explanation or a timely answer to that, she said, 'Fuck off home to your mother, Michael – before I call the Guards.'

The door slammed in his face. Michael turned on his heel. The town felt a much greater distance from him now. He took a couple of exploratory steps and then began the long walk home.

*

Izzy had agreed to have lunch with Teresa Heffernan in the clubhouse after their game and she was beginning to regret the decision. They'd both played badly, mostly, Izzy believed, because of Teresa's gossiping. The wind was high, and, determined to be heard, she had shouted continuously as they rounded the course. Bert Harvey had built an extension on his house without planning permission and now the County Council was getting ready to tear it down. Fionnuala Dunleavy's son had written off the car – driven it straight into a wall. 'Off his head on drugs,' Teresa had said. 'A miracle – not a scratch on him.' Izzy had begun to think it tactical, this method of distraction. She'd lost four shots on the back nine and Teresa had won, and Izzy was thick with herself. But now, sitting in the crowded clubhouse, staring across a table cluttered with scrunched-up paper serviettes and teapots and little metal baskets filled with half-eaten sandwiches, she was more annoyed that she was still listening to Teresa, whose seemingly inexhaustible stream of chatter had arrived at the subject of Colette Crowley.

'And you believe that?' Izzy asked.

'Well, Andrew's friends with that apprentice he has working in the butcher shop and he told him that he went up there last Friday

74

night and she let him in. And several people saw him heading in that direction after the Reel Inn closed,' Teresa said. 'And she certainly has form.'

'Are you honestly telling me,' Izzy said, 'that you believe Michael Breslin went walking up to that cottage in the middle of the night, and Colette let that obese eejit climb up on top of her?'

'Don't shoot me,' Teresa said, her smile collapsing. 'I'm just telling you what I heard.'

'Well, it would suit you better than to go around spreading rubbish like that.'

'Hang on now,' Teresa said, 'sure it's only a bit of craic.'

'A bit of craic? That poor woman must have been scared out of her wits. Imagine if some fella came banging on your door in the middle of the night?'

'Chance would be a fine thing,' Teresa said into her cup.

'Jesus, is there only one person working in this place today? Here,' Izzy said, 'try and grab that one's attention.' She held out a stack of empty sandwich baskets to the waitress striding past, her ponytail of black curls flapping behind her. 'Walking away empty-handed every time,' Izzy said, dropping the baskets back onto the table.

'Well, of course,' Teresa said, 'you know Colette better than I do.'

'And I know she wouldn't have anything to do with a gobshite like Michael Breslin. That fellow's a scourge when he has a drink taken.'

'Well, right so,' Teresa said, 'forget I mentioned it.'

And talk turned to Christmas, and visitors, and Teresa's brother coming from Australia for the first time in fifteen years, and things to be bought, and cooked, and cleaned, but Izzy found herself unable to think of anything but Colette.

*

The dry air in the hall scraped Izzy's throat. It was too warm for the jumper she'd worn and so she'd discarded it on the chair beside her and now she sat there in a cream satin blouse feeling fussy and overdressed, the material staining at the armpits. She looked across at Colette in her long tartan skirt, with one enormous safety pin that seemed to hold the whole thing together. It looked like an old blanket she'd pulled off the back of a settee. Her legs were crossed and she tapped at the air with her black high-heeled boot, and Izzy could see where the leather came apart from the sole and gaped open like a little mouth.

It was the fifth workshop. Numbers had peaked at eight and reduced again to five. There was still Eithne, and Fionnuala, and Thomas. Helen Flynn, a retired schoolteacher, had joined them in week three but she rarely said a word or made eye contact with anyone. And when she did lower her notebook from her face and peer out at them from her round, rimless spectacles, all she had to contribute was some plaintive offering about how difficult she'd found the homework.

Class, as usual, began with housekeeping.

'Colette,' Eithne said, 'I know I asked last week that the radiators be turned up, but I really feel they've reached an unhealthy temperature.' She was perched on her chair with one bare foot placed on her knee in a kind of half-lotus position, gently rocking back and forth and fanning herself with her notebook. 'It's a cold night out there and it's not good for the human body to go from one extreme to the other.'

'Your body's going through extremes because you're bloody menopausal,' Fionnuala said.

'And that's as it may be, Fionnuala, but this heat is not helping.'

'Have you been to see your GP?' Thomas asked.

'Oh Jesus, I remember when I was going through it,' Helen said. 'It was a curse.'

Eithne ignored them and continued to fan herself.

Colette closed her notebook and gave a wan smile. Her eyes appeared to smart, like she'd just woken up and hadn't yet adjusted to the light. 'Now, I do apologise for the heat this evening. I went around and I tried to turn the radiators down but they seem to be stuck, so I'll have to have another word with the caretaker and see what he can do for us for next week.'

'Perhaps, Colette,' Thomas said, 'if I had a look at them there might be—'

'I think if we get on with our work, Thomas, that should be enough of a distraction. Now, how did we do with the exercise?'

Izzy had struggled with her homework. Since starting the workshop she'd written a few poems and short pieces. She thought them to be among the stronger work in the class, and Colette's comments reflected that. But this particular challenge required something more from her, and several times she'd sat down at her kitchen table to attempt the task and then abandoned it.

Orla's comments hadn't helped. Orla came home from boarding school in Sligo every Friday evening, unless she went off to one of her friends' houses. It was rare for a weekend to pass without some argument, and often that had to do with Izzy sharing her opinion on Orla's appearance. She did not want to hurt her daughter's feelings but she felt that if she said nothing Orla might not realise how fat she was getting. And so her concerns expressed themselves in sideways swipes that she chastised herself for as soon as she'd said them. 'That pocket money we give you is for stationery, not junk food,' was how she'd responded when Orla complained that her jeans no longer fitted. Orla had returned to school that Sunday with the avowed promise that she'd never speak to her mother again.

Getting her to think seriously about her future was another challenge, and Izzy loved to threaten her within earshot of James – 'Do you want to be stuck in this town for the rest of your life married to some eejit?' She was bright and could do what she wanted, within reason. She probably wouldn't get the points for medicine or veterinary or any of the really big courses but she could be a solicitor or an accountant or one of those nice, clean jobs.

But where Orla lacked opinions about her career, she was full of chat about everything else. Izzy had hidden her workshop notebook in a drawer in the kitchen but Orla had gone rooting for something and found it.

'What's that?' Orla asked.

'That's my homework,' Izzy had said with a note of forced preciousness in her voice.

'Your homework? Are you doing another one of those classes? How many is that now? Oil painting, watercolours, yoga, tai chi, knitting—'

'Ah, will ya mind your own business. It's my writing workshop, if you must know.'

'A writing workshop?'

'Yeah – have you never heard of one of those? You'd want to get a life, Orla.'

Orla laughed. She opened a tiny yoghurt pot and licked the foil lid then began to eat it with the handle of a dessertspoon. There was a little spot of yoghurt on the tip of her nose.

'What did Daddy say about that?'

'Oh, he doesn't mind as long as I don't write anything about him.'

'And what *do* you write about?'

Izzy crossed her arms on her chest and gripped her shoulders. She closed her eyes. 'We write about nights of wild passion and abandon, when in the first throes of romance we ripped off our clothes and—'

'Mammy, stop!'

Izzy's eyes flew open and she flashed a smile at her daughter.

'Seriously, what do you write about?' Orla asked.

'We write about anything and everything. It can be ordinary enough. Thomas Patterson writes love poems to his wife – quite sexy stuff, actually. Fionnuala Dunleavy writes about doing the dishes, when she bothers to write anything. Eithne Lynch writes about auras. Just what you'd expect, I suppose. Colette sets us writing exercises and we have to respond to them.'

'Colette Crowley?'

'Yeah.'

'Crazy Colette Crowley – poet laureate of Ardglas?'

'Why do you say it like that?'

'Ah, the state of her – going around in those big wool skirts and Aran sweaters, and the head on her – she looks like she cuts her own hair.'

'Ah, will you stop – she's a very attractive woman, Colette – that's just what those bohemian types are like.'

'And what kind of homework does she give you?'

Izzy hesitated. 'Well, this week, she's asked us to write a eulogy – it can be for ourselves or for a fictional character—'

Orla's eyes widened as she withdrew the end of the spoon from her mouth.

'Or if that's too much of a challenge we have to imagine what would be written on our gravestone.'

'Fuck off!' Orla said. She gave each word its own emphasis.

'Orla, I warned you, if you use language like that again, I'll give you a slap in the mouth.'

'She's asked you to write a poem about your own death?'

'Well, we can respond to it in whatever way we want but—'

'Jesus, I thought it'd be all writing about flowers and sunsets and *my heart is low because I have to make the dinner* – that sort of thing!' She placed the yoghurt pot on the counter. 'Ugh!' she said. 'Housewives sitting around writing poems about their funerals . . . and then you all have to read them to each other?'

And later in bed when she'd relayed this conversation to James, in a tone of mock affront, he'd only laughed. When she'd put out the light, he'd turned to her and slid his hand over her stomach and said, 'Shall we do what poets do?' in a silly sing-song voice. She'd roared with laughter and rolled over on top of him.

Sitting in that airless hall now, with her blouse sticking to her, and Thomas Patterson reading a story about finding a tombstone with his name engraved on it, she could see why her daughter thought her to be ridiculous. It was an exercise in vanity, the whole thing – the clever, sophisticated lady had told her she was interesting and so she'd kept doing her homework, showing up, performing. Until the day Colette had stood in her sitting room, listening to her showing off about her ornaments and her golf trophies and Izzy had felt herself to be empty and exposed and not up to the task. Still, she could not relinquish this new version of herself Colette had presented her with, so she was back to make another attempt, to prove to a woman she barely knew that she had been right in bestowing her praise and favour upon her.

'I'll have to stop you there, Thomas.' Colette held up her hand

and smiled at him. 'We have to keep it to no more than ten minutes for everyone or else we'll run out of time.'

Thomas muttered something and folded over the pages he'd been reading from.

'Now,' Colette said, 'does anyone have any initial thoughts on Thomas's piece?'

Izzy had been so bored she'd stopped listening after a couple of minutes. 'I mean, it was very descriptive,' she said. 'The bit about the crow leading him to the gravestone and landing on it was very—'

'It'd scare the life out of you,' Helen said, shooting Thomas a look of disgust.

'Well, Helen,' Colette said, 'fiction is a safe way to explore the darker reaches of the mind. It reminded me a little bit of Edgar Allan Poe – the sense of foreboding, the imagery, the classic set-up of a man faced with his own mortality.'

'The classic set-up that's like a hundred other things I've read before,' Fionnuala said.

'Now, Fionnuala,' Colette said, 'could you frame that differently?'

Thomas was staring at Fionnuala.

'Well, it's always the same thing in these horror stories, isn't it – *man sees a ghost of himself, man thinks he's alive but he's dead, man glimpses his own death . . .*'

'Yes,' Colette said, 'we've discussed this before – the use of archetypes – the limited number of stories that are available to us and how it's up to us to make something original out of the components we've been given—'

'And if I'd been allowed to finish, you'd have seen that this story goes in a very different direction to what you're expecting,' Thomas said.

'The date of his death is written on the gravestone, it's a date in the future, and he ends up dying on that date,' Fionnuala said.

'Well, I didn't see that coming,' Helen said.

Thomas tossed his pages onto the table. 'And where is the groundbreaking, original work of fiction you've written, Fionnuala?' Thomas asked.

'I haven't had a minute's peace all week. I have two teenagers at home and if one of them's not slamming every door in the house then the other needs driving to football training. I have no time to be sitting around writing stories.'

'I've said it every week,' Colette said, 'you don't have to present work to attend – you're always welcome here, but I would ask that you keep your comments as constructive and respectful as possible. Now, let's move on.'

Eithne Lynch read her poem 'Life After Death' about the 'multiple selves' within her, and the number of times she'd been reincarnated and the number of times she'd be reincarnated again. She was a 'vessel' for these different lives and would finally 'take refuge in her own womb'. Nobody really knew what to say about that. Fionnuala moved around in her seat a lot, pulling at the hem of her jumper. Then Helen read her poem 'Deirdre of the Sorrows', about the great turmoil that resulted from her death. The rain poured, the wind howled, animals cowered – generally nature was all askew. But despite the great impact her death had, no one showed up at her funeral. It was typical of the kind of thing she wrote, and after Colette had offered feed-back and she had asked if the rest of the group had anything to add, Fionnuala, no longer able to stay silent, told Helen that she needed to go home to her husband and have a good ride. Even Helen laughed at that.

'And would you like to share with us what you've written, Izzy?' Colette asked.

Izzy looked down at the notebook. 'I'm afraid I struggled a bit with this one,' she said.

'That's all right.'

'I mean, I've written very little, I really couldn't think of anything.'

'It's OK, you don't have to share but it really doesn't matter how short it is, we're not here to judge.'

That's precisely what you're here for, Izzy thought.

'Well, I just kept coming back to the same thing over and over again and so I tried to do something with it, to shape it into a haiku, in the way that you'd shown us.'

'Ah yes, they're trickier than they look, aren't they?'

'But in the end, all I could come up with was two lines – the second line and the last line.'

'That's fine, Izzy. Why don't you just read that to us.'

Izzy looked around at the faces of her classmates staring so intently at her. She looked down at the page again. 'On her gravestone was written / "She was found wanting",' Izzy said. And then a silence seemed to swell around her, to expand beyond the confines of the hall to take in the night outside, and she felt herself to be falling through vast, soundless space. She could feel Colette's eyes upon her and when she met her gaze, she was looking at her with such focus, like Izzy was the horizon, the point she'd had to fix upon to steady herself.

'I think that's very beautiful, Izzy,' Colette said. 'Does anyone else have any thoughts on that?'

Her classmates began to shift in their seats.

'I don't think there's anything you can add to that,' Fionnuala said, looking down into her lap. 'That says it all really.'

'There you go, Izzy,' Colette said. 'You've silenced us. Although I might suggest that you try something else with it. What if you reduced it further? What if you just said, "Found Wanting"? That could be your title and you could use it as a jumping-off point. Removing the pronoun, or whoever the "she" is, from the poem might allow you some distance from it, a greater freedom to explore images connected to this idea, and give you a greater depth of meaning. But well done.'

When the class finished Izzy stayed behind. Colette was placing one red plastic chair on top of the other when she suddenly stopped. She stood to her full height and placed the fingers of one hand to her bottom lip.

'You know, Izzy – I think I will remember those words for a long time,' Colette said.

Izzy set down the chairs she was carrying. 'Colette,' she said. 'On Saturday I'm going to take the boys to Bundoran. I'll let them have a couple of hours at Waterworld and afterwards I'll take them to the Great Northern for a bite to eat. I don't suppose there's much else to do around there this time of year – the funfair might be open for a bit in the afternoon. Anyway, we'll be in the foyer of the Great Northern at four o'clock.'

Colette bowed her head and closed her eyes. 'Thank you, Izzy,' she said.

Izzy picked up her canvas bag from the floor and bid goodnight to Colette. She stepped outside into the cold night and as the door of the hall shut behind her, found herself adrift in that silence once again. A little unsteadily, she made her way through the darkness to her car.

CHAPTER 9

When a fourth envelope addressed to Colette dropped through Donal's letterbox, he got angry. He opened the door just as the postman was getting into his van. 'Here, you,' he said, holding up the envelope, 'can you not read or are you too lazy to go up there and deliver this yourself?'

The postman just stared at him, wide-eyed, but made no movement to suggest he would get out of the van and reclaim the letter.

'Forget it,' Donal said, slamming the door.

He took the other three letters from the drawer in the hall and headed to his van. He laid the envelopes out on the passenger seat, all written in the same hand on the same grey, marbled stationery – he'd held on to them for weeks.

The cottage had become somewhere to be avoided. He'd invited enough trouble upon himself lately. He'd been doing the wiring on an extension for a woman in Donegal Town and he'd recognised the unhappiness in her as soon as he'd walked through the door. After her husband left in the morning and the kids went off to school, she floated around the place like she was haunting her own life. When he'd calculated the risk of starting something, he'd reasoned that she had as much to lose as he did. But after they'd slept together a few times, she'd started getting notions. When the job ended, he told her that this was a natural conclusion to things, an opportunity for them to save their marriages before any real damage was done. He tried to make it sound like the sacrifice he was making was so great that she'd have no other choice but to match his bravery. Still she'd clung to him and pleaded until he'd grabbed her wrists, removed her hands from his chest, and thrust them back at her. What he saw in her eyes then, he'd thought, was just the right amount of fear.

Too close. Too close for comfort, he thought, as he looked up at the cottage and a light rain speckled the windscreen. These things began in a rush of excitement and ended with phone calls to the house, with Dolores staring at him as she listened to the silence on the end of the line. They became administrative, something to be managed, and elicited the same stress he felt when on a Sunday night he thought of all the work he had to fit in that week. Distance was crucial, he'd decided, and there would be no more women from Donegal Town or Ballybofey, or even Letterkenny. From now on he'd be in the next county before he'd even think about starting anything.

You kept trouble away from your own doorstep at least, and that was why he didn't allow himself to think too much about Colette; this strange woman who behaved like a teenager – who rolled her own cigarettes and left her bedroom in disarray. She was not so much his type anyway, too tall for a start, and she was growing

stout with age. She was attractive all the same; there was no denying that. But he was not stupid enough to get involved with his
tenant, even though he could see how a woman like Colette, the
pure conundrum of her, could make a man behave in stupid ways.
She'd fooled a shrewd customer like Shaun Crowley.

He found the envelope with the oldest postmark. He turned it
over, dug his thumb in at one corner, and ripped it open. He withdrew a handwritten letter on numbered pages that went all the way
up to twelve, the final one signed 'John'. He could barely make out
the writing but certain sentences and phrases were clear to him,
and they detailed this man's heartbreak over the loss of Colette and
used words like 'bereft' and 'crestfallen'. One line read, 'The curve
of your breast is like a planet in orbit.' There were verses, some of
them with lines crossed out. There were single lines hanging in the
middle of the page. They were clearly written by someone who was
losing his mind. He had never read anything like it. She'd made a
mockery of this poor John fellow as well. And these were only the
letters that had accidentally come to his house. He put the letter in
the glove compartment. He'd throw it in the bin later. She'd never
even know it had existed, and besides, it could have been lost in
the post. At least this way he wouldn't have to explain to her why
he'd kept it for so long.

He turned up the drive to the cottage. Colette's car was there but
the curtains on the bedroom window were drawn. He peered into
the kitchen. A thick wedge of envelopes in the same grey stationery
sat on the table, held between the vase and a candlestick. Perhaps
she'd gone out for a walk on the beach, as he knew she was in the
habit of doing, or perhaps she was still in bed. He thought of her
coming to the door in some old dressing gown, drawing aside the
mussed-up strands of hair, sleep still heavy upon her, the warmth

of it rising from her body. He lifted his fist to knock on the door and at once thought better of it. He pushed the letters through the slot and heard the soft pat as they landed. And when he stepped back from the door, he saw that she'd fixed a little wooden sign to the front of the house that read 'Innisfree' in white lettering.

He looked in again as he passed the window, trying to absorb as much detail as he could, aware that inside somewhere she might be watching him, waiting for him to leave. There were a couple of birthday cards beside the microwave, a few empty wine and vodka bottles by the bin. On the counter was a cassette player with a stack of tapes beside it. Sometimes when he looked up at the cottage he could see her dancing, throwing herself about the place, tossing her head from side to side so that her black hair twisted around her face. Whatever she was listening to, she was giving herself over to it entirely. And it made him embarrassed for her; disgusted him a little that she could forget herself like that, leave herself exposed in this way.

He got into his van and drove. Things were getting busier coming up to Christmas and it felt good to be on the road, not stuck in the house with Dolores going on about whichever one of the kids needed new shoes. When he'd told her that morning he had a job to get to in Letterkenny, she'd furnished him with a list of presents to buy at the shopping centre. They had to make a start, get the toys hidden away in the attic before the kids got too curious, she'd said. Like he'd needed reminding that this was what his life was, an endless round of Christmases and christenings, confirmations and communions.

Married at twenty-one – in the wedding photo that hung in his hallway he looked like someone had put a gun to his back and told him to smile. But there was solace too in knowing that once he'd married Dolores, he'd never see a poor day. Mick and Eileen McNally had come down from Howth when the EU was handing out fishing trawlers to whoever wanted one. They were millionaires within a decade. But where the McNallys were vulgar and brash, his own parents were pious and discreet. They were among the most religious people in the town, and it was to be an embarrassment for them when he got Dolores pregnant after they'd only been going out a couple of months. He'd thought about running away to England but instead he got drunk for three days, and on the third day he was at the disco in the Harbour View Hotel when Mick barrelled in and hauled him out by the collar of his shirt. He marched Donal down the alley by the hotel and in near darkness, amid the smell of putrefying rubbish, threw him up against a damp wall, and told him that if he didn't marry Dolores, he'd see to it that his body was dredged up off the harbour floor.

As if to sweeten the deal, Mick paid for the construction of their house. But married life in that house was to be a shock to him. This was it, this was all his life had amounted to, and he felt short-changed and cheated and angry all the time. Often in that first year he'd leave his wife and baby daughter at home and retreat to his mother's kitchen table, where he spent a great deal of time complaining. His mother had always indulged him and his three brothers, overcompensated for their father's coldness with love and care and affection, but even she grew tired of Donal's complaints. She knew Dolores was a good wife, that she cooked and cleaned and took care of their child in a manner that was beyond reproach. Dolores was fulfilling her side of the bargain. And he even resented her for that. Dolores was also a regular attendee of confession and the Stations of the Cross, while Donal only fulfilled the minimum requirement of showing up for mass on Sunday. No matter how much he complained, his parents would never countenance the idea that an alternative life existed for Donal on the other side of his marriage. They actively campaigned against all evils, and chief among them was divorce. Donal could remember, before the last referendum, when they'd boarded a bus to Dublin to hold either end of a banner and parade it up and down in front of Leinster House – 'DIVORCE?' it read, 'JESUS SAYS NO'.

Donal's brothers had all gone on to university and now worked good jobs, and continued to be good Catholics. They'd had the decency at least to wait until after they were married to get their wives pregnant. His father had believed in discipline and education, and if his sons were not going to go on to the priesthood, then they were at least going to be upstanding citizens. Bad school results and bad behaviour were met with a few lashes of the belt, doled out with calm, considered control. All four Mullen boys were handsome and clean and intelligent, and in a town where most grubby-faced teens were just trying to get their hand up a girl's blouse so they could boast to their friends, the idea that their religiosity might make them respectful was to their advantage. Donal recognised the way girls looked at him from an early age, but of all the women he drew to him Dolores was the first who he knew would do whatever he asked of her. But when she told him she was pregnant, he began to think he was the one who'd been had, tricked into marriage by a woman who knew he'd have no other choice.

Donal had completed his electrical apprenticeship and worked hard to grow his business. Buying the cottage had been his first act of financial independence from his father-in-law. But there wasn't much demand for holiday homes in Donegal outside of the summer months, so when Dolores had told him she was pregnant again, it seemed like a good idea to rent to Colette. But she was starting to cause him bother, coming down to the house and asking stupid questions about the fuse box and rousing little fights between him and Dolores. And now she'd screwed that sign to the front of the house, and he'd never hear the end of it.

Donal turned off the radio. He couldn't get his thoughts in any order. He was tired of the chatter of the presenters and the afternoon quizzes and the same songs being played no matter what station he turned to. But it had been like this all day, his mind flitting from one thing to the next, and he was driving through Barnesmore Gap before he knew what was happening to him. The broad valley rose up around him as he drove a clean line through it, and he was thinking about Colette. He had her on the table in the cottage, her legs wrapped around him, the dirty soles of her otherwise snow-white feet placed upon his back. He was so distracted it was all he could do to keep his mind on his driving and he pulled over onto the hard shoulder and drove into one of the car parks that had been made for tourists to take photos of the Gap. But on this day at the end of November his van was the only vehicle parked there. He looked up at the valley, the grey sky, the pine forests wrapped around the slopes. And he placed his head against the steering wheel and came into a tissue and shuddered so hard that he felt the van shake. He rolled down the window and tossed the tissue out. It's been a while since that happened, he thought.

CHAPTER 10

Izzy expected Carl to come bounding out of the house as soon as she and Niall pulled up. She'd never had to knock on the door, had never even been inside the house. The noise of the car coming up the long gravel driveway was always enough to announce her arrival when she'd come to collect Niall. But she had asked Niall many questions about it – she couldn't help herself. He'd told her that there were five bedrooms and every one of them was en suite. There was a utility room upstairs and a utility room downstairs connected by a laundry chute. Izzy had thought that a very clever idea. Sheila Sullivan came every weekday to have food ready for Carl and Barry when they got home from school, which Izzy thought an even better idea. And Sheila cleaned the house as well. Izzy had a cleaner herself but she came only once a week and Izzy could have been doing with her more often.

'But what is Colette doing when Sheila's cooking Carl's tea?' Izzy had asked.

'Writing,' Niall had said, as though that was self-evident.

Colette Crowley had had full-time help so that she could sit about all day writing poems, and this Izzy could not get her head around at all. 'Writing?' she'd repeated.

She beeped the horn and they waited in silence. Niall had barely spoken a word to her since the night before when she'd announced in her most enthusiastic voice that she had a surprise for him – she'd be taking him and Carl to Waterworld the next day. She'd watched the colour drain from his face. He'd been full of questions then about whether she had actually spoken to Carl or just his father. He'd said that Carl wouldn't really want to go and his father would make him. He was furious with her. She should have asked him first, he'd said.

When she'd phoned Shaun at his office to arrange the meeting, she told him she'd been meaning to call for some time. The weeks had gotten away from her. She said that Niall was very sorry about the fight and that it was a shame how the boys had grown apart. She suggested they might broker some kind of peace between them. Shaun made little noises of assent that barely amounted to a handful of coherent words. It was as she'd expected – that she could count on Shaun to be unfailingly amenable.

And just as she was about to beep the horn again, the front door opened and Shaun ushered Carl forth with his hand on his back. Shaun was a very tall man and he had to stoop in the doorway to smile and wave at Izzy. She waved back but he was already withdrawing into the house, and that was his way whenever you met him – he was never quite looking at you. And she remembered then Shaun and Colette as a young couple – or at least Colette had seemed young, whereas stolid, serious Shaun had always seemed middle-aged – and him shepherding his fiancée around the town just a half step behind her, his hand ever on the small of her back. Such a handsome couple, and Colette, tall as she was, still had to tilt her head back to look up at him. But Shaun always had his eyes averted and his smile turned inward, like he was trying to conceal the extent of his happiness, like if anyone knew the fullness of his pride in her she might be taken away. And whatever misgivings Izzy had had about this glamorous blow-in arriving in a town where she knew no one, to marry a man ten years her senior, were banished when she saw the protectiveness Shaun showed her. And any problems Colette might encounter, she'd have enough money to do something about them. And money, Izzy had always believed, was a great comfort.

Carl hopped into the back of the car all bundled up in a black puffer jacket.

'Yes,' he said, burying his chin and mouth in the collar of his jacket.

'Yes,' Niall said.

The boys did not talk to each other much during the journey. Izzy tried to bridge the conversation between them. She asked Carl questions about school and he gave brief, polite answers.

'Are you going anywhere nice on holidays this year?' she asked. The Crowleys went on lots of holidays and usually had deep tans in the middle of winter when everyone else was bright red with the cold. But it was Colette who usually went away with the boys and Izzy was sorry she'd asked.

'No, not this year,' Carl said.

She tried to cover this up. 'You're a good swimmer, aren't you, Carl? I'm trying to get Niall to go for swimming lessons in Ballyshannon.'

'I can swim,' Niall moaned.

'I know you can, it's only to improve your technique.'

'I'm going to go,' Carl said.

'What day of the week is it?' Niall asked.

'Saturday,' Carl said. 'There's a bus going from the Diamond.'

When they got to the water park Carl took a £20 note from his pocket and offered it to her. It was typical, she thought, of someone as well-mannered as Shaun Crowley to have told Carl to do this even though he knew Izzy would never take money from him.

'Don't be silly, pet. You give that back to your father.'

She paid the entry for the boys at the front desk and pointed them in the direction of the changing rooms and then went up to the viewing deck with her book. The glass-fronted seating area looked over the swimming pools and slides that filled the enormous metal-framed building. The place was packed with wet little bodies sloshing about and ruddy teens climbing one on top of the other and dunking each other's heads under the water. She waited until she saw Carl and Niall emerge from the changing room in their red swimming caps and take a few tentative steps into the shallow end of the pool before she opened her book.

She pulled out the bookmark – it read, 'My other book is *War & Peace*'. Brian had left it inside the book when he'd lent it to her. She knew this was supposed to be funny but she found the books he pressed upon her challenging enough and hoped he didn't have plans to progress to Russian novels. This most recent one, *The Remains of the Day*, was very serious. Nobody in it seemed to have a sense of humour at all. In fact, the only funny thing about it was how the main character, a butler in a big old stately pile, was always going on about loyalty and dignity and duty when it was clear that all he really wanted was to marry the housekeeper. Or at least that's what was becoming apparent to Izzy, because at first he had seemed so passionless – and she tried to turn this thought over in her mind a few times so that she might remember it when Brian asked her what she thought of the book. Brian always asked her what she thought of the books he gave her. And often her feelings were the same – that she enjoyed the writing but if she had been asked to describe a single significant or dramatic event she would have struggled. And yet she couldn't put this one down and she had to keep reminding herself to look up every few pages to check on her son. On the hour a horn sounded and she watched everyone rushing to the same pool where the wave machine was starting to churn the water, and after a minute or two the boys were jounced together in the swell.

She closed the book. She tried to imagine explaining to Brian what she was about to engage in, and the silence she'd be met with, the blankness in his expression, carefully reserving judgement, waiting until she'd said what she needed to say before he'd make any comment whatsoever. Just speaking things in the light of his gaze had become her way of knowing how she truly felt. Even when she'd spouted that rubbish to him about Colette's brazenness, painting her as some kind of scarlet woman, she'd known then in her heart that this was not really what she thought of her. And she knew now there couldn't be anything wrong with a mother as kind and loving as Colette spending time with her child, and the righteousness Izzy felt about this unsettled her sometimes. Colette, for her part, would be in her car now, on her way, anticipating this meeting with every breath in her body. There was no question of that, no chance on earth that she would back out of this arrangement. And Izzy wanted to be equal to that determination.

At 3 p.m. she saw Niall look up at the clock and watched the two boys dutifully making their way to the changing rooms. By three thirty they were in the foyer of the Great Northern Hotel. She instructed the boys to order quickly from the children's menu and she ordered a sandwich and a pot of tea for herself. She stared around her at the busy foyer, at the disgruntled-looking golfers in rain gear crowding the reception desk, and she was thinking this venue a very poor choice now because people from her own club often played on the hotel course. But perhaps that was a good thing; this made it precisely the kind of place you would accidentally run into someone you knew.

She sank down in her seat, hoping the wingback armchair might provide some cover for her. She turned her attention to the boys, who were in good humour, a little listless from swimming but giddy in that tired way children could be, and she thought that if the only outcome for the day was that their friendship was renewed then that was enough. And as she thought this, her resolve vanished. She began to pray for Colette not to appear.

'Come on, Niall, eat that up,' she said, 'we need to get on the road.'

Izzy noticed that Carl had left some food on his plate and she thought about telling him to finish it, and then all of a sudden she was beside them, so tall, she felt her presence before she saw her. They all looked up at her at once. But Colette's focus was on Carl, who was turning the last of his food over in his mouth, this process slowing to a halt as his eyes widened to take in the full shape of his mother. His face froze, his lips parted slightly, flecks of burger flew out with his breath.

'Hello there,' Colette said.

Niall beamed up at her like he'd just been surprised by an old friend. Carl finally downed his food with a hard swallow.

'Hello there, Colette – how are you?' Izzy said, her enthusiasm ringing false in her ears.

But Colette just looked at her. Izzy watched her try to raise a smile and that smile buckle under the weight of the effort. Her eyes pleaded with her not to be forced to participate in this conceit. 'Can I?' she said, holding out her hand to Carl.

Carl looked at Izzy then, and when she nodded, he slid off the sofa and walked right past his mother.

'I'll have him back to you in an hour,' Colette said, and followed Carl.

Izzy watched them step into the revolving door at the hotel entrance, and disappear.

'Is she allowed to do that?' Niall asked.

'Of course she is, Niall, don't be stupid – she's his mother. And what's she doing except going for a walk with her son?'

'But does his dad know?'

'Niall, imagine if your father said that I wasn't allowed to see you.' But he was still staring at the revolving door, spinning empty. 'Niall, look at me.'

He turned his face slowly to her.

'You're fond of Colette, aren't you?' she asked.

He gave a solemn nod.

'And I know you like Carl and you want him to be able to spend time with his mother. So the best thing you can do is forget the whole thing. And please, dear God, don't mention a word of it to your father. He'll get all up on his high horse and the only thing that'll happen is Colette and Carl won't be able to see each other, not to mention the trouble it'll cause between me and him.'

She watched his smooth little brow knit with frustration.

'Look, no one is asking you to lie to anyone, Niall, it's just that sometimes saying nothing is the safest thing you can do.'

She picked up her cigarettes and withdrew one from the pack.

'What are we going to do now?' he asked. 'Is she going to drive Carl home?'

'She will not – we'll be driving Carl home. Now, do you want a dessert?'

'Yes,' Niall said, and with that his concerns seemed to vanish.

*

It had rained for most of the day and the grassy area where they queued for the bumper cars was sodden. The funfair was mostly closed out of season, but it sometimes opened for a few hours on the weekend, depending on the weather. None of the rides she and Carl really enjoyed – the rickety old roller coaster or the helter-skelter or the swinging boats – were open today. Even the matte-black floor of the bumper car arena was spotted with little pools from where the rain had dripped through the tarpaulin covering. A teenage boy in a baseball cap collected tickets and mopped the floor between rides.

Colette took a wodge of tissues out of her purse and wiped the water off the seat before she let Carl take his place behind the wheel. The little car was so small they were pressed right up against each other and it felt good to be close to him after so long. She couldn't stop stealing glances at him, trying to drink in every in-cremental change that had happened since she'd last seen him, and commit those to memory before they were parted again. Some of the smoothness in his face had been rubbed away to reveal harder edges, a solidity to his features that hadn't been there before. She wrapped her arm around him and held him tightly against her.

They were buffeted from every direction, and the harder they were rammed, the more Carl laughed and the more determined he became in pursuing the offending vehicle. They loved funfair rides; that was a thing they shared. Shaun would never go on them. Even when they went to Disney World, he'd stayed off all of the rides and she'd accompanied the boys on every single one.

When the bumper cars stopped, she paid the teenage boy to let them go around a second time.

There was a break in the weather. Light blue patches appeared in the sky. The setting sun glinted weakly from behind the low cloud moving in over the bay. Her time with her son was running short and she had maybe ten minutes before they'd be caught in another downpour. Carl was dragging her in the direction of the amusement arcade.

'Let's walk back to the hotel across the beach, pet,' she said, 'that way we can have a proper chat.'

They picked their way over an expanse of wet black rock, holding on to each other for balance. On the beach an icy wind raced sideways at them and they had to pull their hats down over their ears.

'Can you not drive me home?' Carl shouted.

'No pet, I'm afraid I can't. But maybe soon.' A glimmer of light squeaked through the cloud and she looked up. 'Isn't that beautiful? Look at that,' she said, and threw her arms out. 'There's every kind of weather in that sky,' she said. 'Look!' And she crouched down to his height and pointed out to sea. 'In that corner there's a storm brewing, and in that corner it's raining, and over there the sun is shining. And look at that water!' She was exultant. There was a great swell in the sea and the waves were rising up and barrelling down on the shore and each time it was like thunder roaring at them from across the sand.

But Carl was not to be distracted. 'Why can't you drive me home?'

'I don't think your daddy would like that,' she said.

'But if you drove me home, you could come in and talk to him.'

'Oh, Carl, love, I wish it was that easy.'

'But it is easy – you're all just making it hard.'

'Oh, you might be right about that, but I don't think your daddy is ready for things to be easy yet. But he will be someday soon and you and I will get to spend more time together. For now it might be best if you didn't tell your father that you saw me.' She placed her fingers beneath his chin and tilted his face upwards. Those grey eyes staring out at her from an abundance of dark lashes – she had to catch her breath. 'Now, don't get me wrong, Carl, you mustn't do anything that makes you feel uncomfortable or sad, and if you want to go home and tell him first thing then you go and do that. But that might make it difficult for us to see each other again like this.'

'But why aren't I allowed to see you?'

'Carl, your father loves you very much and he just wants your life to be as calm as possible and I suppose I haven't really helped a lot with that. And maybe he's cross with me – but he won't be cross forever. And in the meantime you have Sheila there in the afternoon and I know she spoils you rotten. And Barry is there.'

'Barry's an arsehole.'

She slowed her step. She tried to summon the energy to reprimand him. 'Why is Barry an arsehole?' she asked.

'He fights with me and breaks my stuff and kicks me off the sofa—'

'And have you told your father?'

'Yeah – but he's not there all day and there's nothing he can really do about it anyway because Barry doesn't listen to him. And he smashed a window out at the school.'

'What?'

'He smashed a window, in the science classroom, during break. He said it wasn't him but the school think it was. Because he'd accused the science teacher of bullying him.'

'And what did your father do?'

'He told Barry he wasn't allowed out for two weeks but Barry just heads off with his friends every afternoon and he doesn't listen to Sheila either.'

'Oh, Barry,' she said, and reminded herself to phone the school again. Master O'Connor had made her feel like a nuisance last time she'd called, like Barry's truancy was none of her business. 'But Sheila, does she stick up for you when Barry's acting the mick?'

'Yeah.'

'And Mrs Diver – is she good to you? Do you like her?' She had promised herself that she would not ask questions about Ann Diver.

'Yeah – she's all right. She buys me sweets and stuff. But sometimes . . .'

'Sometimes what, pet?'

'She's always telling me what to do. She tells me to stop watching so much TV and to brush my teeth and she makes me go to bed at half nine and you used to let me go at ten.'

'And does she stay over in the house much?'

'Not much – maybe once a week.'

Ann Diver, in *her* bed, beside *her* husband. Ann Diver, who was so nice and holy and good. She had Shaun going to mass again, which had been something he did only at Christmas and Easter. Did they even have sex or were they bound in some kind of chaste and sacred union? On the rare occasion when it happened, Shaun enjoyed sex, was connected to her and his own body during the act in a way you'd never have guessed from his usual awkward demeanour. Still, it was hard to imagine anyone getting enthused about having sex with Ann Diver.

The tide was coming in fast and they were being forced back off the sand and onto the shelf of stone that shored up the coastal wall.

'Carl,' she said, 'I suppose the real reason I wanted to speak to you was because I need you to know that when I went away that time, it was never my intention to be away from you for so long. I wanted you to come to Dublin and live with me, and—'

'That man?'

'Carl – that man is not a part of my life anymore and he is not going to be. That's all over.'

Carl had picked up a long stick. There was a pool of water in a dip in the rocks. He began to poke at a pile of ink-black seaweed, lifting it on the end of the stick and lowering it into the water.

'Carl – are you listening to me? I just want you to know that none of it is your fault.'

'You said that before, that time when you came home and left again.' He was pointing the stick at her. 'And Daddy says that too. So it must be *your* fault or else why am I not allowed to see you?'

'This is what I'm trying to say to you – mammies and daddies fight and go through problems and sometimes they are complicated and they can't be fixed that easily, but it doesn't mean that anyone's to blame.'

'But why can't you just come home and be in the house? It's where you live. You can't just be kicked out of your own house.'

It hurt to hear her son speak this injustice so plainly. 'Carl – I made the decision to leave. But I didn't make the decision to leave you. Just know that if it was up to me, I would be back home with you in a minute and that I spend every waking moment thinking about you. And remember – the only men in my life now are you and Barry and Ronan.'

'But not Daddy?'

'Carl,' she said, lowering herself onto one knee. She felt the fabric of her jeans grow damp against the rock. 'We don't have long left and I don't want to spend that time getting at you but I just wanted to say one more thing . . . The school told me that you've been fighting.'

His head bowed and he puffed out his cheeks and two perfectly round tears trembled on his lashes and spilled down his face.

'And what have we always said about anger?' she asked.

His mouth opened and closed a couple of times. He was trying to get the words out but his breath was catching on the sobs rising in his throat. 'That – it's – a . . .'

'That it's just another way of showing we're hurt, and I know you're hurt, pet. I know you're angry and you're hurt and you have every right to be but you mustn't take it out on the people around you,' she said. 'Do you know what I do when I'm angry? It's a new thing I've learned.'

He raised his head and looked at her.

'I go down to the beach and I scream. I roar at the top of my lungs. Will we try it?' And before he could answer she grabbed his wrists and threw back her head and strained her mouth open so wide it pained her cheeks and she let out a shout that came from the very depths of her stomach and drew every breath from her. She rocked a little, unsteadied, emptied by the effort of it. But she was laughing too, taken over by a breathless gaiety. And when she looked at Carl again, she could see the confusion in his eyes and he began to let out a moaning sound, low and fearful. She tried to catch the pitch of it, to match it with her screams, and Carl's cries grew louder, bolder, until the two of them were roaring with abandon and she had to grip his wrists tighter to hold their bodies in place. And the wind was such that it swallowed the noise, wrapped it up and carried it away, so all she felt was a dull ache in her ears, a low hum in her bones. Their shouts imploded into laughter and she held his body tight against her and closed her eyes. And when she opened them again, she saw two figures on the steps to the coastal wall so bundled up in coats and hats and scarves that it took her a few moments to recognise who it was standing there staring at them. She watched as Izzy slid her arm over Niall's shoulder and drew him against her.

CHAPTER 11

As Collete pulled up, the bottles gave one last triumphant rattle in the boot of the car. She sat there in darkness watching the place where she now lived – it looked so makeshift, so temporary. A sense of emptiness emanated from it, like it had been abandoned long ago and all that was left was the shell of a dwelling, its dead eyes gazing back at her. 'Fucking fool,' she said out loud.

She walked around to the boot, lifted out two plastic bags. The handles, stretched thin by the weight of the bottles, scored deep furrows in her fingers. She managed to unlock the door and set the bags down beside the counter, turning on the little light over the cooker. She pulled a bottle from one of the bags and drove a corkscrew into the neck, watching the foil splinter.

She should eat, she told herself, and then she should sleep. She was exhausted. She had barely slept the past few nights anticipating this meeting with her son. And she had not been prepared for the shock of Carl's anger. It was there in his eyes, leaping out at her. She had tried to soften it with explanations that sounded hollow even as she'd spoken them. This project of easing his pain had been nothing more than an attempt to comfort herself, and she'd failed at that. She felt none of the peace she'd imagined. She'd simply been desperate for him – that was it. She had wanted so desperately to see him that she had convinced herself of the rightness of the act. And now the emptiness she felt was so vast, she would do anything to fill it. She thought of Michael Breslin, the pounding of her heart as she'd answered the door, him stinking of drink, his great gut straining over his belt. Bashful, he was, retreating before she'd even dismissed him. But tonight she would not have sent him away. She would have taken him in and placed a drink in his hand and gladly spent the night fending off his advances if it meant that she didn't have to be alone.

She downed her wine, refilled the glass, and took a seat at the table. A notebook lay open in front of her with words written down the length of the page in pencil, like a shopping list. Titles, for poems she might one day write. She had begun to set lower and lower expectations for herself. Each morning she climbed back into bed with a mug of tea, sweet enough and strong enough to strip the hangover from her. By midday she was at the table, but it was so difficult to put down even a word that sometimes a single line could be enough for her to call it a day. Often, when her concentration failed her, she found herself walking to the kitchen window. She watched for any sign of the Mullens. She seldom saw Donal and Dolores together, but sometimes they headed off in the car with the kids. Dolores would sit in the passenger seat while Donal placed the children in the back and fastened their seat belts, circled the car closing the doors. He often kicked the tyres. The whole performance was so absurdly proprietorial, but what she saw was a man concerned with the safe conveyance of his family.

It was new to her, this feeling of being unsafe. In all the years she'd lain beside Shaun she'd never thought of the fact of his presence as any kind of protection. Then John had lain beside her. Now she imagined into that empty space the body of one of these men, and newly conjured was the figure of the man next door. But it was more than protection she was summoning. She had so little else to compare it with, but the sex with John she could have best described as serviceable, just another regret heaped upon the affair. Donal Mullen was a different prospect altogether, and she could not deny the pure fact of his attractiveness, how brutally uncomplicated he appeared. That first time he had shown up at the cottage, the deliberate ease with which he'd moved around the space – it was all she could do to occupy herself with that letter, the temptation to lay her eyes upon him was so strong.

He could either be a snow day, an escape from the routines and rituals that now comprised her life, or the cold shock that would wake her up. She was prepared to suffer either eventuality. And whenever she walked to the window and saw Donal emerging from the house, she counted *one, two, three* – and every time, he looked up at the cottage.

In the afternoons she walked the beach, and did her best to tamp down her fears over her dwindling finances, staving off the day when she would have to go to Shaun, cap in hand, and ask for more money. There were so few hours of daylight that it was dark by half four and however early darkness fell that always seemed like an acceptable time for a drink. She prepared herself a meagre supper and listened to the radio. She could just about manage to read a few pages of a novel. She could only read poetry that was new and unfamiliar to her. The collections that had offered her solace in the past could now undo her with a single line. She no longer needed Elizabeth Bishop to remind her that the art of losing is a skill so easily acquired. And then she meted out the medication she'd stolen from her mother, bit off half of one of the bitter blue tablets. She drank until her thoughts could no longer rise up against the tide of her exhaustion, and she was dragged down into sleep.

She closed the notebook and pushed it across the table. It knocked into the envelopes she'd leant against the vase. They fell forward, one sliding across the oilcloth, delivered to her. She turned her eyes away from it. The weak light above the cooker barely made it to the corners of the room, crept far enough only to give an impression of things, and for a moment she felt as though her entire known world was held within the scope of that light. She'd had so much, had been offered everything. Shaun had said, keep that apartment in Dublin, go there as much as you want. He hadn't even suggested she get rid of John. Keep your marriage, keep your family, keep your home. Everything. *You're not listening to me, you're not listening to me* – that was what she had said over and over, that night she had driven back to Donegal to tell Shaun she was leaving him and he had carefully responded with a diluted version of the future she proposed. It was like he had anticipated the conversation, had been preparing for her withdrawal from his life for some time. And she realised now how thoroughly she had been understood.

More than that – she had married a man who had offered her the financial means and freedom to conduct her life, her career, exactly as she wished, and who had looked on with humble adoration. How many women could say the same – they had been adored by their husband? For her part, when it came to leaving him, she'd told him she wanted nothing. She had been magnanimous – and wasn't that a cheap trick? No wonder he'd hardened against her so fully when the time came, no wonder he had turned to wholesome, simple Ann. And how like every other man he'd behaved, as soon as he believed something belonging to him was threatened – that was a great disappointment to her. She didn't know if she could forgive him for that.

When she'd phoned from Dublin and told him she wanted Carl to stay with her for the summer, he saw that it was her intention to have him come and live there. He'd stopped paying the rent on the apartment, and two days later a van driven by one of the men from the factory arrived from Donegal with forty-seven cardboard boxes containing everything she owned. Standing in that cramped apartment, towers of boxes surrounding her, she'd picked up the phone and called Shaun at his office.

'You never forgave me,' she'd said.

'You never forgave yourself,' he'd said.

Seventeen years since she'd gone to give her son Patrick his morning feed and found him cold and stiff in his cot. She had collapsed entirely, had needed her mother to move up from Dublin to help with Ronan, who was still only a toddler at the time. Shaun had returned to work a week after the funeral. She had wanted to die and was lit by rage that he seemed capable of living. She drank herself to sleep every night. And then she found out she was pregnant with Barry and she began to see a way to survive. It baffled her that at a time when she had no interest in living, she wanted to bring a child into the world, and yet it was the only thing that made sense to her. And over the years she had watched Shaun kiss and cuddle each of their sons, read them bedtime stories, had taken great pleasure in seeing whichever of the boys needed most help at the time, sitting at the dining room table, with Shaun offering instruction on their homework. Shaun did not frequent pubs, did not play golf like so many other men in the town. He enjoyed the company of his children. He was a busy man but what little time he had, he spent with them. Yet she'd continued to underestimate his love for their sons, and having lost one already, she'd thought he was just going to give Carl up because she'd asked him to.

She'd calculated everything so carefully. In many respects remaining in Dublin had made a great deal of sense. She'd spent her entire adult life in a cultural backwater where opportunities to advance her career were limited. She could get more teaching work if she stayed in Dublin. If she returned to Donegal, very soon she'd find herself alone in that house with Shaun, and with little practical purpose as a mother. Ronan was already at Trinity, Barry already at boarding school in Dublin, and in a year's time Carl would be joining him. But when she'd told John that Shaun had stopped paying the rent, that they'd need to find a bigger place so that Carl could come and stay with them, he was all talk then of his responsibilities to his wife and his daughter and his unpaid mortgage.

'Fucking fool,' she said again, to test her voice, to hear its sound. The cottage was the place where she had started to converse with herself aloud. She had said things before of course, sung songs and cursed when she stubbed her toe. But in this house she had begun to say fully formed sentences out loud. It felt like tempting fate. *That is the kind of thing a mad person would do* was one of the things she said sometimes. Once she had spoken this, she felt like she had breached some boundary, and she began to say things when she was out walking on the beach, testing how close she could get to another body before she would make herself stop. And what would be the end of that?

She poured another glass of wine and wandered into the bedroom and stood before the full-length mirror. However thin her life had felt wandering around that flat in Dublin and during those cruel months she'd spent living with her mother, now it felt like it had no substance to it at all. She raised the wineglass and clinked it against the mirror. 'Cheers,' she said.

There was the noise of an engine and she walked to the window and looked down just as Donal's van pulled up and the sensor light went on above his front door. He stepped out of the van and she counted aloud – *one, two, three*. He looked up at her and at once lowered his eyes, just like the other day when he'd dropped off a letter, making a point of telling her that Dolores and the kids were going away for the weekend. They were down in Roscommon seeing her sister, he'd said, all the while staring down at the doormat and trying to straighten it with his foot.

Colette ran out the front door and over to the wall. The wind whipped her hair across her face, the rain spat at her.

'Donal!' she shouted down to him just as he was stepping through the front door. Her words were carried away on the wind, reduced to nothing. She shouted again and he turned and looked up at her, crowned in a halo of light from the porch. 'Would you mind coming up to me for a second?' she asked.

'What?' he shouted back at her.

'There's a problem,' she shouted.

He shuffled in the doorway a bit, wiped his feet on the mat. 'Aye – just give me one minute and I'll be up to you then,' he shouted.

She ran back inside and shut the door behind her. 'Fuck, fuck, fuck,' she said. She sat down at the table and downed the glass of wine. She got up, took off her shoes. She crossed the cold stone floor and went into the bedroom and turned the lamp on beside the bed, turned off the main light. Standing before the mirror she smoothed her hand over the ends of her hair a few times so it fell evenly around her shoulders.

There was a knock on the door and she felt the noise of it sift down through her. She answered it and looked at him but she did not move and for a moment he just stared at her.

'Is something wrong?' he asked.

'No,' she said and moved aside to let him pass. 'Everything's fine, Donal, but the heaters, I'm having terrible problems with the heaters.'

'Are they still not coming up to temperature?' he asked, walking to the window.

'That's right,' she said, and sat back down at the table.

He was wearing a big black padded jacket not dissimilar to the one Carl wore. It rose up on his back as he crouched down to check the pipe so she saw a crescent of white flesh exposed. Dark hairs sprouted at the base of his spine.

'Well, there's good heat coming out of that one now?' he said. He looked up at her with curiosity and she nodded. He rose and moved closer to her at the table. 'You should put a few decorations up in here, make the place look a bit more festive.'

She looked up at his face to see if this was meant as some kind of joke, but it was impossible to read anything from the expression he wore.

'What do you be listening to?' he asked.

'What?'

'When you're dancing. What do you be listening to?'

'You've seen me dancing?' She gave a little laugh.

'You know I have.'

'Do you really care what music I play?'

She watched him narrow his eyes at her then – it was a change so slight and sudden but there was frustration in it, and it gave her pleasure to unsettle him just a little.

'I don't think that's what you came up here for, Donal – to talk about my record collection.'

'I came up here because you asked me.'

'I did, yes.'

She looked down at the table. 'Will you have a drink?' she said and rose suddenly just as he took a half step towards her. His face was inches from hers but she would not look at him. She stared down at her bare feet, toe-to-toe with his black work boots, blotted with mud. And she could smell the night upon him, the cold air that clung to him. There was a smell of cigarettes on his breath, which was strange because she had never seen him smoke, and just beneath that was the low hum of alcohol. She looked him dead in the eye and before she turned away an agreement was made. She walked into the bedroom and stopped beside the bed. His footsteps behind her were so soft and she began to count their slow progress across the floor – *one, two, three* – until he was close enough to her again to feel the chill that rose off his body. His fingertips grazed her skin as he pushed aside her hair. The cold air kissed the back of her neck.

CHAPTER 12

Izzy heard the front door open and turned down the heat under the pots and pans that crowded the cooker. The little television on the worktop was showing the news, and it was all about the newly formed government. Ministers who'd lost their jobs kept their head down as they exited government buildings, and the new ministers waved and smiled to the cameras as they walked through the gates. But the change in power hadn't led to a ministerial position for James. He had seemed the natural choice for Minister of the Marine. He'd phoned from Dublin the day before to deliver the news and he'd tried to disguise his disappointment with weak dismissals. The man he'd been passed over for – his family had been involved in Irish politics for generations. 'He was handed that job by his father,' James said, the only hint he gave of his bitterness. But she was disappointed for him, knew how much he had wanted this, and how it would only serve his belief that the country was run by better men – better educated, better connected – than himself.

Izzy turned down the volume on the television.

'Hello, Daddy,' she heard Niall calling from the living room.

'Come in here, Niall,' she shouted. 'Your tea's ready.'

James was standing in the doorway wearing that padded anorak she hated – the way he wore it over his suit, like a teenager going for his first job interview.

'Hello, love,' she said and brandished a smile at him. He looked lost, she thought, like he'd wandered into the wrong house. She poured him a measure of whiskey and handed him the glass.

'Hello,' he said and walked straight to the end of the table, where he hung his anorak on the back of the chair.

Under the stairs, she thought, *under the stairs*. They had the same conversation every evening about him hanging his anorak under the stairs. But she would not engage with any of that now. She took the plates from the oven and served up the food. She carried James's dinner to him just as he pulled some letters and his diary and keys from the pocket of his anorak and piled them on the table. *Say nothing*, she said to herself, *say nothing*.

'Now,' she said, placing his dinner before him. She'd prepared lamb chops, carrots, and parsnips – his favourite.

The phone rang and she heard Niall bounding into the hallway. She put the pot of creamed potatoes at the centre of the table and James leaned forward, his nostrils flaring.

'Colette's on the phone,' Niall called.

She wiped her hands on her apron. 'Tell her we're just sitting down to the dinner and I'll give her a ring back later.'

It was the third time Colette had called that day. They had a trip planned. The next day they were driving into the North, to Enniskillen, to do some Christmas shopping. Izzy was bringing Niall and Carl and they would meet Colette. There were other towns that were closer, but on a Saturday just before Christmas they were likely to meet half of Ardglas out shopping and so Colette had convinced her to drive a little farther afield.

Colette had phoned several times a day since the trip to Bundoran. If James asked, Izzy told him it was her other most frequent caller, her friend Margaret Brennan. Sometimes Colette would use the pretence of discussing the workshop – she would ask Izzy if she thought the exercise she'd set had been effective, if the class had responded well to it. But always she would move the conversation on to her gratitude to Izzy for helping her, and the loneliness she was feeling as Christmas approached. When Colette suggested the shopping trip, she said that it might be the only opportunity she'd get to see Carl over the Christmas period, and Izzy had agreed to it with the addendum she placed on every discussion of the subject – that these meetings were not a solution to anything and they'd have to stop.

'Turn off that television, Niall,' she said as he walked through the kitchen door.

'Leave it on,' James said. 'It's good to know what's going on in the world.'

She saw that the news had moved on and now they were showing a report on the ceasefire in the North. She blessed herself. Two months old and so far it seemed to be holding. But there was no end of talks between political parties and factions and paramilitary groups, and none of them ever seemed to be happy with the outcome.

'Jesus,' James said, 'you never know when it's going to all kick off again.'

'Oh now, we have to be grateful for every bit of good news we get.'

'They'll never be satisfied – shower of bastards.'

Izzy watched Niall struggle to dislodge the ketchup in the bottle, then with one violent shake of his arm half the contents slid out onto his lamb chops.

'Look at that waste, you could put most of that back in the bottle,' she said.

'It was an accident,' Niall said, and already she could see tears in his eyes.

'What does Colette want?' James asked.

'Sure, I don't know, I didn't speak to her.'

'She phoned the other night too, when you were at bridge.'

'You never told me.'

'Ah well, she said she'd phone back.'

'And she has done, several times. She usually phones me up to ask something about the creative writing class and then keeps me on the phone for hours. But it's only an excuse. It's sad really. She's lonely.'

Niall was looking at her and she tried not to catch his eye. He had scraped up every morsel on his plate but had not run off to watch television like he did every other evening.

'You may be excused, Niall,' she said.

He stood up and began to walk slowly towards the door.

'Niall,' James said. He took a £20 sterling note from his wallet and handed it to him. 'That's for Enniskillen tomorrow.'

'Thanks, Daddy,' Niall said, slipping the money into his pocket.

'Now don't lose it,' Izzy said.

'I won't.'

'Do you want to give it to me to look after?' she asked, but he was already running out of the room.

She glanced at James, who still had one eye on the television. There was a story on the Russian soldiers moving into Chechnya. Men in winter camouflage, guns propped on shoulders, marched in perfect unison through driving snow. It was a beautiful sight really, or beautiful and terrifying at the same time, and she thought she might include this image in some way in her writing. Her poems so far had so much to do with her own life and she was getting bored of herself.

'It'd break your heart, the whole thing,' she said.

'Oh sure, the world's in a terrible state.'

'I'm not on about the news,' she said. 'I'm on about Colette.'

James lifted another pile of creamed potato from the pot, the spoon giving a loud clack as he brought it down on his plate. 'Oh, you'd want to be careful there,' he said.

'How do you mean?'

'I'd just steer well clear of that whole situation.'

'Well, what am I supposed to do if she's ringing up the house every day pouring her heart out to me? I can hardly hang up on her.'

'No, but you wouldn't want to get too involved in another family's business like that.'

She was silent for a time. 'And all the things you get involved with that have nothing to do with you.'

'That's my job.'

'And you don't know the half of it. Shaun won't let her see the kids.'

'Sure, I know that. Everyone knows that.'

'But no one says anything. Did you know that she hasn't seen Carl in six months? And did you know that he's cut her off?'

'What do you mean?'

'What else would I mean? Financially. The woman hasn't a

penny – it's a disgrace. Why else do you think she's living up in that cottage – for the good of her health?'

'I still think that you're better off staying out of it – leave the pair of them to sort it out between them.'

She laid down her knife and fork. 'You could help,' she said.

'How in the name of God could I help?'

'You could have a word with Shaun. You could say something like . . . like you think the reason Carl and Niall were fighting was because Carl misses Colette, and wouldn't it be better for Colette to see a little bit of Carl. It could be very casual – you could make it brief, just next time you bump into him. Do it man to man. He might listen to you.'

James held a forkful of food, suspended in midair, just a few inches from his gaping mouth. 'Casual?' he said. 'Casual? What would be casual about me bumping into Shaun Crowley and telling him how to conduct his marriage? And where exactly do you imagine this meeting would take place – would I casually arrive at his office or would I casually corner him on the main street? Shaun and I aren't friends. That man doesn't have friends.'

'I don't see anyone queuing up to be friends with you either. Anyway, you know each other professionally, your children are friends.'

'Casual?' he repeated, shaking his head. 'That's a good one.'

'Oh well, don't bother, I'll ask Father Brian. That's more his area than yours. Isn't that what he does for us anyway – marriage counselling?'

'Sure, isn't he already trying to rehabilitate her, letting her read at mass? Let him get on with it.'

'You're just worried about upsetting Shaun Crowley.'

'I would be worried about interfering in any man's business.'

'Bullshit. If he didn't own most of the town you wouldn't be long telling him his business.'

'Look,' he said, 'there's a lot of gossip going around and I'd like if we didn't become part of it.'

She gave a loud tut. 'Oh, some hope of that. It doesn't matter what you do, people'll still be talking about you.'

'Are you that bored? Have you so little to do that you need to go sticking your nose into their marriage?'

'Oh, would you listen to you – this is coming from the man who couldn't stomach the idea of me managing that property on the main street, and now you're worried I have too much time on my hands?'

'Well, next time you come up with a hobby can you think of one that won't cost us twenty thousand pounds? I'd stick with the painting and the yoga.'

'I bet Shaun Crowley doesn't leave his money lying around in the bank doing nothing.'

James threw down his knife and fork and they clattered against the plate. 'Is this what you want? Do you want a fight before Christmas? Do you want us to fall out over Shaun and Colette Crowley like we haven't enough fucking problems of our own?'

She folded her arms and looked at the back of his chair. 'No wonder they wouldn't let you be a minister,' she said, 'going around in an anorak like that.'

He placed his hands flat on the surface of the table with a loud clap and pushed himself up out of his seat. She followed the blank shape of his back as he walked towards the hallway. He would take himself off to the good sitting room and she wouldn't see him again for the rest of the evening. She collected the plates and as she turned to the counter she saw, through the open door of the living room, Niall lying flat on his stomach, his feet kicked up in the air, swinging them back and forth. He always lay right in front of the television no matter how many times she told him to sit farther away. And she thought then of the trip to Bundoran, of how they'd stood watching Carl and Colette screaming at the sky, and she'd sworn to herself she'd never place him in that situation again.

She put the plates down and walked to the phone in the hallway. She'd tell Colette that she would be unable to help her tomorrow, or at any time in the future. She would not make excuses, or be mealy-mouthed; she'd simply put these facts to her and hang up the phone. She took her little phone book from the drawer and found Colette's number, and when she looked up, she could see James through the glass doors of the sitting room, holding the newspaper wide so that the entire upper half of his body was masked by it. Each time he turned the page he threw out the spine with a great snap, like the entire world was an affront to him. She placed the phone book back in the drawer.

CHAPTER 13

Ann Diver picked up the red jumper for the fourth time. She held it out in front of her by the shoulders like she was about to dance with it. Another woman came along and grabbed one of the jumpers and did exactly the same thing, and Ann thought she'd best hang on to this one or there'd be none left. The shop was jammed. She checked there were no loose threads or holes under the arms. If she was going to spend good money on it, she wanted it to be right. She turned over the little cardboard price tag. She'd quickly given up trying to calculate the difference between the punt and the pound. There was nothing in it. You maybe got one extra penny for every punt you spent but anyway, that wasn't the reason she'd gone to the North to do her Christmas shopping. She wanted to get something special for Ronan and Carl and Barry. There were brands you could get in the North that you couldn't get at home, and they were that spoiled it would take the extra effort.

'Do you need any help there?'

She turned around and swung the jumper into the face of a shop assistant. 'Jesus, I'm sorry.'

The girl smiled at her.

'Oh, I'm having trouble making up my mind,' Ann said.

The girl's neck was streaked with fake tan. She was pretty though, with bright eyes and a gleaming smile of perfectly even teeth. But too much make-up, Ann thought, and her eyes and mouth out-lined in dark pencil. 'BRONAGH', her name badge said.

'Is it the size you're having trouble with?' the girl asked in her strong Northern accent.

'Oh, it's the whole lot if I'm being honest. Would this be suit-able for a fella of twenty?' Ann asked, guessing the girl could be no more than sixteen or seventeen herself.

'It'd be perfect – sure, I bought one for my brother, it'd go with anything. How tall is he?'

'He's around six foot.'

'And is he . . .' The girl puffed out her chest and cheeks and lifted her arms from her sides.

'He's broad on the shoulders but there's not a pick on him.'

'God, he sounds lovely,' the girl said, 'send him in to me. Is he blonde or brunette?'

'Oh, he's tall, dark, and handsome.'

'That'll do me grand,' the girl said. 'Take the large and if there's any bother keep the receipt and he can just exchange it.'

Ann sighed and looked at the price tag again.

'It's lovely and Christmassy too, the red,' the girl said.

In the atrium of the shopping centre was a fountain surrounded by plastic palm trees. Small children tossed coins into the water. Above the fountain hung a sign listing all the shops and what floor they were on. Ann craned her head back and read through the list to see if there was a shop that might sell wrapping paper. She thought it mean of that boutique to charge her £40 for a jumper and not offer to wrap it. A lot of shops were offering that now, the free gift wrap. She'd spotted some paper behind the counter, but she'd been too shy to ask and there was a queue building up behind her and so she'd taken it from them wrapped in a bit of tissue paper and placed in a stiff cardboard carrier with string handles, the logo of the shop, 'Taylor's', emblazoned on the side. Still, the smart bag would look good under the Christmas tree and all she'd have to do was buy a bit of paper. But she couldn't see a shop on the list that might sell gift wrap. She stared up at the three floors of shops that surrounded her.

Ann took a piece of notepaper from her handbag and unfolded it – eleven names. They were mostly nieces and nephews, a few of her friends who worked at the hotel, and now Shaun and his kids had been added to the list. Next to Carl she'd written 'sketchpad and pencils'. Next to Barry, she'd written 'aftershave'. Barry was the most difficult and surly of teenagers but he was certainly easy to buy for. He'd just started going to the disco in Glenties on a Friday, and whenever he left the house, the sweet, overpowering stench of cheap deodorant drifted off him. And then she spotted Shaun's name at the top of the list with nothing written beside it.

When she'd spoken to him on the phone that morning, he'd told her he would invite Colette to the house for Christmas Day. She could come in the morning for a couple of hours, open the presents with the boys. By the time Ann came around three o'clock, Colette would be gone. He was doing it for Carl, he said. In the past couple of weeks, he had started playing up, crying at bedtime and agitating for a meeting with his mother. He had asked Shaun,

'If you knew Mammy wasn't living with that man in Dublin anymore would you let her come home?' But of course Shaun already knew Colette and that man were no longer an item, it was the first thing she'd told him when she came back to the town. But it had gotten Shaun thinking. Carl's questions were getting right to the heart of the matter, and Ann could tell Shaun was finding it more difficult to blame Colette when she'd told him herself that she'd made a terrible mistake.

He'd said he was sorry and he hoped this didn't cause her any upset, but she told him that he had to do what he thought was right and it could only be a good thing to allow the boys to see their mother. She'd disagreed with his insistence on keeping Colette away from Carl, but didn't feel it was her place to say anything. Whatever he decided, she would fall in with his plans, she said. And to her pat responses, he'd said, 'I love you.' It was the first time he'd said it. His tone was flat, with no pageantry to it, the way he might have made any plain statement of fact. Yet she couldn't bring herself to believe it, angry that he had chosen this moment. All she'd offered by way of response was a lie. She'd told him that she was driving down to Mayo for the day to visit her aunt.

She loved him, she was certain of that. She would not spoil all of this with her need and jealousy and anger. She had too much to be grateful for. For the past twenty-five years her Christmases had been spent at the table of some relative or friend and now she had someone who cared for her, who was as good a man as she could hope to find, and she was going to spend the day with him or part of it at least. But she had spent so much of her life at the behest of other people that she knew how quickly things could change. His next call might be to tell her that he and Colette had reconciled. And then all the presents that she'd bought would stay huddled in the hall cupboard in her little house as a reminder of her foolishness.

Ann looked at the list again, then stuffed it back in her handbag. She would focus on the boys. Shaun would be happy with whatever she bought, but the right present could improve her standing with his children, who for the moment suffered her presence with a poorly concealed impatience. Carl was a talented artist. She saw the pictures he brought home from school. He had a real facility for drawing and yet he spent all his time playing computer games, and nobody commented on this. She checked the sign again and saw that there was an art shop on the second level, and she made her way to the bank of escalators that zigzagged between the floors.

Ann lifted her leg and withdrew it a few times before she felt confident enough to place her foot firmly on the escalator. She had difficulties with escalators, getting on them and getting off them – they gave her a kind of vertigo and she always felt like she was going to go toppling forwards or backwards. She held on firmly to the rubber banister, and as someone passed her on her left-hand side, she clutched the strap of her handbag. She wore the strap across her body. Claire from the hotel had been to Dublin and was minding her own business walking down O'Connell Street when some young fella grabbed the bag off her and tore a few ligaments in her shoulder while he was at it.

As she stepped off at the top of the escalator an announcement came over the loudspeaker and she felt her heart seize up for a moment. She swayed in place. *'Could Hilary Carlisle please come to the main desk in the atrium, where her son is waiting for her.'* And then it was like everything steadied all at once and her mind was alert to each sound and movement happening around her. The danger had not arrived. Every time the loudspeaker went she was anticipating a bomb scare. You saw it on the news all the time – droves of people being ushered out of churches and cinemas and shopping centres. And not just scares, real bomb attacks that killed and maimed dozens of people. There was a ceasefire at the moment but usually if you listened to the radio or turned on the television at all you'd think the roads in Northern Ireland were ripped to shreds by bombs. All she could see when she looked around her were people going about their business, laden down with shopping bags. There were a lot more people than she was used to, and there might be a civil war of sorts going on but everyone seemed to be well off. And she supposed that fear was a thing you got used to in the same way as anything else. Like grief or anger or shame – you either moved past it or you lived with it for so long that you didn't know the difference anymore.

Was that what had happened to Colette? Ann had known Colette for years. You couldn't miss a woman like Colette in a town like Ardglas. Colette of the black hair. Colette of the blue eyes. Colette of the long bones – always to be seen in an outfit that seemed intended to make her look as dowdy as possible. But you couldn't mask a beauty like Colette's. So handsome, and she always seemed to be in good humour. She had a smile for every person she met and asked questions and was interested in people. Some people carried their grief with them – and that was not Colette. Some you could tell how much they'd suffered just by looking at them. Ann did not doubt that she must feel the pain of what had happened to her. Sometimes when Ann had run out of things to pray for, when she had worked through her own list of grievances, she would pray for other people. She would pray for her niece who had had four miscarriages and who sometimes took to her bed for days at a stretch. She would pray for Ellen Lafferty, whose son had made his bed the night before his final exams and hanged himself from the tree in the back garden. Now Ellen was hardly fit to move, she was so bowed by grief. Then there were the three Callaghan children, whose parents were killed in a car accident when they were teenagers and who'd practically had to raise themselves. But not once in her life had it occurred to her to pray for Colette Crowley. She'd never entered her mind. And now Colette was all she thought about.

She'd been in the bookshop in Donegal Town a couple of weeks ago, stocking up on Christmas cards, when in the corner of her eye she saw a sign for 'local authors'. One of Colette's books was face-out on the shelf. She checked to make sure no one was looking and took the book down. She admired the faded black-and-white photo of Colette on the back. It was like looking at her through parchment paper. There was one poem called 'Cycle' that was clearly about menstruation. There were a number of poems about how the responsibility of raising children had thwarted her creative ambition, which Ann thought a bit rich. Shaun said they'd always had a childminder and a cleaner. In a second volume that had been published over ten years earlier there was a poem about a beautiful young hero who drowned himself because he mistakenly thought the woman he loved had forsaken him. It was written like one of the old Irish legends, with all of nature being called upon to convey the sorrow and heartbreak of the woman. Ann thought it a right old dirge.

Shaun had removed Colette's belongings from the house so there was little there to remind her. Still, Colette's choices were everywhere and so some idea of her hung around. The china in the cupboards, the linens on the bed, the tiles in the bathroom, were all of such a particular and peculiar taste they could only have been the choice of one person. Shaun rarely mentioned Colette, but one night when they were lying in bed, Ann had felt brave enough to ask him what their marriage had been like. He told her it had ended the day their son died. Cot death, he'd said, and even though she'd known that already it had sent a chill through her to hear him say it. Colette went into shock, refused to accept what had happened. She took to her bed. She could hardly feed herself for the first few weeks. There were days, he'd said, when he honestly thought she was going to die too, that she'd never get past it. Nobody was allowed near the house and if they showed up she ran them from the door. And he didn't know what to do for her. She began to drink heavily but when she discovered she was pregnant with Barry she stopped. And when they did begin to emerge from it, they could barely look each other in the eye, they were that ashamed of how they'd behaved, of their complete failure to provide each other with even a morsel of comfort when they'd most needed it. Since then, they'd shared a home and a bed, raised their sons together, but they were like guests, politely inhabiting each other's lives.

And then he spoke of how strange and new it felt to exist in the world without Colette. For twenty years, wherever they went, the fact of Colette's presence drew attention to them. And then she was gone, and he was invisible. And because of his proximity to her for so long he had never really considered what this had been like for Colette. Was it any wonder she expected life to just make way for her, to adjust to her shape? He had lived like the custodian of a prize, he said, and it felt good to be free of this responsibility, to be nothing other than himself for once.

After Shaun told her all of this, she spoke about her husband, Robert, and how he'd liked to swing his fists – how he only ever hit her on her body so that no one saw the marks. And then he went out on the boat he fished on one Sunday night and never came back. The Guards arrived at the door to tell her that he'd gone overboard in bad weather off Tory Island. The search and rescue operations they conducted back then weren't up to much, and because the body was never recovered she couldn't even have a proper funeral for him. The council provided her with a small house but even the upkeep on that cost money and she had to feed and clothe herself and make a life. She managed to stay out of trouble, to never complain, to appear happy but not too happy, and to hold on to some kind of respectability. This was her currency. People felt sorry for her. She could see it in their faces. But the truth was she was glad to be free of her husband and she did not miss him. She'd felt ashamed about telling this to Shaun.

Ann stepped onto the next escalator and held her breath. She began to count as she glided upwards towards the glass ceiling of the shopping centre and everything around her became bathed in a new light. She caught sight of herself in a shop window – just a brief glimpse of a middle-aged woman in a bright yellow ski jacket. She'd had her highlights done the previous week and the colour had settled a bit and she was happy with them. She was slim, she always had been, and running around the restaurant all day had helped her to maintain her figure. She'd been the recipient of many a leer down through the years from male customers who knew of her extended widowhood and thought she was game. But Shaun Crowley was known as a quiet, even-tempered man and she'd been surprised by the matter-of-fact and straightforward way he went about the whole thing. Not a bit shy. It was like he asked women out all the time.

Eight, nine, ten – the second floor of the shopping centre was quieter and the shops were of a different sort, smaller units selling fabrics and picture frames and stationery. She felt the tension in her body easing as she approached the art shop and then she heard the clinking of cutlery and crockery. The café on the top floor looked so warm and inviting under the glass roof and the blue sky and she thought a cup of tea would fortify her before she carried on with the rest of her shopping. There was just one more escalator and she stepped onto it with purpose.

The girls behind the counter wore little white trilbies with a black band and green-and-white striped aprons. They looked like they worked in a butcher's, she thought. They were all pink in the face from the steam rising up out of the enormous bains-marie. She collected a tray and queued and ordered a small pot of tea and a donut. The place was nearly full but there was an empty two-top at the back. She sat facing away from the counter first but then she was looking directly at the escalator and getting eyeballed by every person it delivered to the top. So she switched seats but then she was looking around her at the busy café. She felt self-conscious sitting there on her own. She reached into her handbag for the crossword cut from a copy of *The Irish Times* she'd found in the hotel. She never bought *The Irish Times*, *The Independent* maybe, but Shaun bought it every day and they did the crossword together in the evening. She loved doing puzzles but *The Irish Times* crossword was a bit more challenging than what she was used to and she thought she'd need a bit of practice. There were a few answers filled in already but she was having difficulty with eight down, eight letters, 'Euphemism for hardships'. She took a sip from her tea and looked up and there was Izzy Keaveney standing in the queue with the boys. Carl had his back to her but she knew it was him from the little black puffer jacket he wore. Shaun had told her that Izzy was taking the boys away shopping but he had said nothing about them going to Enniskillen. But that was not the kind of thing Shaun would think to ask. And then Carl turned and smiled and she almost didn't recognise him because Carl never smiled. Clever Carl, the fairest of them all. Carl, the love of his father's life. And he was smiling *at* someone – a tall woman approaching them with a Taylor's carrier bag swinging from the end of her finger.

Her cup clattered down onto the saucer and tea spilled over the table. The crossword soaked into the beige Formica surface, the blue letters dissolving into inky blotches. She kept her head down. The tea spread slowly, pooling at the raised metal edge that skirted the table. She looked up from under her brow. There was a plastic fern on the ledge in front of her, a poor camouflage. The down escalator was on the opposite side of the café so she'd have to walk past them to get to it, or wait until they'd left. But she'd managed to avoid Colette for the three months since she'd been back in the town and she was not going to allow this to be their first encounter. She could hide in the toilets, she thought, and she looked over her shoulder and beside the door to the ladies was an elevator. Elevators made her claustrophobic but she decided she might have no other choice. She looked over at them again and saw that Colette and Carl had gone ahead to find seats. An elderly couple getting up to leave offered their table to Colette and she thanked them and sat down opposite Carl, smiling at him. Ann saw that Colette was so absorbed in her son she could have stomped past them shouting at the top of her voice and Colette wouldn't have looked up for a second. And then Colette reached into the Taylor's bag and with a flourish ripped something out of it. She was like a matador, dangling a piece of red material in front of Carl's face. A jumper – the exact same one Ann had bought Ronan. Ann lifted her handbag and brought the strap down over her body. She edged out of the seat slowly and kept her gaze lowered and headed in the direction of the elevator. As the doors closed, she shut her eyes and counted to ten. It was only when she opened them again on the ground floor that she realised she'd left Ronan's present under the table in the café.

CHAPTER 14

Colette laid the piece of gift wrap flat on the kitchen table and stood the bottle of whiskey at its centre. She had no idea what to do. Should she lift the paper up and smother the bottle in it and fasten a ribbon at the top like she was wrapping a hamper? She took a sip from her wine and stepped back and surveyed the table once again. She approached, placed the bottle on its side, rolled it up. She twisted the excess paper and put a ribbon at each end and what she was left with was a kind of demented-looking Christmas cracker. There was something about this that pleased her. Shaun wouldn't care about the wrapping anyway.

Shaun had been the hardest person to buy for. Whatever she brought had to be a carefully selected peace offering. Anything too extravagant or too sentimental could upset the balance in the relationship she hoped to re-establish. Shaun liked a single measure of a rare and expensive whiskey while he watched the nine o'clock news. As a gesture it was ordinary enough to be dismissed as meaningless and intimate enough to suggest something.

She refilled her wineglass and checked her watch. It was a quarter to two and she would stop drinking by four. She had some pasta that she could reheat in the microwave for dinner and she would drink plenty of water. She would be well-slept and clearheaded when she went to visit her sons the next morning. It was the excitement of seeing them really that had made her want a glass of wine, the festive feeling that had come over her while wrapping their presents.

There was a knock on the door.

'Who is it?' she asked, and she heard a small, high-pitched voice give a response she couldn't make out. 'Give me a second,' she said and went to the bathroom mirror. She ran her tongue over her front teeth and scratched off the dark dregs that were stuck to her lips. She placed her wineglass in the kitchen sink and opened the door to find Madeleine Mullen chewing on her thumbnail and leaning on one hip and mouthing something Colette had to get her to repeat several times. Finally she pulled her thumb away from her teeth and with some aggression said, 'Mammy says there's a phone call for you down at the house.'

'Oh God, Madeleine, I'm still in my dressing gown, could they not leave a message?'

'No, she said it's urgent.'

Shaun or her mother, she thought, they were the only two people who ever called her here. Her heart began to pound.

'Right, I'll be there in one moment,' she said, but Madeleine was already walking away.

Colette ran into her bedroom and grabbed a pair of old jeans that was thrown across the end of the bedframe. She pulled them on under her dressing gown and threw a jumper on over that and knew she must look quite mad with the dressing gown flapping around her like a torn skirt and the cord hanging from her waist. There was a pair of plimsolls by the door that she put on without any socks, and as soon as she passed through the gap in the wall and began descending the hill, she felt the shoes and the ends of the jeans dampening. When she reached the bottom of the hill Dolores was standing at the front door staring at her.

'Oh, Dolores!' She laughed. She pulled the ends of her hair out from under the neck of her jumper and tossed her head. 'You'll have to forgive me – Madeleine caught me in my déshabillé,' she said in an exaggerated way, repeating the phrase her mother used when she opened the door to some unexpected visitor.

Dolores stood there blinking at her.

'Is something wrong?' Colette asked.

'Your husband's on the phone,' she said, and disappeared into the house.

Colette stepped into the hall and picked up the receiver. 'Hello, Shaun?'

'Don't come to the house tomorrow,' he said.

She looked down at the black and white tiles of the hallway and they seemed to swim away from her, to melt into a grey blur.

'What are you talking about, Shaun?' She tried to laugh but it came out breathless with desperation. She wrapped the cord of the telephone around her finger. 'Has something happened?'

'I think . . . given the circumstances . . . it would not be appropriate for you to come to the house tomorrow.'

Colette looked around her and saw Dolores standing in the living room doorway with her back to her, bouncing the baby on her hip. Every doorframe in the hallway and every picture frame she could see was fringed in gold tinsel, including the wedding photo of Donal and Dolores that hung above the hallstand. Colette turned to the wall. She gripped the receiver with both hands and pressed it close to her mouth. 'Jesus Christ, Shaun, please have the decency to tell me what's going on,' she whispered.

'I didn't think it possible . . . I didn't think . . . of all the things you've done, to ask our son to lie to me . . .'

Cartoon gunfire rang out from the television in the living room.

'Shaun, please, just let me bring the presents out to the house in the morning, we can talk about all of this.'

'If you had seen how upset he was . . . asking a child to keep a secret like that. What were you thinking?' He was spitting the words out. 'Shopping trips, and walks on the beach – you were having a right old time, weren't you?'

'I am not going to defend myself for needing to spend time with my—'

'You've been drinking, haven't you?'

'Shaun . . .'

'I will thank you to stay away from the house tomorrow and not go spoiling Christmas for the boys.'

'Shaun, you can't keep—' She was shouting but the line was dead and Donal was standing at the end of the hallway staring directly at her. He was half in shadow, half in the light from the kitchen. He gave one slow nod. She looked at the receiver in her hand, still so close to her face she could hear the dead tone ringing off. She hung up and turned around and Dolores was facing her now, but she was not looking at her. She was staring at the tiles where Colette saw that she'd left muddy footprints all the way from the door to the phone.

'I'm sorry, Dolores,' she said, and she hated the sound of her voice, smothered in its own soft obsequiousness. She walked slowly to the door, her feet making a squelching noise in her sopping plimsolls. She looked up at the cottage and saw the roof of her car just visible above the wall, and she thought about grabbing her keys and driving out to Shaun. She would confront him. They would have this out. A wind caught the cord of her dressing gown and lifted it and she looked down at her wet feet. She remembered then that she'd been drinking. How much she could not say, but too much to get in a car and arrive on the doorstep for a fight with her husband that would likely frighten their eleven-year-old son.

But none of this made sense to her. When she had last seen Carl in Enniskillen, he had seemed so happy and content, and he would have been looking forward to her coming the next day.

'Will you close that door, you're letting the heat out,' Dolores said.

'Dolores, I need to make a phone call.'

Colette heard her tut – the gall of the woman.

'You're making a wild lot of phone calls recently. I might have to start charging you for that,' Dolores said.

Colette ignored her and lifted the receiver. She knew the number off by heart.

'31470 – who's speaking, please?' Izzy answered in that pretentious way of hers, the shrill little uplift at the end of the question.

'Did you tell him?' Colette demanded.

'Excuse me?'

'Did you tell him?' Each word was fired from her mouth.

'What are you going on about, Colette?'

'Shaun knows. He knows about all of it. He said it was Carl who told him but somebody else must have said something. We were supposed to see each other tomorrow, why would he go blabbing to his father now?'

'Oh, Colette,' Izzy said.

'Was it you who told him?'

Izzy sighed. 'Well, as God is my witness, I never said a word to him, and what desire would I have to go bringing trouble into someone's house on Christmas Eve?'

'Well, all I know is that I was supposed to be spending tomorrow with my sons and now I'm banned from my own house.'

'But you knew the child was going to say something eventually.'

'I knew no such thing.'

'Colette – I don't know what to say to you. Go home and sober up.'

Her throat felt hot then, so many words trying to crowd their way into her mouth.

'Colette, I'm not an idiot – anyone would know from talking to you that you have drink taken. Get some rest. Have you enough food in the house for tomorrow?'

She slammed down the receiver and when she turned around Donal was standing just a few feet away, his arms folded, staring at her. She'd rarely seen him in anything other than work clothes and now he was wearing a smart shirt and jeans. He was clean-shaven and his hair was slicked back with gel.

'Is there some kind of bother?' he asked.

She noticed that the living room door was closed now but she could still make out Dolores's slight figure through the panes of frosted glass.

'No, Donal. There's nothing wrong. I'm sorry for disturbing you. Happy Christmas. I hope it all goes well tomorrow.'

She walked out the door and then she heard him say her name, and turned to face him.

He moved closer. 'You're half-cut,' he said. 'Don't come down here again like that.'

She was still staring at him when the door slammed shut in her face.

It was difficult to maintain her balance climbing back up the rain-soaked hill. Near the top she pitched forward onto her hands and felt them sinking into the wet ground. She dug her feet into the well-worn footholds and clawed at the earth to stop herself from sliding back down. When she tried to move forward, the mud sucked off one plimsoll, then the second. She finished her journey barefoot, and as soon as she got into the house, she tore off her jumper and dressing gown and jeans and stepped into the shower and turned it up to the highest temperature. She let out great gasps as the heat engulfed her. But the hot water lasted only a minute or two, and she turned off the tepid dribble and stepped out of the shower, leaving a pool of dirty brown water to drain away. She wrapped a clean white towel around her and walked to the kitchen sink to retrieve her glass of wine but then she saw Shaun's present lying on the table. She tore off the paper and un-screwed the lid, filled a glass tumbler almost to overflowing, and took a long draught. She stared out the window at the beach. The sea had almost absorbed the last of the weak blue light that lay over it like a shroud. She felt steadied, watching the water soaking up the last of the day as the whiskey warmed her.

She walked to the bed and lay down. In the morning she could, if she wanted, get in her car and make the four-hour drive to her mother's house. But she still lived in hope that Ronan would visit her. And then she remembered how happy her mother had been when she'd told her she was spending the day with Shaun and the boys. She had made plans then to spend Christmas with her sister and her husband and their teenage daughters. And Colette would not do that. She would not sit with her sister and her mother judging her for an entire day. That was something she could not suffer. She closed her eyes. She would rather sleep until St Stephen's Day.

When she woke again the sky beyond her window was a featureless black canvas. She heard the soft crunch of stones on the road outside. Footsteps stopped at the door and then she heard the three slow, steady knocks, a key sliding into the latch. She looked down the length of her body, wrapped in the towel. A draught passed through the room and her skin came alive with the cold sting of it. She heard the front door close and then saw the full shape of him through the open bedroom door. He wore the hood up on his coat and he looked taller and broader, almost taking up the whole doorway. He panted as he bent to unlace his boots and then there was the sound of one boot dropping on the stone floor, the second. She thought about moving, of making some effort to stir, but a leaden stillness held her down on the bed.

CHAPTER 15

On the second Monday of January, it was with some relief that James placed the key in the door of his constituency office. The room smelt stale and even though outside the air was cold and heavy with damp he opened the two large windows that overlooked the pier. His office occupied the bottom floor of one of the oldest buildings in the town, and the smell of age was embedded in the walls and the plaster cornicing and the old fireplace that seemed to heave dead air into the room every time so much as a breeze passed over. Still, it was a handsome, well-proportioned room, and he'd had the old wooden floors carpeted recently to lend some warmth to the place. James placed the bundle of newspapers he was carrying on his desk and hung the new blue overcoat Izzy had bought him for Christmas over the back of his chair. He walked to the door to retrieve the post he'd stepped over on his way in. His back was not what it used to be and he had to get down on one knee. He swiped the envelopes together and just then the door swung open and almost knocked him sideways.

'Jesus, James, I'm sorry,' Cassie said, poking her head through the door.

'Hello, Cassie,' he said. He struggled to his feet and tossed the post onto her desk. If there was one thing he could set his watch by, it was that his secretary would be five minutes late every single day. He'd mentioned it to her a few times but it wasn't an argument he wanted to get into on their first day back at work. 'Are you all right?'

'I'm great, James,' she said. 'I was well looked after at Christmas.' She held up a new handbag.

'Oh, you're spoiled is what you are,' he said. And he knew too that not so long ago her parents had bought her a car so that she could make the ten-minute drive from the family home to work each morning, and really with so few impediments it was impossible for James to fathom why she couldn't be on time. But again, he told himself to drop this argument. He'd had trouble holding on to secretaries in the past and Cassie had been with him for nearly three years. Her father was a skipper on one of the boats who'd begged James to take her on after she left secretarial college. He liked the idea of someone untested coming into the office so they could be trained up to work the way he wanted rather than bringing notions with them from other places. It was an undemanding job. She had to handle his correspondence, do some basic bookkeeping. If James was in Dublin all she had to do was answer the phone. In the early days he'd had an open-door policy. But he had ones coming in to tell him that their neighbour was parking in their spot or that the binmen had forgotten to collect their rubbish. Now Thursday mornings were the only time of the week when people were allowed to come by without an appointment. Other than that, they needed to make arrangements through Cassie. He felt like she could do with reminding sometimes that she had a nice, clean job in an office when she could just as easily have ended up working in one of the fish factories.

'How was your Christmas?' Cassie asked.

'Christmas was a success, Cassie,' he said, and really that was the only way he could think to describe it. There had been no fights was what he meant. They'd come close when on St Stephen's Day Izzy sat down at the kitchen table with a pile of winter-sun brochures and began to read the descriptions of the hotels out loud to him. He could be doing with a holiday, she'd said, after all the stress he'd been under, and he'd told her that there'd be no holiday for him until July at the earliest. If she wanted to go away with her sister for a week, she was welcome to. And he'd retreated to the sitting room then before she could think of a retort. All over the Christmas period he'd managed not to shout at Niall, even though Niall's bottom lip was set quivering over the slightest upset and the sight of it angered him. And although there had been no significant altercations between Orla and Izzy, the threat had been ever present. A sense of peace had descended over the house when Orla had returned to school the night before.

But he had not enjoyed it. That was what it boiled down to in the end. Not that he had ever really cared about Christmas. It was a sentimental season and he was simply not a sentimental person. Yet he was aware that there was some pleasure he was supposed to have gleaned from it – having his family around him, the rest and relaxation, the indulgence of it all. He had felt tired all the time and then some nights he had been unable to sleep. He had always been a prodigious sleeper – it was one of his gifts. It had infuriated

Izzy that even at times of great difficulty in their marriage, he had been able to drift off to sleep with such ease. But now all the concerns that usually occupied him during the day crowded in on him at night. He lay awake, keeping sentry over them. He worried that he'd left the handbrake off the car, forgotten to pay the electricity bill, that Niall was sleeping with his electric blanket on, or that his indigestion was some pernicious disease eating away at him. He'd decided that in the new year he would go to Doctor D'Arcy and ask him for a sleeping tablet of some kind. But then he'd thought that all he probably needed was to get back to work. Besides, on a recent visit Doctor D'Arcy had suggested he might be overworked and that his problems were 'more in his head' – that was how he'd put it. And when doctors started saying things like that you were only a few questions away from being offered different kinds of tablets. Telling him that he was having trouble sleeping would only inspire him further. And then there'd be two of them in the house on tablets and Izzy wouldn't be able to accept that at all. She'd say he was just looking for attention.

A cold air rolled in from the fireplace and the newspapers on his desk rustled.

'Will you shut those windows now please, Cassie,' James said, putting on his glasses and picking up the first newspaper on the pile. 'And while you're at it, you could kind of de-Christmas the place.'

'What do you mean de-Christmas the place?' she asked.

This had been a bone of contention between them. She'd wanted to hang decorations and he'd objected.

'Well, you know, you could throw out the cards.'

'Aye, that'll take all of two minutes,' she said.

James perused the cover of a week-old *Irish Times*. The newspapers were always thin on real news this time of year and any political stories were about the machinations in the newly formed government. James had read most of them already but he wanted to skim through to make sure he'd missed nothing. Roles were changing hands so often. You could be an ordinary member of government one day and be made a minister the next. You had to keep your wits about you. Izzy liked to say that he couldn't see farther than the end of his own nose. His wife often said cruel things like this. It seemed strange to him that she could say whatever she wanted and he was expected to remain calm, but on the rare occasions when he did respond in anger she was so instantaneously wounded. If he had tried to explain the unfairness of this to her, she would have said, 'Ah, it's a pity about you.' Anyway, James didn't see how he could be such a short-sighted underachiever when he'd left school at fourteen with no qualifications whatsoever and was now an elected member of government – even if he hadn't been made a minister.

And he would be nursing that wound for a while. It was hard not to take it as a personal slight. He'd received no warning that the decision wouldn't go in his favour. Before he knew it, he was shaking hands with the new minister, congratulating him on his appointment. It wasn't that the man had more experience – James outstripped him on every front except his family name. And it didn't seem to matter that a few years previously a newspaper exposé revealed he'd put some of the renovations for his house on his tax return. James had kept quiet about other people's misdemeanours – in this regard at least he knew how to play the game – but for his own part, he had never so much as asked for a parking ticket to be quashed. When you came from nothing, you could be held to a higher standard. But he was beginning to wonder where all this good behaviour had got him.

Cassie placed a mug of tea in front of him.

'Thank you, Cassie,' he said.

'There's not much going on down there today.'

He looked up from his newspaper to see Cassie standing at the window staring down at the pier.

'Oh, they'll not be going anywhere for a while yet,' James said.

Most of the fleet was still tied up. The sea and the sky were of the same dark, even grey today, the low winter sun trying to break through the cloud hunkering at the lighthouse. The wind was up and the water churned and despite their size, these great hulking vessels seemed to roll in the tide. James watched the ropes that tethered them to the pier, slacken and tighten, slacken and tighten, and he felt his stomach lurch.

These boats were like cruise ships compared to the one he'd gone to sea in. Two years he'd spent rolling around in a seven-berth trawler called the *Assaro*, where nausea sent him diving below deck and into his bunk, which he discovered was the worst place to escape seasickness. But the other men said they'd make a man out of him yet. He was indignant at the suggestion that there was something lacking in his character and complained about the poor pay they received, about the dangerous conditions they worked in. And one night they received a mayday call from a boat with four men on board that was taking in water off Rathlin Head. The swell was so great that they couldn't get anywhere near them. All they could do was watch as little by little the boat was pulled under, until finally it was like the depths of the sea opened up and sucked it down with its last breath. A sheet of white foam sluiced gently over its absence.

He found another job as soon as he could and took up a position as foreman at the fisheries co-op shortly after getting married.

And he continued to complain. Fishermen were getting a bad deal and James organised a strike until a regulation was put in place for a minimum price on the sale of the fish. When the next elections for local council came around, he was encouraged to stand. He feigned reluctance but won easily and when he ran for Dáil Éireann the first time, he lost, but made it in on his second attempt a few years later. There he was able to lobby the European Parliament and effect serious change that meant fishermen could catch more, earn more, work in safer conditions. And those around him grew richer and richer. And this was what Izzy meant, what she was constantly lamenting, that James's narrow thinking had limited them in this regard. But he had a house and two cars and a daughter in a private school. He enjoyed a holiday in the sun every year. He had more than he'd ever expected to have. It was Izzy who was never satisfied. It was the only thing he really disliked about her. Even the cruel jibes he could live with because the thing about his wife was that she was funny, and when that wit was directed elsewhere it made him laugh. But she was grasping, and she made a very good job of counting other people's money. According to Izzy, everyone had more than they did. And it did seem to James, when he looked around him, that every one of his contemporaries had become a millionaire except him. And what was more, he had helped them to do it.

'What will I do with these?' Cassie asked.

She was standing in front of him with a small cardboard box half full with Christmas cards.

'How many did we print?' he asked.

'Two hundred.'

'And how many did we send?'

'Around a hundred.'

'Ah, shite – that was a waste of money. Could they be reused for something?'

'No. They're Christmas cards. And they have 1994 printed on them.'

'OK. Well, throw most of them away and keep a few for the archive.'

'What archive?' she said.

'Cassie, where do you file old documents?'

There was a knock on the door and Cassie placed the box on his desk and went to answer it. One of the cards was taped to the outside of the box. It was a photo taken last summer at the annual dinner held by the Ardglas Fisherman's Organisation. President Mary Robinson had attended and she was standing in the front row of the photograph. Surrounding her were the boat owners of the town and their wives, and Izzy and James. His wife was wearing a black dress with pearl earrings and a pearl necklace. Her fair hair was held back by a black velvet Alice band. She was sitting with her legs crossed and her hands clasped around her knee. The fact that his wife was attractive, and admired by other men, and always looked the part when they attended official functions was something he took pride in, and he liked to think that he expressed this admiration to Izzy as often as he could. He tried to remember if they had fought that night.

'Happy New Year to you,' Cassie said to the tall man with his head bowed standing in the doorway. He was taking an inordinate amount of time wiping his feet on the mat and allowing cold air to blow into the office. James stood up and saw it was Shaun Crowley, and his irritation turned to curiosity.

'Hello, Shaun, how are you?' James said.

'Will I make tea?' Cassie asked.

Shaun was moving slowly across the room, patting the pockets of his coat and looking around the floor like he'd lost something.

'Well, I'll have another cup anyway. Shaun?'

'I won't be stopping long,' he said.

'Well, take a seat.' James gestured to the chair opposite him. 'What can I do you for? How did you get on this Christmas?'

Shaun dropped heavily into the chair and sat back, slouching and loose-limbed. He removed his glasses case from the pocket of his wax jacket, took out a tiny white cloth, and began to clean his glasses with great concentration. James noticed that the hem of his trousers was about an inch too short so you could see the dark hairs on his legs just above the bands of his red socks. He wore expensive handmade shoes, the leather dull for want of a good polish. His flannel shirt was unbuttoned to his chest, where his white vest was visible, and yet more hair sprouted.

Cassie placed another cup of tea on his desk and James watched Shaun cast a suspicious eye at her, not neglecting the cleaning of his glasses for a second.

'Cassie – will you go over to Doherty's and get today's papers, please?' James asked.

She nodded, took her coat from the stand and her keys from her desk, and left the office.

'Now, Shaun – to what do I owe the pleasure?' James had his elbows on the leather panel of his desk, his hands joined just below his chin.

Shaun placed his glasses back on his face and it was as though the gift of sight renewed his vigour. He blinked a few times, taking in his surroundings. And then he stood up and strode to the window with some purpose. He held his hands behind his back and stared down at the pier, shaking his head a few times.

'Twenty years ago, there were fifteen boats in that fleet, and now there are nearly fifty,' Shaun said. 'And twenty years from now there won't be a fish left in the water.'

'Never a truer word was spoken, Shaun. They're leaving nothing for the next generation. That's why I'm always saying it – tourism's the future of this town.'

And then Shaun looked over his shoulder at him like he was surprised by his presence in the room. He returned to the seat and sat himself squarely in front of James, pinching the knees of his trousers so that the material rode up another inch, exposing his bony white shins.

'Well, what was it you wanted to discuss?' James asked.

'Christmas, James. Yes, Christmas. Christmas was hard, James.' He made a noise of assent then, like he was agreeing with himself. 'I don't mind telling you that Christmas was a difficult time. Carl was very upset all over Christmas because he didn't see his mother, who as I'm sure you're aware no longer lives at home. The fact that she no longer lives there is a decision she made herself. She decided to live in Dublin and to leave her home and her sons and to begin a new life.'

Shaun began to rummage in his wax jacket. He withdrew his fist, opened his hand, glared at the scrunched-up white tissue lying in his palm, and then returned it directly to his pocket.

'Shaun, I'm very sorry to hear all of this but—'

'But I would say that I am as entitled to a fresh start as Colette is. Wouldn't you?'

'Shaun—'

'And I would say that my sons are entitled to a calm and stable existence – doesn't that seem fair?'

James folded his arms and leaned back in his chair.

'But Colette has certainly not contributed to that, and neither has your wife,' Shaun said.

'What?'

'It seems they've struck up quite the friendship since Colette's return to the town, which is odd really, considering they never had much to do with each other before.'

'Izzy goes to Colette's writing classes, what of it?'

'I would never really have pictured them as friends. I wouldn't have thought they'd have shared any of the same tastes or interests. And Colette didn't have many friends, which was a thing I never paid too much attention to at the time. I thought it was just because she was a blow-in, you know, and that perhaps people thought she was odd because of what she does.'

James could feel something inside him tightening, like a clenched fist at the centre of his chest. He looked down at the silver letter opener shaped like a mackerel that lay on a square of marble between him and Shaun.

'But your wife's a blow-in too,' Shaun said. 'I know she's not from far away, but really it's the same thing. In a small town an outsider's an outsider. But I always said to Colette that Izzy was one of the nicest women who ever came into this town. It's a shame she's been dragged into all of this, but it doesn't surprise me that Colette would use her as some kind of . . . go-between—'

'Get to the point, Shaun.'

'The point is that your wife has been facilitating meetings between Colette and Carl. There was a shopping trip – to Enniskillen of all places. I thought that was an unusual choice.'

'She took the boys to the North to do a bit of Christmas shopping – so what?'

'And she arranged to meet Colette there and they had a right old time buying presents and gadding about together.'

'Where are you getting all of this from?'

'Oh, they were seen.'

'By who?'

'That's of no importance.'

'If you're coming in here launching accusations at my wife then you should have the balls to say who told you.'

'Not accusations, James – facts.'

'A mother was seen doing a bit of Christmas shopping with her son, those are the facts – and I'm supposed to go home and reprimand my wife over this, for what?'

'I would say what you do with this information is your own business. I'm not going to tell you how to conduct your marriage. But what I will say is that often it's difficult to see something that's happening right under your own nose.'

'Right, Shaun, you've said your bit, now I'm fully aware that my wife went shopping with Colette.' James put his glasses back on his face and reached for the newspaper. 'Thanks for filling me in. You can show yourself out.'

'That wasn't what I was referring to.'

James dipped his eye and looked over the rim of his glasses. 'Then what are you saying?'

'That the parish priest's car is parked at your house more often than his own. It appears Izzy's made another new friend in the past few months.'

'I'd be very fucking careful about where you're going with this,' James said.

Shaun jammed his little finger into his ear. He grimaced and shook and then removed his finger, examining the tip.

'Just because you failed to pay attention to what was going on with your own wife,' James said, 'doesn't mean you get to tell me what to do with mine.'

'I'm just telling you what people are saying.'

'Do you think I pay a blind bit of notice to what people are saying about me?'

'I think you care a great deal about what people think of you, James. And maybe if you cared a little less, you might have had some real success. I think you play a careful game, and that you have more respect for your constituents than for your colleagues. That's why you've managed to hold your seat for so long but . . . well, with all the changes that are going on in the government at the moment, it wasn't difficult to spot that you've been passed over again.'

The door opened and Cassie struggled to close it against the wind. 'Oh Jesus, it would skin you alive out there,' she said.

'Good day to you, James.' Shaun rose from the seat, head bowed once again. He almost collided with Cassie as he walked out the door.

'Goodbye now, Shaun,' she said, wiping her feet on the mat.

James could hear a ringing in his ears, growing louder and louder.

'Is everything all right?' Cassie asked.

He looked down at his desk and there was Shaun's glasses case with the little white cloth he'd used to wipe the lenses spilling out of it. Taped to the inside was a piece of lined paper with his name, address, and phone number. James threw the case in the bin beneath his desk. He took the bin and walked to the fireplace, passing along the mantelpiece. 'I told you to get rid of these fucking cards,' he said, tossing each one in the bin as he went.

CHAPTER 16

If asked by anyone about the greatest trick the Catholic Church played on its congregants, and there were many, Father Brian Dempsey would have said the act of confession. It was the idea of it as an anonymous exchange that was most misleading. There was in fact enough light in the confessional to make out the shape of the person sitting on the opposite side of the grille, and so if you had some familiarity with that person, it would be possible to recognise them. And in a small town like Ardglas where there were maybe only a thousand inhabitants, and only a few hundred of those who regularly attended confession, it was even easier to discern who was speaking. You could recognise them by their voice alone. People had some idea of this themselves, and that was why they did not give detailed accounts of their sins but rather a sanitised version. 'I told my wife to fuck off' became 'I used bad language towards my wife.' 'I rode my neighbour's wife' became 'I was coveting my neighbour's wife.' 'I beat my wife black-and-blue' became 'I was impatient with my wife.'

He was thinking about these things while he listened to Dolores Mullen's confession. The enclosed space, the dead air, had a soporific effect and he was often half-asleep listening to other people's sins or drifting off in some kind of reverie. People's confessions were mostly so routine and dull, like their dreams, interesting only to them. But Dolores's sins were growing less vague the longer she went on.

'I feel such anger towards my husband,' she said. Her voice shook with every word.

He had known it was Dolores from the moment she stepped into the confessional. Not only was she a religious woman who came to confession regularly – the mother and father and five sisters were all religious – but she had a head of hair on her so outsized it almost filled the entire compartment. He could see the haze of frizz in what little light filtered through the darkness.

'He is unfaithful, Father,' she continued. 'He has been unfaithful many times. But this time I think that it's with . . . well, I know that . . . I know that it's with one of our . . . neighbours.'

Brian tried to think who in the vicinity of Donal Mullen's house he might be riding. There were no other houses that close as far as he could remember.

'He used to at least have the decency to do it away from home, to do it far enough away from me and our children, but now he has so little respect for me that he doesn't even care if I know he's going next door for it.'

And then he knew exactly who it was. She'd phoned him not two days previously to tell him she was no longer able to read at mass and hung up on him before he'd had a chance to respond.

'And I think some night when he's sleeping, I'm just going to get the knife out of the drawer in the kitchen and stick it in his back.'

It was amazing what people were trying to tell you if you really listened. Dolores was not so much concerned with being absolved of her sins as letting him know that her husband was not a good man. He might come to mass on Sundays and bounce his children on his knee, but Dolores was here to let the priest know that any positive impression that might give was false. And it was what Izzy was trying to tell him with that anecdote about the flower shop. She was saying, you know that man who laughs at your jokes and breaks bread with you and plays golf with you on the weekends? Well, that man is capable of selfishness and cruelty and because he will not confess to that, I'll do it for him. And by going to the parish priest they were going straight to the top – they were telling the moral arbiter of their lives that their husbands were bad men. It astonished him, the deference priests were still shown, that even in this day and age men like Donal Mullen and James Keaveney would be mortified about the parish priest knowing what bastards they were.

As if he hadn't guessed already.

And so he thought that one of his main roles in the parish was as a conduit for people's resentments. Through him the powerless were able to wage some small revenge.

'Oh, Dol . . . Dear, have you tried speaking to your husband about your suspicions?'

There was a silence then so long and pervasive that he looked through the grille to be sure she hadn't left.

'I'm five months pregnant, Father,' she said.

'Well then,' he said, and began to bless her.

'What about my penance, Father?' she asked.

He sighed. 'Oh, I wouldn't worry about that,' he said. 'I'd say you have enough on your plate at the moment.'

'Thank you, Father,' she said.

He thought that Dolores might be his last confession but he waited a few minutes. He couldn't go sticking his head out the door to see who was there or else the illusion would be broken. When he was confident that no one else was coming he stepped out of the confessional and left the church.

As he walked up the driveway that connected the church grounds to the parochial house he thought about Donal and Dolores Mullen – *May she slice him into ribbons while he sleeps*, he said to himself. During his time in the Guards he'd dealt with more incidents of domestic violence than he cared to remember, and now he was a priest all he did was deal with domestics.

As he unlocked the door of his car a few flakes of snow began to fall. He sat in the seat and closed the door and stared up at the little icy clumps, gliding down so slow and separate it was like some invisible hand was casting down each one. The sky had been threatening it all day, in its flat grey frigidity. There came more snow, fuller, faster, but each flake vanished as soon as it met with the wet ground, and he decided to continue with his plan.

He had not seen Izzy all over the Christmas period. It was a family time, but he guessed that at this stage James would be back at work and the kids would be back at school. Whenever he heard an interesting confession the first person he thought of was Izzy. He wanted to relay the details to her, to discuss it with her, to laugh over it – but his conscience forbade him. Izzy was great fun, and irreverent, and the only person in the town who didn't treat him like a priest. When you first arrived in a new parish every person of note would invite you for Sunday dinner, and he was not surprised when an invitation was extended by the local politician. What he had not expected was how close he would become to the Keaveneys, Izzy in particular, in the short time he'd been in the town.

It had not taken him long to realise something was off in the fabric of the Keaveneys' marriage. Even at the first lunch he shared with them, they had bickered openly, and if they couldn't even remember to put on a good show for the parish priest then things must really be bad. But their behaviour towards each other varied so much from week to week, it was hard to know what to expect. On the good occasions James seemed to take pride in his wife's quick wit, and at such times Izzy accepted his deference with a coquettish bat of her eyelashes. At other times James was impatient with his wife, bristled when she spoke. There was a theatrical quality to Izzy's character that seemed to embarrass him. Izzy, on the other hand, found her husband to be pompous and insincere and followed up his statements with snide remarks. And Brian admired her tenacity. It fell just short of open hostility, but how unlike the other meek housewives of the parish she was, who in the face of far weaker opponents than James Keaveney spoke of nothing more contentious than the weather. It was uncomfortable, however. Still, Izzy was a good cook and the conversation was less stilted and the atmosphere less stuffy than other homes he had been in. And he'd obviously passed some kind of test, because not long after they first met, James invited him to play in a four-ball at the golf club.

They had both hit balls into the rough and were separated from the other players when James, head down, taking practice swipes at the ball, explained that things were not good between him and Izzy.

'She has the depression,' he said, not looking up. 'It comes on her from time to time, and when it does, I'm to blame for everything. She's like a briar. There's no talking to her.'

He'd waited for James to say more.

'Maybe you'd have a word with her. Don't say that I said anything. But she won't listen to me.'

He was surprised by James's openness. But again, he listened carefully for what he was really being told. *That woman you think is hilarious, housewife of the year? She's mad in the head.* It was his experience that a man often thought his wife insane when she expressed unhappiness with her lot. Brian told James that he would speak to Izzy. He was glad to have an excuse to spend more time with her.

Izzy was sharp. She guessed that the priest had been sent to pull her out of her funk. And so she was more open about her problems than she might otherwise have been. If her husband had told the parish priest that she was being difficult, then she was going to be equally open about his shortcomings.

On one occasion she told him, 'James likes you because you're a man's man. The last priest we had in the parish was a bit . . .' She extended her arm and let her hand flop down from the wrist.

'That doesn't surprise me, the seminary was full of them.'

'Oh yeah – that's where you'd meet them, all right – but anyway, this fellow, Father Slattery, you might know him, he made a bit of a show of himself. He wasn't into the priest bit at all. All he did was go around the parish eating and drinking in people's houses and gossiping with women. He was mad for a party. Well, he took an awful shine to me altogether, thought I was great craic, and he was calling to the house the whole time. James ran him a few times because he thought he was keeping me from making the dinner. Anyway, we used to have the most unmerciful rows over him.'

'Why? Did James think he was some kind of threat?'

She laughed. 'He did not – he said to me one day, "Izzy, that man is as bent as a hoop" – may God forgive him.'

They both laughed then.

'So what was the problem?' he asked.

He remembered her eyes at this moment, the keenness in them, the way her look seemed to tilt at him. 'That was the problem,' she said. 'He was ridiculous. And James was worried he would make him look ridiculous, that people would be laughing at him behind his back. That's James's biggest fear – embarrassment, being made a fool of.'

As his car budged its way across the narrow bridge that led to the road where the Keaveneys lived, he could barely see through the snow, his entire vision filled with its slow, continuous cascade.

Pulling up in the driveway, he imagined the conversation he would never have with Izzy about Donal and Dolores Mullen.

'And he's riding Colette Crowley and Dolores is going to kill him.'

'Ah, will you stop,' she'd say, or, 'Well, wouldn't it be good enough for him.'

Through the snow he could just make out James's green Toyota parked at the side of the house and only then did he realise how much he'd been hoping to be alone with Izzy. They had probably heard his car coming up the drive, so he would have to go in and say hello, but he decided that he would not stay for very long.

He checked in the back seat for his coat but realised he'd left without it and when he looked through the windscreen again the snow had reduced to a few flakes falling so slowly it was like they were suspended in midair. He was about to make a dash to the front door when he saw the shapes of two figures through the kitchen window, like shadows playing on a wall, miming aggression, coming together and drawing apart. And then the taller of the two broke off decisively and disappeared and a moment later the front door opened and James was standing there staring at him. He waited for a moment but when it became clear James had no intention of moving, he stepped out of the car and approached him.

'You've come at a bad time,' James said.

'Is everything all right?'

'Yeah, we'll be fine.'

'Is there anything I can do?'

'Yeah,' James said, curling his finger, indicating for him to move closer. He took one step towards him and James spoke into his ear. 'Fuck off and interfere in someone else's marriage.'

The door slammed in his face. He heard James shout something and Izzy responding, and then there was silence. He lifted his fist to knock on the door but his hand fell limp at his side. He walked to his car, and just as he started the engine, he saw the curtains on the kitchen window sweep closed.

CHAPTER 17

Colette extended her leg beyond the bed covers and pointed her toe at the ceiling. Donal pulled the sheets across her hip and wrapped his arm around her. She placed her mouth on his and slowly lowered her leg back down onto the bed.

'Another one,' he said. 'Come on.'

'No!' She laughed. 'It's cruel.'

'Ah, go on, sure it's only the pair of us.'

'It's still cruel.'

'What he doesn't know won't hurt him.'

'Are you banking on that philosophy?'

'Don't go getting all serious on me now.'

She felt around on the floor beside the bed for another letter and handed one to him.

He began to read: '"Dublin, the twelfth of December 1994." Two days since the last one – Jesus, does he not have anything better to do? "Colette – today I saw a family returning from a day out."' He read in a breathy voice. '"They pulled up on the street outside with an evergreen poking from the boot of the car. I watched them haul the tree from the boot, a collective effort, spraying pine needles everywhere as they went." For fuck's sake, this fellow needs help. "I thought about what we would be doing this time of year if you had stayed. I look at the people who surround me and my life now and I think of how lacking in colour and texture it is" – well, that's enough for me.' He shredded the letter with his fingers and threw the scraps up in the air so they cascaded down upon her.

'Will you stop,' she shouted and laughed and rolled up onto his chest, looked him straight in the eye.

'Next!' he roared and pushed her over onto her side of the bed and placed his weight upon her. He reached for another letter.

'No,' she screamed. She tried to wrestle with him but he pinned her arms down with his elbows and placed the letter right in her face.

'The twelfth of Never 1994,' he said. 'Oh, Colette, I am dreaming of your breasts. Every night I see them dangling in front of me like ripe peaches covered in soft, downy fuzz—'

'Donal – I asked you to stop.'

'And I am driven so wild by desire that I practically explode all over the walls of the house – the house that you abandoned me in.' He tore the letter in half and threw the two parts aside with a flourish.

She watched him pick a tiny scrap of paper from her hair and present it to her on the tip of his finger.

'Make a wish,' he said.

She puffed out her lips and the scrap floated down onto the bed covers. She stared up at him, drew a knuckle along his jawline, felt the scrape of stubble, and touched her finger to his mouth. 'That was very good,' she said. 'You really captured his voice. In fact, I would say you were even better than him. Now, let's leave the poor man in peace.'

'Was he good for something, at least?' he asked.

She sat up, sighed, looked around for her tobacco. 'Passable,' she said.

'Only passable? That's some report.'

'What do you want me to say – that the earth moved?'

'No.' He shook his head. 'I don't want you to say that. Describe him to me.'

She wrapped her arms around her knees. 'Well, he was a professor of linguistics and—'

'Ah no, I don't care about any of that shite. What did he look like?'

She considered this for a moment, tried to make her memories of him coalesce in her mind. 'Well, he was tall. And he had a thick head of hair but it was almost all grey. But a nice shade of grey – not a wizened-old-man grey, it still had some life in it. And he wore glasses with black frames, and he had a kind of beaked nose—'

'Jesus, he sounds like a real looker – go on,' he said, 'more detail.'

'Oh look, Donal, I told you already I don't want to talk about this anymore. We've had a good laugh at the man's expense, now can we just drop the subject?'

He shifted onto his elbow, and she felt the full force of his attention round upon her.

'Riddled with remorse, are you?' he said.

She tried to focus on the pale yellow sunlight streaming through the window.

'We both know the only reason you came back to this town was 'cause you bet on the wrong horse,' he said.

'I told you already that—'

'Ah yeah – you told me you were unhappy, that you were bored. Join the fucking club, Colette. Do you think that makes you special? It doesn't mean you run off and ride the first poor fucker who comes along.'

'It's what you've done.'

He gripped her arm and she felt his fingers bed down deep in her flesh.

'Don't you get high and mighty with me,' he said. 'I have three children and I know where each of them is right now. Can you say the same?'

'You wouldn't understand.'

'Why? Because I'm not a professor? I understand that there are some mothers who'd tear the eyes out of anyone who tried to keep them from their kids. That they'd do anything to be with them. And all you do is lie here with me in the middle of the day. So don't expect me to feel sorry for you.'

'I never came to you looking for sympathy.'

'No, Colette, you've only ever come to me looking for the one thing. So let's not make this complicated.'

He let go of her wrist and she felt his hand slide across her stomach. She gasped at the coldness of his touch, shut her eyes.

'Now,' he said, 'tell me what he looked like.'

Like being rocked on a current of air, she felt herself glide back down onto the bed.

'Why do you need to know this?' she asked.

'So in case he ever shows up here, I'll recognise him. Now, go on.'

'And what would you do if he showed up?'

He reached down between her legs. 'What would I do to him if he showed up on my property?' His breath was hot against her face. 'What would I do if he came sniffing around here?' He placed his mouth so close to her ear, it was like his voice was sounding from inside her head. 'I'd fucking kill him. Is that what you want me to say?'

'That's not what I want.'

'If he showed up here, I'd pull one of the stones off of the wall out there and cave his fucking head in.'

'That's not what I want.'

She stared up at the ceiling and tried to remember what she had wished for just seconds ago. But it had left her; all sensible thought had emptied out and pleasure had filled its place. She closed her eyes and gave herself over to it.

*

'Have you brought your letters?' Colette asked. 'For the new people in the class – I told everyone before Christmas to write a letter as a fictional character to a fictional character. The idea is to wholly conceive of two individual lives and then to imagine how those people might communicate with each other. Let's hear from one of our more seasoned students first.'

Colette looked around at the blank faces staring back at her. Numbers had almost doubled since the last class. There were even a few people who weren't from the town. People often made resolutions of this kind, to do something different in the new year, but whether they'd be there next week or not was another story. Still, ten students meant £80 and that was £80 she was in need of.

The door opened and Colette looked over her shoulder, hoping for Izzy to appear, but Helen Flynn came hurrying into the room, head bowed, shoulders bunched together. Helen looked up momentarily and Colette watched the briefest of smiles vanish from her face. It was extraordinary, she thought, how Helen always managed to appear hostile and apologetic at the same time.

'Don't worry, Helen,' Colette said. 'Just take a seat anywhere.'

Ever since Colette's outburst at Christmas, Izzy's tone had been more formal, more matter of fact when they spoke on the phone. Izzy was maintaining a distance and Colette didn't blame her. But in the past few days Izzy had stopped answering her calls altogether. She'd been looking forward to seeing her in person so she could apologise properly.

She cast her eye around the room again. Eithne was sitting straight-backed on the edge of her seat looking over the rim of her glasses at the pages in her hand. 'Eithne,' she said. 'Would you be kind enough to start us off?'

'Well, Colette,' she said, removing her glasses. 'I tried to imagine my characters as whole beings, as complete entities in and of themselves with independent lives and thoughts and feelings . . .' She was waving her glasses around in the air as she spoke.

Colette felt herself withdrawing. She looked down at the four mauve circles that marked the underside of her wrist. She kneaded at the bruises with her thumb, and that small discomfort was enough to render her present.

Eithne placed her glasses back on her face and cleared her throat. 'Dear Eithne,' she began, 'I have been observing you for some time; in fact your passage through life has been of great interest to me—'

She has not done what I asked, Colette thought, she has

completely ignored the very point of the exercise – the woman is incapable of writing anything that is not about herself.

'I know that the journey has not been easy,' Eithne read, 'but you have fought hard and won many battles and the greatest battle of all has been with yourself. The doubts and fears that slowed your awakening, that meant it took sixty-seven years before you truly realised who you—'

'Stop,' Colette shouted. 'Please, stop.' She brought her fingers to her lips. Her hand was shaking.

Eithne was frozen in place, still holding the pages in front of her, her eyes now fixed on Colette.

'I'm very sorry to interrupt you, Eithne.' She tried to smile. 'It just occurred to me that we're missing someone today.' Everyone was staring at her as though she were about to make some great revelation. 'Does anyone know if Izzy will be joining us this evening?'

Eithne flashed a look around the room then as if this news of Izzy's absence was a great surprise to her. 'I have no idea,' she said.

'But has anyone seen her recently?' Colette asked.

'I saw her here and there over Christmas,' Fionnuala said.

'I was chatting with her at the vegetable man on Saturday,' Thomas Patterson chimed in, 'and she seemed in good form, ready to get the creative juices flowing again.'

'Right so,' Colette said. 'Something must have come up for her.'

'May I continue?' Eithne asked.

'Of course,' Colette said. 'In fact, would you mind starting from the beginning again, I want to feel the full impact of it.'

And then she listened to Eithne's account of her birth and her schooling and her various lovers and her spiritual awakening. She registered the waning interest on the faces of the new attendees and regretted having asked Eithne to read first. Helen Flynn wore the look of horror that seized her face when even the remotest sexual reference was made. But no matter how much she told herself to concentrate, Colette could not stop glancing at the entrance where the illuminated exit sign blinked above the door.

CHAPTER 18

Standing outside the Bishop's Palace in Letterkenny, it struck James that there was little palatial about it. Lacking any splendour whatsoever, it could have passed for a reformatory, or an orphanage, or a sanatorium. The priest who answered the door surprised James with his youth and energy, welcoming him in with a flourish. 'You're very welcome, Mr Keaveney,' he said, his eyes shining and alert. James guessed he wasn't long out of the seminary. He followed the priest down a long, tiled hallway, lined with dark wooden side tables holding cut flowers in tall vases. The priest's jovial chatter accompanied their journey. He spoke of the weather and the approaching spring and the match between Donegal and Meath that was coming up that weekend. 'Do you follow the football, Mr Keaveney?' he asked, skipping along with such a lightness of step, like at any moment he might lift off the ground and take flight.

'If you don't mind taking a seat there, Mr Keaveney, while I let Bishop Hartigan know you've arrived.'

The priest disappeared behind the door and all his warmth and vitality went with him. His noise was replaced by the ticking of the grandfather clock that stood beside James, detailing the passing seconds. The air smelled of furniture polish and boiled vegetables. On the wall opposite, a portrait of a cantankerous-looking clergyman stared out at him. He posed against an indistinct background of light and fog. A bishop or cardinal, he wore a black cape around his shoulders, a heavy gold cross on a long chain rested on his stomach. James turned his eyes to the floor, began to examine the ecclesiastical patterns in the tiles, then made himself look back at the portrait again, to confront the thin-lipped, forbidding face.

His whole life spent in the same town as Shaun Crowley and he'd had little reason to concern himself with the man. Shaun had always set himself apart. Most people in Ardglas had grown up poor, but he'd inherited the fish factory from his father and was as close to old money as they came. He was quiet and reserved whenever you met him, but people talked, of course, calling him a 'shark' for buying up the smaller, failing businesses in the town. And then that Monday morning Shaun had visited James at his office, and for the first time he'd seen for himself the threat Shaun Crowley could pose. James knew he'd appeared for no other purpose than to condescend and undermine and humiliate. But James prided himself on the control he maintained over every area of his life, and Shaun Crowley had alerted him to the fact that he'd taken his eye off the ball. For that at least, he could be grateful to him.

The smiling priest emerged, leaving the door ajar. 'His Grace will see you now, Mr Keaveney.'

An expanse of thick green carpet lay between James and the

carved oak desk where the bishop sat with a pen in one hand, rubbing at his forehead with the other. There was a bay window behind him and three tall sash windows reached up to the corniced ceiling. He had turned one corner of the document on his desk towards him and was eyeing it with some hostility. As James crossed the room, he waited for the man to look up at him, to rise to greet him, but he was standing right in front of his desk before the bishop said, 'Thank you for waiting, Mr Keaveney.'

James had expected the full regalia, like the man in the portrait, but he was dressed as any ordinary priest would be.

'Now, Mr Keaveney, I am trying to remember if we've met before.'

'Oh, I'm sure we've met somewhere down through the years – or we've been in the same room on some occasion anyway. You would have done my daughter's confirmation a few years back.'

'But I am thinking of some event to do with the Donegal Chamber of Commerce where you gave a speech.'

James remembered the event – it was held in the ballroom at the Central Hotel and there was a lot of free alcohol served to businessmen and local dignitaries, and a complimentary three-course meal – bishops loved that sort of thing.

'And of course,' the bishop continued, 'I heard you on the radio the other morning talking about the Spanish boats invading Irish waters. You spoke very well and I agree that it is important to take a strong position on such things—'

'Thank you,' James said, 'but that's not what I came to talk to you about.'

'No, no, I didn't expect that you had.' And then he began to move things around on his desk as though he was preparing himself to focus fully on whatever James was about to say. 'But before we go any further, Mr Keaveney, might I be permitted to ask you a quick question?'

'Go on.'

'Well, I hear murmurings from the direction of Dáil Éireann that there is to be another referendum on the matter of divorce.' The bishop sat back in his chair, joined his hands over his stomach.

'It seems inevitable that will come around again at some point, yes.'

'But it wasn't so long ago that the people of this country voted overwhelmingly to protect the sanctity of marriage.'

'That was nearly ten years ago, the country's a very different place now.'

'I think I understand what you're trying to say, Mr Keaveney. So I can take it that your own party's policy would be that—'

'That in a modern society a man and woman who have spent a suitable period of time apart and who are unable to reconcile should be allowed to end their union if they wish.'

The bishop smiled. 'Ah, you're really toeing the party line. But tell me, what do you think is to become of the children of these broken families?'

'I imagine that will be the decision of their parents.'

'And what are your own personal views, are they in line with those of your party?'

'It's interesting that you should raise the topic of marriage, because that's exactly what I've come to talk to you about.'

The bishop began to turn the fat silver ring on his finger, an emerald cross fixed into the head. 'Well, Mr Keaveney – present your case and I'll see if I can be of assistance in the matter.'

James stared at the man sitting there with his hands clasped together on his desk, waiting for him to hold forth. A sky of deep, even blue filled the windows behind him. A great light seemed to emanate from this small, elderly man. *Present your case*, James thought, grinding the words together in his head.

'You know, it's just occurred to me, Bishop—'

'Your Grace.'

'That we have very similar jobs. When I'm at home, I open my constituency office for a few hours every week for people to come in and voice their concerns. Anyone can come in, really. It's more or less an open-door policy. So maybe that's where we differ a little bit. Getting an audience with you was like getting an audience with the pope.'

A brief smile passed across the bishop's face, a lazy lifting of the mouth that was more akin to a yawn.

'When I tried to look for your phone number, I was told that it was ex-directory and so I called someone that I knew would have it. And do you know who that was, Bishop?'

The man said nothing, just allowed his eyelids to wither in a gesture of irritation.

'Well,' James continued, 'I phoned Dave Mulligan. I've known Dave for years—'

'Mr Mulligan is a good man.'

'And a good friend of the church, I'm sure – no doubt you've had dealings with each other down through the years. I'd say the church owns a great deal of land in this area, and some of that was sold on to Dave when the coffers were empty, ha? But that's by the by,' James said. 'People come to me to present their case, as you put it. It's often tedious stuff – people complaining that the council aren't collecting their bins, that sort of thing. But it can be about more complex issues as well. And if a person is honest and straightforward and in need of genuine help, then I will do everything within my power to help them.'

The bishop nodded slowly.

'But if they are dishonest – and let me tell you, I can smell bullshit from miles – then they get short shrift from me. So I'm not going to bullshit you today. The parish priest you've placed in Ardglas is making my life difficult and I want you to have him moved to another parish as soon as possible.'

There was a long silence and something in the bishop's face unclouded. 'Could you elaborate a bit more on the nature of this problem, Mr Keaveney?' He parted his hands then in a gesture of magnanimity that made James want to break his fingers. 'It is important for me to be aware of the character of my clergymen.'

James had expected there would be some moral posturing of this kind, but was determined not to be drawn out on the details.

'For them to be able to offer spiritual guidance to their parishioners,' the bishop continued, 'I need to be able to offer spiritual guidance to them.'

'Oh, you don't need to worry about that, he's full of guidance and advice and in particular advice about my marriage.'

'So this is something of a personal nature, Mr Keaveney?'

'Oh, I would say it's personal, all right. I would say coming between a man and his wife is a personal matter.'

'And when you say that he has come between you and your wife—'

'He's making a nuisance of himself, there's nothing more you need to know than that.'

And he was certainly not going to tell him that he had invited this man into his home, shared meals with him, invited him into his marriage to some degree, and how often when he'd returned to his house this man's car was parked in his drive, and he'd come upon him and his wife in the kitchen, in a cloud of cigarette smoke, laughing.

'I'm afraid, Mr Keaveney, I'd need to know a great deal more if I am even going to consider transferring one of my priests to another parish. So let me clarify – Father Dempsey has been offering you marriage counselling of a kind—'

'Yes, and he seems to know a lot about marriage for a priest. But then he's not like the rest of you, is he? He's had a whole other life before all of this. Imagine what he got up to? And now he's in your fold and he's going around telling people how to conduct their marriages and he has my wife's head filled with nonsense.'

'Mr Keaveney, do you have reason to believe that anything untoward has happened between Father Dempsey and your wife?'

'Not with my wife, no, but if you believed half of what you heard around the town . . . he's a bit of a ladies' man, apparently. Big on house calls, if you know what I mean. And he has all sorts of new-fangled ideas. There's a local woman – ran off with a married man and left her husband and kids behind. Well, now she's back in the town and he has her reading at mass. You can imagine how that's going down with the locals, hearing the good word from a woman with that kind of a reputation.'

'Mr Keaveney, if I was to take action every time idle gossip was—'

'I don't care what you do with him, send him on sabbatical – isn't that one of your words?'

'I would have to give the matter a lot of thought and look into your claims more—'

'Look here – this doesn't have to be complicated. I know this isn't the first priest you've had to move. They get shifted around all the time. If some mother phoned the Guards to say her child had been interfered with you wouldn't be long moving him on then. I'd say there's some who are constantly on the move. It's just been scandal after scandal for you lot at the moment and I don't think you need any more trouble.'

'Even if your concerns were enough of a reason to transfer a priest to another parish, these things take time. I would have to find a suitable situation for him.'

'You know how this works as well as I do. You might need something from me one day and I'm a man who's in a position to help you. But if you don't do this then I might find that my hands are tied when you come looking for a favour. And I have a very long memory. Now, I want some indication from you before I leave this room that you are going to move forward with what we've discussed.'

The bishop was staring down at his hands, fists unfurled, lying limp on his desk. 'The issue will be dealt with, Mr Keaveney.'

'Good,' James said. 'Then you'll sort it. I want him gone by the end of the month.'

James rose from his seat and walked out of the office into the high-ceilinged hallway, where the young smiling priest seemed to have been waiting for him.

'Ah, Mr Keaveney,' he said, 'are you on your way?'

'I am. I can show myself out.'

James lengthened his stride, trying to keep ahead of the man. Sun shone through the stained-glass panels on the door at the end of the corridor, shedding pools of colour onto the tiles.

'I'm afraid I have to show you out – house rules,' the priest said.

'You don't have a lot to do up here, do you?' James said.

'Ah, we keep busy enough.'

James pushed open the front doors and a shock of cold air hit him. He stood atop the steep stone steps and looked down at the cathedral and the town and over the entire surrounding landscape, to where the hills rolled up to meet the sky. He wanted to run down the steps and jump in his car and drive home as quickly as he could, and then he remembered the silence that would greet him there.

'Good day to you, Mr Keaveney,' the priest said.

James turned to him. 'Tell me this – if you had someone in your life who refused to speak to you, what would you do?'

The smile disappeared from the priest's face. 'Well, I suppose I would tell you to pray for them.'

'Apart from that?'

'Is this someone you're close to?'

'Yes.'

'Well, the irony, Mr Keaveney, is that with people we love these things are even more difficult. We want to be forgiven but only God is capable of that and so we have to focus on what is possible. And what is always possible, even if it can be a great challenge at times, is to show love and kindness and compassion to others.'

'Kindness?' James asked, puffing out his lips.

'Yes, Mr Keaveney.'

'OK – I'll give that a try,' he said. 'Thank you, Father.'

James descended the steps, lifting his face to the pale winter sun.

CHAPTER 19

It was a quiet Tuesday night in the restaurant of the Harbour View. There were only two other tables seated and Izzy did not recognise any of the diners so she guessed they must be people staying in the hotel. The only waitress on duty was Ann Diver, and as she approached, Izzy sat back from her empty plate, looked up at her, and smiled.

'God, Ann, you're the only familiar face in here tonight.'

'Isn't it quiet?' she said.

Margaret Brennan, Izzy's dinner date, handed her plate to Ann with half her steak untouched. 'It was gorgeous, Ann, but I wasn't fit for it. You wouldn't wrap it up in a bit of tin foil for me and I'll bring it home? It'll be lovely for my lunch tomorrow.'

'I will surely. And can I get anything else for you?'

'Two coffees,' Izzy said.

As Ann walked away Izzy became aware of the silence once

again. She'd hoped for the restaurant to be quiet. She did not have the wherewithal for smiling and small talk. Even chatting with docile and affable Ann had required effort, although Ann's infrequent presence had provided the only reprieve from the solemnity of the evening.

Izzy lifted her wineglass and took a drink and then watched Margaret copy the action in a slow, mechanical way.

Margaret had said little all evening, and this was unlike her. Izzy had thought she could rely on Margaret's usual lively chatter to see them through the meal. She and James had not spoken a word to each other for weeks now. It had been their biggest row to date.

'Colette is my friend,' Izzy had said to James.

'She is a useless fucking trouble-maker who has never done an honest day's work in her whole life, and you let yourself be impressed by her.'

'You can talk,' she'd said. 'Why don't you fuck off and kiss Shaun Crowley's arse – it's all you're good for.'

And it seemed that it wasn't enough for Shaun to come telling tales on her and Colette, but that he'd needed to let James know the whole town thought she was having an affair with the parish priest. And she couldn't resist goading James a little over the ridiculousness of that, and for allowing himself to be so easily manipulated.

'You're right – I have a confession to make. I have been riding Father Brian. We've done it in every room in the house and I'm surprised you haven't noticed with the beds sundered and me in a state of disarray when you arrive home.'

'Ah, will you shut up, I'm trying to have a serious conversation with you.'

And she was very serious then in telling him that while not even the briefest of romantic moments had ever passed between them, the feelings she held for him surpassed those of friendship. He was a man who listened, who took her seriously, who was interested in what she had to say. He didn't ignore or dismiss or belittle her. And while she wished it were her husband who played this role in her life, that was not the case. His visits were the thing she looked forward to most every week. 'And when I hear you put your key in the door in the evening,' she'd said, 'I feel like I'm just going to go and throw myself off the nose of the pier.'

So began the usual round of manoeuvres that had come to characterise their fights. She'd moved into the spare room, although on this occasion James didn't even pretend to be surprised. When Orla had arrived back from school that Friday, Izzy had collected her from the bus stop and warned her of the atmosphere that awaited her at home. Orla had sunk down in the seat and sighed, folded her arms, and turned her face to the window. 'Again?' she'd asked. Niall had grown more withdrawn and sullen, and everything he did seemed to infuriate her. But in particular, he had developed a new habit of playing with his hair. He would take the hair at its longest point on his crown and twist it tightly around his index finger or use both hands to fiddle with it until he had managed to tie a few strands into a wispy knot. She often found him doing it while staring at the television, or in moments of distraction, but no matter how often she told him to stop, the next time she saw him he was pulling at his hair again.

And each evening she tried to come up with a new way to escape the house, to be away from all of them. A meal with Margaret had seemed like something she could manage. She had not expected that Margaret would be the one who needed to be drawn out on her problems. It was a poor substitute for her talks with

Brian, where she could give full vent to the depth of her unhappiness, but with Margaret she could discuss the failures in her own marriage with relative openness. Margaret knew what it was to experience shame. Her marriage had lasted less than a year. Brendan, her husband, had been a skipper on one of the boats and was out at sea all the time. Margaret had just given birth to their son, Daniel, and struggled with being alone so much. Brendan was maverick and ambitious and would go on to own his own trawler, and while Margaret was good-looking, she was also prim and plaintive. They were a poor match. One evening Brendan came in from fishing and told Margaret that it was a mistake for him to have married. He simply had no interest in the kind of life that could be shared with her. Margaret learned later that he had a girlfriend in Galway he'd kept all through their courtship and marriage.

Brendan moved out of the family home. A change in the law a few years back had meant they were able to legally separate, although what material difference that made to Margaret's life Izzy could never tell. Brendan had always supported Margaret and Daniel, only now he was legally obliged to do so. And still, neither Margaret nor Brendan could ever remarry. So Margaret was in the position, unique among all the women Izzy knew, of having the financial support of a wealthy husband while being completely blameless for the failure of their marriage. And yet Izzy had felt nothing but pity for her in the twenty years they'd been friends. Margaret had lived her entire adult life like her husband's mistress, dependent on him for hand-outs, keeping away from other men, staying thin, denying herself so much so that she might remain alert and ready for when he finally returned to her.

Margaret pulled her shawl off the back of her chair and gathered it around her shoulders. She had lost more weight and it had aged her, Izzy thought. She had also stopped dyeing her hair. It was usually jet black but tonight it was tied up in a neat bun, a swirl of grey and black that she'd skewered with what looked like a wooden knitting needle.

'Is she coming with those coffees?' Margaret asked.

Izzy looked up just as Ann was backing through the kitchen doors. 'Here she comes now,' she said.

'She's a bit distracted this evening,' Margaret said.

'Oh, sure that woman's in love,' Izzy said.

They both tried to conceal their smiles as Ann placed the coffees in front of them. Margaret had her arms folded on the table and was staring down into her coffee, and as soon as Ann was far enough away, she looked up at Izzy, her tired eyes sunken in her head. 'I'm a bit worried about Daniel,' she said.

Margaret usually spoke a lot about her son but so far this evening he'd been absent from their conversation. Margaret and Daniel had lived alone together for his entire life until the previous September, when he'd moved to Galway to attend college. Daniel had been Margaret's sole focus, a stand-in husband. She fussed over him and fixated on him in a way that Izzy thought unhealthy. He still drove back from Galway every weekend with a boot full of washing for her. The fact that he was intelligent and driven, that he was so much like his father, had always been a great source of pride for Margaret. She was ambitious for him. But problems started when he was an adolescent. He was prone to obsessions. Around the time of his exams there came a phase of cleaning his hands until they were raw from scrubbing. And that seemed harmless enough until he started to think he had swallowed glass, that every time he ate there was glass in his food. He lost so much weight they had to send him to see a psychiatrist.

The boy was depressed and Izzy didn't know why Margaret couldn't just come out and say it. Half the country was depressed, including herself. But Izzy believed you needed a reason to be depressed, and really the source of Daniel's problems was a mystery to her – he had grown up in a way that was unlike the other boys and girls in his school, certainly, but he was intelligent and athletic and attractive and spoiled by his father and mother, and there was no end of friends calling to the house for him.

'Has something happened?' Izzy asked.

Margaret lifted her cup and placed it back on the saucer. She sighed and closed her eyes tightly.

'Come on, Margaret, talk to me now, you're scaring me.' Izzy reached out and touched her fingertips to the back of her hand.

Margaret flinched, then sat back in her seat and lifted her chin. 'Oh, it's nothing that won't get sorted out, but he's had a bit of an episode. We've had to take him out of college for the time being. He's at home with me at the moment but we have an appointment in Letterkenny next week to see the psychiatrist and we'll know more then.'

'And when you say he had an episode . . . ?' Izzy asked.

'A complete mental breakdown, a full-blown collapse . . .' Margaret almost shouted the words. She lowered her voice. 'It's the same problem. He gets these thoughts, preoccupations . . . dark things,' she whispered, 'and once he starts to think them, he can't get them out of his head and then he can't sleep and . . . it's a whole cycle . . .'

'And Brendan's being good about everything?' Izzy asked.

'Oh, couldn't be better. When we got the call from the college, he went down and collected him and brought all his stuff back. He's with Daniel now, to give me the night off.'

It always astonished Izzy that despite his leaving her and their child all those years ago, Margaret only ever referred to him in the saintliest of terms, like it was some small miracle that he cared enough to look after his own son.

'I think it was the stress of living away from home for the first time,' Margaret continued, 'he couldn't handle being out of his routine, living with other people, not being in control of everything.'

Niall, just before she'd left the house, was fussing and fretting over where she was going and whether or not he could go with her, and when he'd hugged her, she'd looked down – a pale, mottled bald patch about the size of a 5p piece, where he'd pulled the hair from the crown of his head.

'But he's young, and you've done something about it, he'll get over this,' Izzy said.

'It's just hard to see him wasting his life.'

'And you've sat on that now for weeks. Why didn't you pick up the phone and give me a ring?'

'Now, ladies,' Ann said, placing the bill between them along with a small foil parcel.

They looked up at her in surprise and sat back in their seats, drawing away from each other, their intimacy undone. Izzy noticed they were the only table left in the restaurant. They split the bill without any of the usual fuss about one paying for the other.

In the foyer of the hotel, they stood staring through the glass doors at the pouring rain outside, neither of them too keen to walk back to her car. They both agreed then that they should do this once a week, that with the weather as bad as it was it would give them something to look forward to. Izzy made Margaret promise to let her know how Daniel got on with the psychiatrist. They were standing beside the door to the bar, and each time it swung open, for a brief moment, music and chatter poured out and was silenced again.

'It's stopping,' Margaret said, looking out at the rain and fastening the buttons on her coat.

A man stepped out of the bar and walked to the cigarette machine and Izzy peered through the closing door. A few people sat huddled around tables, and a lone drinker, a woman, was keeping the barman company while he polished glasses. She was slumped over the bar, trying to engage him in conversation. The door opened again and Izzy recognised Colette. She was wearing jeans and trainers and had her hair tied up in a ponytail like she'd just gone out for a walk and casually decided to have a drink by herself.

'Jesus,' Margaret said. 'Is that Colette Crowley? She looks like she's had a few.'

'Margaret, I'll say goodnight to you here,' Izzy said.

'Are you sure?'

'I am, yeah – go on now, I'll be grand.'

'Well, Izzy, good luck to you.' Margaret smiled at her and walked away already clutching her car keys. She tipped up the hood of her coat as she stepped out the door.

As soon as Izzy entered the bar, she could hear Colette over every other voice.

'Do you see your mother often, Conal?' she asked, her words fumbling their way out of her mouth.

Izzy stopped about a foot away from Colette, who was so focused on the barman she didn't notice her.

'Oh, I do,' the barman said. 'I visit her all the time, Colette.' He held a glass up to the light as he spoke.

'You must, Conal. It's so important to be good to your mother.

You only get the one. Mine's an auld bitch.' She placed the pint glass to her mouth and it swallowed the tail end of her sentence. She spat some of her drink back into her glass. 'Ah no, no, no, I don't really mean that.' She was rising up and down off the stool, rocking back and forth, as though she was trying to gain enough momentum to launch herself across the bar. 'And are you going to college, Conal?'

'I told you, Colette – I'm starting at the Tourism College next year.'

She thought Colette was going to fall off the stool and she placed her hand firmly on the small of her back. Colette looked up at her then and a smile spread slowly across her face, like Izzy was the answer to a question she'd been mulling over for some time. Izzy laid her hand on Colette's arm and Colette reached out and held it. But she said nothing, just kept smiling and looked down at the floor. Then she pulled her hand away and slapped the edge of the bar. 'Izzy Keaveney,' she said. 'Here, Conal, get Izzy a drink – what are you having, Izzy?'

'I won't have anything,' Izzy said to the barman. 'I'm driving.'

'Oh,' Colette said, gulping at the air like a fish.

'Do you need a lift home, Colette?'

'I do not – sure, I'm grand. I'm just going to finish my drink here with Conal and then I'll head off out the road. The walk'll do me good.'

'It's a bad night, Colette.'

Colette had her arms folded in her lap now and was massaging her forearm with one hand. She reached for her glass and brought it to her lips and out of the corner of her mouth, she asked, 'How are you getting on with that priest?'

'Come on now – they're closing up in here,' Izzy said.

'Aye, Colette,' Conal said, 'I'll be kicking everyone out in a minute.'

Colette folded her arms again and looked down into her lap like a sullen child. 'You stopped coming to the classes,' she said.

'I have a lot going on.'

'I'd say you have, all right. So busy you can't answer your phone. Conal!' she shouted, suddenly very animated. 'You wouldn't know this – Izzy Keaveney.' She pointed at Izzy. 'Very, talented, poet.' She wagged her finger at Izzy with each word. She reached out and grabbed Izzy's arm and pulled her to her. 'Have I told you that, Izzy?' Her voice was shot through with concern. Izzy tried to prise Colette's fingers from her arm.

'Come on now, Colette, we'll go. I'll drive you home.'

Colette's body suddenly slackened and she slipped off the bar-stool, with Izzy steadying her as her feet met the floor. Izzy was aware that everyone in the bar was watching them. A man she did not recognise, a burly, bald-headed man, approached them and offered his assistance.

'We'll be grand,' Izzy said, smiling at the man. 'I can get her home from here.'

'Izzy's got it all under control,' Colette said to the man.

She linked arms with Colette, stiffening her elbow to bolster her. Izzy tried to appear stately in the face of Colette's imminent collapse. She felt like she was leading a drunk bride to the altar.

On the pavement at the front of the hotel, Colette shouted again, 'Izzy's got it all under control.'

Izzy dug her elbow into Colette's side. 'Shut up now, Colette – you'll wake the whole town.'

They meandered across the road to the car park, buffeted as

Colette's weight pulled them from side to side. When they got to the car Izzy opened the passenger door and pushed Colette in.

'Put your seat belt on there, Colette,' she said, getting in on the driver's side.

She flashed the wipers a few times to clear the windscreen.

Colette was pawing at the seat belt but couldn't quite get a purchase on it.

'Give me that,' Izzy said, reaching across her. She pulled the belt out and clicked the clasp into the buckle.

They passed along the Shore Road and through the industrial estate, where the tall streetlamps beamed a lurid yellow light over the factories. It was such a quiet night, not another car on the road, and Izzy was conscious of every sound – the gentle shush of the tyres moving along the wet road, the hum of the engine, and Colette's breathing deepening to a jagged rasp. She glanced at Colette, who had her eyes closed and her head back against the headrest.

'Come on now, Colette, don't fall asleep on me – you'll be home in two minutes.'

She reached out and jabbed Colette in the thigh. Colette made a gulping noise and sat up.

'You're not going to be sick, are you?' Izzy asked. 'Because if you are let me know and I can pull over.'

Colette leaned forward and blinked at the windscreen.

'Don't get sick in the car, Colette – all right?'

Izzy could hear her taking long, slow breaths. The car began the steep climb up the Coast Road. The moon came into view, a disc of pure white light hanging low over the bay.

'Look at that,' Izzy said. 'A full moon. Well, that makes sense, doesn't it?'

Colette huffed.

They turned into the driveway of the cottage and as the head-lights swept the road in front of them, Izzy saw a tall figure in an anorak. The figure looked up at the approaching car and Izzy saw Donal Mullen staring directly at her. He put his hood up, passed through the gap in the wall, and descended the hill. She stopped the engine in front of the cottage and they sat in silence.

Izzy looked down at Mullen's house. A light flashed on as Donal approached his front door.

'Does he do that often?' Izzy said.

Colette began to brace against the seat belt like she was being tied down.

'Nightly visits?' Izzy pressed the buckle and Colette relaxed. 'I won't open my mouth, Colette. It's your life and you may destroy it if you want to. You seem to be doing a good enough job of that by yourself. But why do you need to drag another man and his wife into it?'

'He didn't need too much encouragement.'

'I'd say as much – because you really came to the right house if you were looking for trouble.'

'I'm not looking for anything from him – I just want my life back.'

'And that's the way to go about it, is it? To have him throwing his leg over you every night? You know he's had half the women in the town?'

'And I'm getting the full benefit of his experience.'

'So that's what it's about, is it?'

'I wouldn't expect you to understand.'

'What? You think I can't see the appeal of a man like Donal Mullen? I'm not blind. He'd be a welcome distraction for any woman. I'd say he'd show you a good time but—'

'Ha,' Colette shouted. She smiled and shook her head like she was trying to rid herself of some bitter memory. 'You have no idea,' she said, and in that moment it appeared to Izzy that Colette had become entirely sober and lucid, before her eyes glazed over again. 'Now, let me out of this car,' Colette demanded.

'The door's open, you silly bitch.'

Izzy followed Colette to the door of the cottage, where Colette stood patting the pockets of her coat.

'Have you lost your keys?' Izzy asked. She heard a rattling sound and stuck her hand into Colette's pocket.

'You can leave me alone now,' Colette said.

'Oh, that's a good one, all right – and then I hear tomorrow that you've choked to death on your own sick and I'm never able to forgive myself. Get in there and get into your bed.'

Izzy unlocked the door and ushered Colette inside. Colette careened off, struggling to unbutton her coat. She turned on the bathroom light and Izzy saw her confront her reflection in the mirror, before turning and heading to the bedroom. Izzy looked around the kitchen. The table was covered in newspapers and books and an overflowing ashtray, and she was aware then of the smell of stale smoke and cigarette butts. She walked to the other side of the table and opened the window just a couple of inches and the hush of the sea rushed in. She lifted the ashtray and brought it to the bin, which was surrounded by empty bottles of beer and wine and spirits. A pile of dirty dishes lay on the sideboard. She took a glass and rinsed it out, filled it with water, and carried it to the bedroom, placing it on top of the books stacked beside the bed. Colette had managed to pull her coat and her trainers off and had discarded them on the floor. Otherwise, she'd deposited herself on the bed fully clothed, and was writhing, kicking the bedclothes down to the foot of the bed. Izzy decided that she would be OK sleeping this way. She had no desire to wrestle her out of her clothes.

Colette flopped onto her back and let out a moan.

'Come on now, Colette,' Izzy said. 'You can't sleep on your back. Roll over onto your side.' She leaned over and put her hand behind Colette's shoulder and pulled, and her body relented. Once Colette was on her side Izzy walked back to the kitchen and found a bowl under the sink. She placed it on the floor beside the bed. The agitation in Colette's body had quelled. She'd drawn her knees towards her chest, but still it was like her whole body was softly rolling, like she was trying to shed her skin. Izzy smoothed Colette's hair away from her face and went and turned the bathroom light off. She sat in a chair by the window and looked at the sea and watched a thin strip of cloud creep slowly across the moon. She listened out for the little moans released by Colette, growing further and further apart. And the memory of Donal Mullen's face, looking away, flashed across her mind, before her thoughts turned to Daniel Brennan. Every time she had ever met him in his whole life, he was smiling politely, but he was always looking at the world askance. And she wondered if he was asleep at that moment – if it was even possible for him to fall asleep. Or was he always just thinking, turning those thoughts over and over in his mind – trying to keep himself awake in case the darkness consumed him entirely.

*

The next morning she awoke in some confusion, surprised to find herself still sleeping in the spare bedroom. There was a dull light filtering through the thin curtains and she expected that beyond them lay another grey day. In her mind hung a vision of Niall in his school uniform, quietly creeping towards her. Then she heard an engine start, the car pulling away from the front of the house. James would be taking Niall to school and then he would be off to Dublin for work.

When she had returned home last night, she'd forgotten for a moment that she was not sleeping with James, had not spoken to him for weeks, and had placed one foot on the bottom stair before she remembered. But the momentum had remained in her body, the desire to propel herself upstairs and wake him and tell him that really they were lucky – to have their home and their children, and yes, to have each other. Really, they had so much. And what was the good in screaming the house down and blaming and making each other so unhappy over two people who had nothing to do with them? They could move on from this, was what she wanted to say to him.

She sat up in the bed, reached out for the book on her night-stand, but her hand just rested on its hard cover. She could not bring herself to lift it, to open the pages, the investment required felt too great. And she could not spend another day alone in the house. There was only one person she wanted to speak to, to be in the company of, and the need for him felt so strong that it smoth-ered any other concern. She showered and dressed. She put on an Alice band, pushed the wizened ends of her hair behind her ears. Before she left the house she checked herself in the hall mirror, in her brightly coloured jumper, the collar of her white blouse peek-ing up from underneath. She wore her pearls. She applied a slick of lipstick so similar to the colour of her own lips it was like wearing nothing.

It was unusual for her to go to the parochial house to visit Brian and so she brought the three novels she'd borrowed from him to give her some excuse. It had been at least six weeks since they'd spoken to each other and she had not tried to phone him and he had not, as far as she knew, tried to phone her. The only time she'd laid eyes on him was when he stood before her at the altar on a Sunday morning. Driving along the bridge into the town, she tried to think of what she would say to him. The sky held the same dull uniformity it had all week, so unusual for this time of year, when you could expect every type of weather in a single hour. There was no variation between one day and the next. And surely she would lead with something like this. 'Well, will it ever end, this winter?' she could say, smiling and shaking her head, before he even had a chance to say hello. He was used to this. She never said what she really meant at first, but she recognised how keenly he saw her. And she would allow herself to be drawn out. She would probably tell him something of the difficulties she and James were having. But she could not imagine speaking in any frank way about her dealings with Colette, about the shopping trips and the fights they had caused.

'*You have no idea.*' She had spent months aiding and listening and investing so fully in the life of a woman she barely knew and all that woman had done was turn to her and say, *You don't understand what desire is.* To be rid of this resentment she felt for someone who had been reduced to nothing, to be free of the smallness and petti-ness of that – and yet the need was present to let him know some-thing of how she had witnessed Colette drunk out of her mind in the hotel bar the previous night. She could hear herself coming sideways at the topic, telling him she was exhausted. *From what?* he'd ask, and she'd mention about having to drive Colette home and about Donal Mullen waiting on her doorstep. 'Adultery' – they talked about so much and yet she could never remember them using this word. Even when it happened in the books they read, they steered clear of the issue. And as she pulled up in the church car park, she warned herself to avoid the subject of Colette – her need to lower Colette in his estimation was too strong. She could simply spend the afternoon with him in silence and it would give her pleasure. She could allow herself to be buoyed upon his warmth, the gentle way he had of poking fun at her; better to spend the afternoon like that than to breathe a single word of Colette. She did not need to help her anymore, she did not need to participate in her life, but it was better to pretend that Colette had never existed than to try to reduce the woman any further.

There was a large white van parked at the front of the parochial house. All of the windows were open like some kind of spring-cleaning was going on, but she thought that a bit premature. She took the books and got out of the car, and as she approached the house two men walked out the front door, each carrying a cardboard box. The priest's housekeeper, Stasia Toomey, stepped out the front door and watched the men load the boxes onto the back of the van. She wore a floral apron tied so tightly her stomach and bosom were pushed together into one great lump. Stasia had noticed her from across the car park, and even from that distance, Izzy could read the look of annoyance on her face. By the time Izzy reached her, she had focused her attentions on the workmen once again.

'Mind that now,' she said to a young fellow carrying another box out of the house. 'Ah hello, Izzy, how are you?' she said, as if Izzy's presence was a great surprise to her. 'Is that the last of it?' she asked the elder of the two workmen.

'No,' he said, walking back into the house, 'there's about a dozen more boxes.'

'You couldn't keep a close enough eye on them,' Stasia said. 'He doesn't have that much stuff altogether but it would all be thrown in the back of that van with no consideration whatsoever if someone didn't direct them. And then of course it would arrive with everything in tatters – and who'd get the blame for that?' she said, poking herself in the chest.

'What in the name of God's going on, Stasia?'

'What's going on? We're getting a new priest,' she said, a note of satisfaction in her voice.

'What do you mean we're getting a new priest?'

'He's gone,' Stasia said, pronouncing the words loudly and clearly for there to be no further discussion of the matter. 'Mind that,' she said to the younger fellow, who was pushing an office chair out the door. 'Ah, can you not lift it? The wheels'll get scratched!'

'Gone where?'

'Well, this stuff is being sent to Claremorris so that would be a good place to start looking, I suppose. Anyway, you'd know more than I would. I was told nothing other than to arrange for his things to be sent on. I came here on Monday and everything was packed up and ready to go. And the new priest arrives in a couple of days and in the meantime I have to get the whole house cleaned and ready for him and you'd swear there were ten of me.' She sighed and folded her arms. 'But all I can say is that he was always a gentleman towards me. I never had any problems with him.' She fussed with the neck of her housecoat when she said this.

Izzy watched the workmen ferrying the boxes from the house to the van.

'Do you want me to take those?' Stasia asked.

Izzy stared at her.

'Those?' Stasia said, pointing.

198

Izzy looked down at the three books she held against her side. 'Oh . . . yes,' she said, placing her palms against the top and bottom of the pile and carefully handing the books to Stasia, who made a great show of taking them into her arms, like they were much heavier than they really were.

'I'll make sure they get to him,' she said, but she had already turned away from Izzy and was supervising the workmen again, her arms wrapped around the books so they were pressed to her chest, their spines peeping out at Izzy. She turned and began to walk, her arms swinging empty and heavy at her sides. Aware that Stasia was probably watching, she steadied her step and lifted her head, focusing her gaze on her car.

Sitting in the driver's seat, fastening her seat belt, she heard the doors of the van slam shut, but she could not bring herself to look over at it. To have phoned that morning – that was the thing to have done. How much easier it would have been to hide her alarm and confusion over the phone instead of making a fool of herself in front of Stasia Toomey. Because the whole town would be talking about the priest's disappearance, and now Stasia would add to that the last-minute arrival of Izzy Keaveney on the scene – how she'd nearly dropped down dead in front of the parochial house when she heard the news. Everyone must have known about his departure already but her. Did James know? she wondered.

She heard the engine of the van starting and some gruff shout echo between the workmen.

Of course he knew, she thought. Of course he knew.

CHAPTER 20

Eric's little body was still warm from his bath when Dolores carried him into the sitting room, swaddled in a towel, and laid him down on his changing mat. The water in the tub had soothed the eczema on her hands and she'd slathered them in lotion, and it felt good now to have them occupied in some activity. She pulled her son's toes and smiled at him and tried not to think of the red welts that bealed between her knuckles.

Madeleine bounded into the room. Dolores knew it was her without looking up, from the frantic swish of her jeans, the breathless energy she carried. Madeleine had been pursuing her all day.

'Please can I go to Glenties on Friday?' she asked, for what felt like the hundredth time.

Dolores had calmly resolved not to get angry with her daughter. There had been so much silence and anger in their house these past few months that, where it was possible, she was determined to be gentle and patient with her children.

'Why can't I go?' Madeleine pushed.

'Because you're too good-looking,' Dolores said. 'They'll all be after you at that disco.'

And she meant this in a way. Madeleine was turning out to be beautiful – a much finer version of herself. Where her curls were dry and dense, Madeleine's were soft and silken. Where Dolores's body tapered, Madeleine's curved. And if she was anything like Dolores, she was probably fertile too.

'So you're jealous?' Madeleine said. 'You can't have any fun any-more, so I'm not allowed to either.'

Madeleine threw herself down on the sofa beside her little sister, who was propped up against a pile of cushions, quietly watching the TV. Jessica slowly turned her wide-eyed gaze on Madeleine, fascinated by this performance. Then as though in a trance she slipped down off the sofa, trailing her blanket after her, and sidled closer to the TV.

'Of course I'm jealous.' She held Eric's ankles between her thumb and middle finger and dusted his arse with talcum powder. 'I'm six months pregnant and you get to go out and have fun while I'm here with two weans. You have it all ahead of you. And that's why you can wait. You can wait until you're sixteen – two more years.'

'But Ciara and Tara go every week and they're the same age as me. Tara's mother won't even let her get her ears pierced and she's allowed to go to Glenties!' And with that she was up again and stamping off down the hall.

Jessica tilted into her eyeline with a listless twirl, having clearly decided that far too much attention was being paid to Madeleine.

She was singing softly, just letting out random notes and sounds as she danced.

'Dolores!' her husband roared.

Madeleine always went straight to her father when she didn't get what she wanted.

'Dolores!' the shout came again.

She sighed and sat back on her heels. She stared down at her son as he chewed on his bottom lip and held out his arms to her, his little fists flashing open and closed. Dolores pulled a white vest over Eric's head and then slid him into his sleep suit, pushing his feet down into the legs and poking his hands through the cuffs. When she snapped the buttons closed it formed the picture of a woolly sheep across his chest. She bent down and rubbed her nose against his. 'Now you're in your sheep suit,' she said, 'and you're gonna be fast asheep in no time.'

'Mammy – look the man,' Jessica said, and Dolores looked over to the window where Jessica was chewing on the windowsill and peering out.

'Jessica, love, if you're that hungry, I think it's time for your dinner.'

Her daughter removed her mouth from the sill, drawing a strand of saliva with her. 'Look the man, Mammy.' She was pointing at an empty sky where the light was draining away.

'What man, love?' Dolores began tossing objects into the baby bag.

'Man up there,' she said – three notes, one high, one low, one high. She jumped up and down and waved her bum around.

Dolores gathered Eric into her arms and groaned as she rose to her feet. She walked to the window and placed her hand on the back of her daughter's head.

'Man!' her daughter said more energetically this time, pointing at the cottage, and Dolores looked out over the waterlogged grass of her front garden and up the hill to where a tall man stood. He had thick grey hair and glasses, and a long camel coat. His nose was hooked, like a crow. He was staring out over the wall with his hands behind his back. And he looked sad. He also looked distinguished. He wore a grey scarf, loosely tied. He obviously had something to do with Colette, and she thought that maybe now she had a fellow of her own she could leave hers alone.

Dolores moved Eric down to her hip out of the way of her bump and rested his bottom into the palm of her hand. She pressed the nail of her thumb into the cracked skin between her knuckles. If she could have gone back to that moment when Colette Crowley had shown up at her house, she would have shooed her from the door like a stray dog. She hadn't thought for a second that that woman, who was at least ten years older than her and looked every day of it, would have been of interest to any man, especially her husband. She'd never met his other women, the ones who phoned the house and hung up, but she knew from the magazines he brought home what his tastes were. He bought cheap, amateur stuff, with strange eighties throwbacks – women with big perms and sweatbands, wearing leotards with no gusset. And his preference was for the palest and skinniest, the ones with the tiniest tits, and this had been some small comfort to her. 'Look at that,' he'd say to her while he fucked her from behind, the magazine laid out on the pillow in front of her face. And if she looked away, he pressed her face down into it. He said it helped him along.

But Colette Crowley was as unlike Dolores as it was possible to be. She was another species altogether. And she wouldn't look at dirty magazines while you fucked her. Or maybe she would, because Dolores had thought a lot about this – you never did know. When that woman showed up on her doorstep in her ugly woollen skirt and her roll-neck jumper and her big mop of black hair with the greys showing – and that fucking saddlebag – she'd thought nothing of her. And then as soon as she told her mother and her sisters that they were renting the cottage to Colette Crowley they started making jokes. 'Oh, she's a fine one to have living next door to you – lock up your husbands – she's man-mad that one.' Her mother also told her Colette had lost a child. Cot death, she said it was. Dolores had gone cold when she heard that, would not have wished it on anyone, but there was the feeling too that this woman up in the cottage was cursed and Dolores had invited her in. And she'd had nothing but trouble since.

And after her mother and her sisters told her these things it was like every time she saw Colette she noticed something new about her. Her blue eyes were flecked with light, like glass shattered into a thousand tiny pieces. Her skin was pale and tired, but so smooth and even and white, like it would cool your hands just to touch them there. And those long, fine teeth, so clean and neat and evenly spaced in her mouth. She came to the house a lot these days, looking for something – Donal, Dolores guessed. And one day shortly before Christmas she had come looking for a spare key for the cottage. She had locked herself out after a walk on the beach, or at least that's what she said. And when Dolores handed Colette the keys, she noticed how long her fingers were. Elegant, that's what Colette was. She could see now too, because she had reason to pay closer attention, that beneath the layers of wool were rounded curves and length of bone and pleasure to be had.

It was that visit that first made her think something was wrong. Colette was distracted, looking over her shoulder. She didn't seem to be at all concerned that she was locked out of her house. She was a little unsteady too and Dolores thought she might have had drink taken. She had that kind of purpose about her, like she'd fixed on an idea and now didn't quite know how to put it into action. Dolores felt that if she hadn't been standing there, Colette would have just barrelled through the door. She noticed too, with some satisfaction, that Colette had gained weight. And watching Colette clamber back up the hill to the cottage, she thought of all the times herself and Donal had gone up there to have sex in the afternoon. He'd start agitating for it and he didn't care if the kids were around. But she did. If she got the youngest two down for a sleep and Madeleine was at home, she'd sneak off up to the cottage with him.

At first, when he'd stopped wanting sex from her, she'd been relieved. She thought it might have been him being considerate for once because she was pregnant again. And maybe it *was* him being considerate. He had to get it somewhere, that's the way he'd look at it, and wasn't it better for him to be off with some other woman than bothering her while she was six months gone? It took a while for the two ideas to marry in her head, that the woman in the cottage was the woman he was sleeping with. But then she came down to the house on Christmas Eve and started shouting at Shaun on the phone. Dolores had watched them from the living room, had heard the cruel way Donal dismissed her from the house. And she said it to herself there and then: *they're fucking*.

It started that some nights he just got out of the bed and left the house and came back an hour later. Sometimes he showered and sometimes he didn't, but either way he was letting her know that he was going to behave however he wanted and he dared her to do something about it. And she knew that even if he led her by the hand up to the cottage and made her stand by the bed while he fucked Colette Crowley, just like every time before he'd tell her it was all in her head – that she was always like this when she was pregnant, that she was nothing but a harpy. Go and cry to your mother and father, he'd say to her. And while she knew Donal down to his bones, she did not know what kind of woman could let a married man into her bed for an hour at a time and send him back to his wife, and then look that woman in the eye the next day and ask her for a spare key, or a cup of sugar, or a word with her husband about the electrics. But of course, Donal's disregard for her meant that Colette knew that Dolores knew. And she must think that Dolores was the stupidest, weakest, most useless woman that ever there was.

Dolores looked down at her hands and saw that her daughter's head was dusted with flakes of skin, the windowsill powdered in it.

'Man gone, Mammy,' Jessica said.

But the man had not gone, he had just turned his back on them and was peering in the window of the cottage, his two hands blinkering his eyes so he could get a good look. Then he withdrew an envelope from the pocket of his coat and put it through the letterbox. He tied his scarf, tossed the ends over his shoulders, and walked off in the direction of the beach. He might have been heading for a walk with Colette, she thought. Colette was always walking. She walked the beach every day, at least once. And she could often be seen walking in and out of the town, even though it was three miles there and back and she had a car. You wouldn't know where you'd see Colette, and sometimes when Dolores spotted her walking with such purpose in some unlikely place, at some hairpin bend in the road, she'd ask herself where the fuck she was going.

Dolores pulled Eric up on her hip and walked down the hall to the kitchen. Donal was sitting at the table eating a fry, mopping up egg yolk with a slice of white bread. He was staring at a football match on the television.

'Here, Dolores,' he said, without taking his eyes off the screen, 'we need to start letting her go to that disco or we'll never hear the end of it.'

'It's turning into a knocking shop up there,' she said.

'Ah, for God's sake – there's only a load of kids at it.'

'I'm not on about the disco, I'm on about the cottage.'

'What's the problem, now?'

He sat back from the table. He held his hands in the air and looked around him. She picked up a dishcloth from the sideboard and threw it to him.

'Her! Every time you look up there, there's a different fella hanging around.'

He wiped his hands on the cloth. He stared at her, turning the food over in his mouth. 'Who?' he asked. The way he shot the word at her was like she'd accused him of something.

'Who do you think? Colette.'

'No. Who's up there?'

'How the fuck should I know? I just looked now and there was some tall fellow in a long coat, moping about, dropping off a letter for her.'

'What did he look like?'

'I told you – tall, grey hair, glasses, long coat, kind of posh-looking—'

Donal shot up from his chair and marched out of the kitchen.

'Will you calm down,' Dolores said, following him along the hallway. 'He's not there anymore.'

207

She watched him standing at the window, staring up at the cottage. 'And who else have you seen going up there?'

'Apparently she had Michael Breslin in one night.'

He offered her a pitying smile. 'Are you out of your fucking mind?'

'Anyway, that's not the point. I want her gone out of that house. Have you seen the sign she's nailed to the front of it? A little sign that says "Inn-is-free". What the fuck's that about? That's structural damage to my property. I want her gone.'

'It says "In-nish-free", you fucking imbecile. It's from a poem.'

'Oh, and when did you get so fond of poetry, Donal – ha? Get rid of her.'

'We need that money.'

'I know what you need,' she said.

And for just a moment her husband looked like a little boy, as fear and confusion and panic passed across his face like shadows, and disappeared. She'd meant that what he needed was some woman to lie beneath him every night. But what he'd understood was that he needed a good beating from her father. Like the time early on in their marriage when Donal had pushed her and she fell and caught the corner of her eye on the mantelpiece. And when her father had seen the V-shaped cut near her temple she hadn't even needed to explain anything. He'd simply waited with her in silence until Donal got home from work and as soon as he'd stepped out of his van her father had escorted him into the living room and shut the door. She'd heard Donal roar. He'd needed three days off work after that until his ribs healed. And he'd never touched her again.

He'd found other ways to punish her. He'd tell her she was too fat, then too thin, and when her sisters showed up at the house, he'd make a point of mentioning how well they were looking since they'd lost weight, or gained weight, or whatever shape they happened to be in at that time. On the rare occasion when they went to a pub or restaurant, he liked to pick out some fair stranger and whisper her virtues into Dolores's ear. He'd say the house was filthy, disgusting, mangy with dirt, and as soon as she'd got down on her hands and knees and scrubbed the floor, he'd cross it in his dirty work boots. He let her know that she was stupid, that she knew nothing, about life or the world. And all the while she held tight to the threat of her father but was unable to do anything with it because Donal was so careful in his behaviours. And so far she'd kept quiet about his affairs. But if she told her father that Donal was keeping a woman in the cottage, he'd kill him this time.

'Just wait until the summer,' Donal said. His look was softer, his tone measured. 'We'll be able to charge more for it then. And if she won't pay, we'll get her out and get holidaymakers in. We can't be losing out on money with another child on the way.'

'I'm going to go up to that house tomorrow and give her a month's notice.'

Donal stepped closer to Dolores and took his son in his arms. He lifted Eric to his face and kissed him on the ear. And then as though he were about to bestow the same blessing on Dolores, he leaned towards her. 'You'll go nowhere fucking near her. If I hear you've been up there messing with her head there'll be trouble. OK?' He pressed the child back into her arms and Eric let out a little squeal of discomfort. 'And do something about your hands,' he said. 'They're fucking rotten.'

She watched him striding down the hall, following the cheers and chants coming from the television in the kitchen. She dropped down on the sofa and held her son closer to her. 'Shush, shush,

shush,' she said, rocking Eric back and forth. The child lay entirely still and silent in her arms. 'Madeleine,' she shouted.

'Yeah,' came the thin call from upstairs.

'Where's Jessica?' she said.

'She's with me.'

She felt the baby turn inside her and placed her hand on her stomach. 'Shush, shush, shush,' she said.

CHAPTER 21

The house was in complete darkness when James pulled up outside. She would be at one of her classes, he thought, yoga or tai chi or painting. This is what she did when they fought – she absented herself. Sometimes she brought Niall with her and he sat in the corner reading or drawing. But he couldn't think what class she would have on a Friday night. And her absence was only a surprise to him because she'd been so present in his mind during his trip to Dublin, and he'd spent the entire four-hour drive home imagining what he would say to her.

He unlocked the door and turned on the hall lights, left his weekend case at the foot of the stairs. He walked to the notepad beside the phone and found it blank. The house was cold. He went to the hot press and turned on the heating. The air in the kitchen smelled fresh, the surface of the cooker gleamed. The fridge was near empty. He checked in the spare room and all her things were there, everything placed in an orderly way – the corners of the bed sheets neatly tucked, the duvet perfectly smooth.

In the sitting room he opened the drinks cabinet and poured himself a measure of whiskey. He turned on the television and started to watch the nine o'clock news but was distracted by the thought that Orla should have been home by now. Was she standing at the bus stop in the town waiting for someone to collect her? But the bus would have arrived hours ago, and Izzy would not forget something like that. Had Orla gone to stay with one of her friends for the weekend? This was the kind of thing Izzy usually found a way to communicate to him – she would have written it on the notepad.

And so he guessed that during his time away his wife had decided to deepen her silence, to punish him further. He had hoped that a bit of time apart would have eased tensions between them, had returned prepared to begin some kind of reconciliation. And he could think of only one reason why in the past week she would have hardened against him more fully. When he'd phoned his office from Dublin, Cassie could not resist telling him the great bit of gossip about Father Dempsey vanishing. She'd begun to relay the details with a modicum of delicacy, knowing that he was a friend of the family, but by the time she'd finished delivering the news she was breathless with excitement – the whole town was talking about it, she'd said. And Izzy was no fool – she'd have guessed that he'd had something to do with it. He'd been prepared to play dumb if the circumstances allowed for that, but it seemed more likely now they would have to have it out over this, that he would have to hold his hands up and admit his part in it.

He switched over from the nine o'clock news to the ten o'clock, watched the same headlines rehashed, turned off the TV. He rose from the sofa, walked to the hallway. He took Izzy's phone book from the drawer and began to look for Margaret Brennan's number. She was Izzy's closest confidante, and he knew she was aware of how much they fought, but still he felt embarrassed at having to phone her to find out where his wife and children might be. And what if he had to call the Guards? He counted backwards in his head – it was five days since he had even laid eyes on his wife and a much greater length of time since they had spoken. *And how were things between you?* And he would have to say that things had not been good for some time. *And is it unusual for your wife to disappear like this?* And while it was not entirely unusual, he had never gone this long without having some communication with her. *And do you have any reason to believe that your wife might be in any kind of danger, that she might have done some harm to herself?*

As he lifted the receiver to dial Margaret's number, he heard the noise of a car pull up. He put down the phone. Izzy came through the door unbuttoning her raincoat. She was out of breath. She looked as old and tired as he had ever seen her – no make-up, but more than this, it was as though some fundamental layer had been stripped from her. She passed him without acknowledgement, took her cigarettes from the pocket of her coat, and hung it under the stairs.

'Jesus Christ – where have you been?' he said.

She walked into the kitchen and he followed. She was sitting in Niall's place, facing the door, her arms folded on the table. She didn't meet his eye when he walked into the room. She wore a plain white blouse buttoned to the throat.

'What's going on?' he asked.

'Sit down, James.'

'You frightened the life out of me,' he said, stepping closer to the table. 'Where are Niall and Orla?'

'They're with Margaret Brennan – they're going to stay there for the night, to give us a chance to talk.'

'You could have left a note. I was going out of my mind.' He pulled out the chair opposite her and sat down. 'So you're talking to me at least – that's a good start.'

But it was bothering him, how prim and formal she looked sitting there in that starched white blouse.

'James, there's something I need to say to you.'

'Well, go on, spit it out. I'm just glad to see you. Honest to God, I thought . . .'

'James—'

'Well, I don't know what I thought, but . . .'

'James,' she said again, meeting his eye, 'I want a separation.'

'What?'

'I want a separation,' she enunciated.

A sharp breath shot from his throat. 'You've said that before.'

'I have. But it's different this time. I've spoken to a solicitor and I'm going to start the process of—'

'You've spoken to Peter?'

'No, James. I've found my own solicitor. But that was no easy task. There were a few who wouldn't even speak to me when they found out who I was married to. I had to go all the way to Letterkenny before I found a woman solicitor who talked me through everything and—'

'Hold on, hold on – you're telling me you've gone to speak to a solicitor, before we've even had a chance to discuss this?'

'James, we've been talking for twenty years. Honestly – what's left to say?'

'But I'm back now and we can hash this out.' He tried to steady the panic in his voice. 'I know I've been preoccupied lately, there's been a lot going on. I've neglected you. But I'm ready to do whatever—'

'Next Friday I'll bring Niall down to Majella's,' Izzy said, 'and on the way I'll collect Orla from school—'

'On what grounds?'

'On the Sunday you'll drive down to Galway to meet us, and we can talk to the kids together.'

'You need grounds for a separation.'

'You'll bring the kids back with you and I'll stay with Majella for a while. I don't know how long. At least a week. I'll need a bit of time to get my head together—'

'On what grounds are you making this application,' he said, jabbing his finger at the table.

She sighed, sat back in the chair. 'It's a complicated kind of description, but what it boils down to is that the marriage has broken down to the extent that a normal relationship has not existed for a period of—'

'Oh, you're well versed in it now, aren't you? But that's not going to wash. How are you going to prove that?'

'There is a process that we'll have to go through and—'

'And what if I just refuse to play ball?'

'You can make things more difficult if you want but the only ones you'll be harming are the kids.'

'I'm not the one who's intent on dragging them through the courts.'

'And I hope that while I'm away you'll do the decent thing and find alternative accommodation.'

'Alternative accommodation?' He shot up from the chair. 'Alternative accommodation? Would you listen to yourself? What are you fucking talking about?'

He watched her staring off into the corner of the room. 'Is this because of that priest?' he asked.

'*Oh, Jesus Christ,*' he heard her whisper.

He walked to the kitchen sink and reached under it for the whiskey bottle, took down a tumbler from the cupboard, and poured himself a large measure.

She folded her arms across her chest. 'Did you think I wouldn't know?' she asked. 'God, I never thought you'd insult my intelligence like that.'

He took a gulp from the glass, felt the sting in his throat. He put the drink down on the table and the dark liquid lapped over the rim. He sat down in the chair. 'I did it to save our marriage.'

'You're a fucking coward, James Keaveney.'

'This is a chance for us to start again, now he's not around anymore filling your head with shite.'

She withdrew a cigarette from the pack and lit it. 'Tell me—' She took a drag and exhaled a train of smoke. 'Was it so embarrassing for you, so scandalous, for me to be friends with the parish priest?'

'Oh yeah – because that's what people were saying, all right – that you were great friends.'

She placed her chin in the heel of her hand, closed her eyes, and smiled. 'God, Shaun Crowley really did a job on you, didn't he?'

'Did she put you up to this?'

'Who?'

'Housewife of the year – Colette.'

'Oh yeah – because I'd really need to be convinced to leave this marriage.'

'Maybe we should follow their lead – they seem to be making a great go of things. I'd say their children are really happy.'

'We would not be the first couple to get separated, James, it happens all the time.'

'Oh really – and how many couples do you know that are separated?'

'Margaret and Brendan have been separated for years and they manage to make it work.'

'Brendan Brennan is a rich man, he can afford to keep two homes.'

'We're not poor.'

'My God,' he said. 'That's the first time I've ever heard you say that.'

'Look, we can sit here all night and try and blame Brian Dempsey, or Shaun and Colette Crowley, but the truth is that any problems we had, we had before they came on the scene. Things have been bad for a long time. Maybe now we can move on and draw a line under it and life can be better for all of us. What do you think it's like for the kids having a mother and father who don't talk to each other for six months of the year?'

'You see, that's the difference between you and me – no matter how bad things got, I would never want a life without you and the kids.'

'Oh, don't start feigning interest in the children now, James. It doesn't suit you. And I don't doubt that if I had your life, I'd be satisfied with it. You have every single one of your needs met. Your children are reared for you, your home is looked after, you don't have to cook or clean or iron a shirt for yourself. You spend half your time on the road to Dublin and when you're here you may as well not be. In the past twenty years I have not been able to rely on you for even that much support.' She pinched her fingers together and held them up in front of him. 'Your job's always been more important to you than me and the kids. I gave up trying to compete with that a long time ago. But any little bit of independence I've ever tried to have you've taken away from me.'

'The shop?'

'Which one – the one you sold on me fifteen years ago or the one you denied me last year?'

'My job has kept a roof over our heads and two cars running and school fees paid and all you've ever done is complain there's never enough. You've made a good enough job of spending it.'

She stubbed her cigarette out, placed her palms against the table, and pushed herself up out of the seat.

'Sit down,' he shouted. 'We're going to talk about this, now.'

She was staring down at the drops of whiskey pooled on the surface of the table.

'Look, we always sort things out in the end,' he said. 'You've been saying for years that you want to leave and you're still here.'

Her hands were still pressed against the table, her whole body bowed. 'I know, I know,' she said. Her arms began to shake. 'Don't remind me. I've wasted my whole life.'

'I love you,' he said. 'Don't you know that I love you?'

'That's an easy thing to say.'

'No, it isn't,' he said. 'Why are you doing this?'

'Because if I have to stay in this marriage for one second longer, I swear to Christ, James, I'll—'

'Well, maybe you need to see a doctor.'

She strode towards the door.

He called after her, 'If it's so easy to say, then let me hear you say it.'

She stopped in the doorframe. Strips of light and shadow fell across the white material of her blouse. Her head drooped forward, her shoulders rounded. And all at once she straightened and walked off down the hall. His body was overcome by a sensation then, like the rattling of an engine. His face was in his hands and his chest heaved, forcing great gasps into his mouth – but whatever mechanism existed within him was so worn and out of use, it could not be called upon to produce tears.

CHAPTER 22

Colette had put her coat on to go for a walk but was distracted by the page again. She sat back down at the table and re-examined the words. The poem in front of her was titled 'Solace'. She'd always loved this word, how it at once spoke of peace and complete desolation. And it sounded so much like the Irish word for 'light'. She wanted there to be some hope. The word was a light at the top of the page to guide the reader through the darkest moment of her life. She'd laid out the details in blank verse – it was important for her to state these words as baldly as possible. Twelve lines in iambic pentameter and a full stop, blunt as a tiny fist, at the end of each one. To wake, and walk to your son's cot and find he was no longer there, that he had been replaced in the night by something cold and unyielding – there was no real way to soften that.

Two days ago she had visited his grave and laid an arrangement of white roses beside a wreath of white roses, which she guessed had been left by Shaun. They had visited the grave together almost every week in the first year after Patrick died. Then they went at Christmas or on his birthday and eventually they stopped going altogether. She'd thought it strange they had both visited so recently, had chosen the same flower. And then, not for the first time in the past few months, she'd wondered where her own body would be laid to rest when that time came. She'd cast aside this thought, focused on the words on the stone: PATRICK CROWLEY – DIED 9 MONTHS – 4 JUNE 1976 – BELOVED SON AND BROTHER. That was it. And she wanted the poem she wrote to be as stark and unforgiving as the words engraved there.

The kitchen table was strewn with handwritten pages. She swept them together and the page that came to the top was covered in numbers. She'd written down her incomings and outgoings, but whatever way she'd tabulated and calculated, the simple fact was there was more going out than coming in. The £474 in her account was what remained of the money she'd borrowed from her mother. Under 'options' she'd written 'sell car, get more teaching work', and finally, 'begin the process of legal separation'. The fact that Shaun had not been in contact via solicitors had given her hope – but Shaun had not paid any money to her since before Christmas, and she knew now that keeping her poor and beholden was part of the protracted punishment he was intent on exercising upon her. And he'd refused to forward her post, which, she was sure, contained invites to readings and festivals that might have provided her with some source of income. There was still £40 a week coming in from her writing workshops but that was barely enough for groceries and petrol.

But she was surprised at how much further her money stretched now that she'd stopped drinking, and at how easy it was to stop once she discovered her body was set to serve a different purpose. But most astonishing was the discovery that at the age of forty-four she was pregnant with her fifth child. She'd thought that her period might be late or that she was beginning early menopause. She'd only ever suffered mild morning sickness, and as it was, she was hungover so consistently that she expected to feel lousy when she woke. And sometimes when Donal had shown up at the cottage, she'd had a lot to drink already. She'd be quiet and listless, pretending to be overcome with desire when really she was incapable of standing up straight. At that point she didn't care what became of her, and Donal had cared even less.

When two weeks had passed with no sign of her period she drove to a chemist in Donegal Town. She didn't have the nerve to walk into the chemist's in Ardglas and purchase a pregnancy test. Even in Donegal Town, where she was far less likely to see someone she knew, she cowered before the white-coated, bespectacled chemist who refused to look at her, instead focusing on taking her money and placing the test in a brown paper bag that she scrunched closed in her fist.

Colette crossed the diamond to the Central Hotel, hurried through the foyer, and went straight upstairs to the ladies, where she pissed on a plastic stick. Over the next few minutes the outline of a child's cherubic face slowly revealed itself. She marched back over and bought a second test from the same mousy chemist, this time standing before her with her arms folded, determined and affronted, as though it was the chemist who had been responsible for the result. She drove back to the cottage and followed the same procedure and saw the cherubic face taunting her once again.

For days she walked around with the knowledge of it sounding in her head, and no matter where she was and what she was doing, that note ringing clear and true was all she could hear. She was alert, yet numb to anything but the possibility of danger – and what that danger was she could not identify. After a few days passed like this, of not being able to articulate a single coherent thought regarding the predicament she found herself in, she'd sat down and tried to write about it.

'I am pregnant,' she wrote. 'At forty-four years old I am pregnant.' But it did not matter how plainly she stated the facts of her living situation and her financial circumstances, she knew that if she wanted to keep her child, there was a way through this. The worst thing that she could have ever imagined had already happened to her, and she'd survived it. Discovering she was pregnant with Barry was what had kept her alive the last time. And what if this was her daughter, what if after four sons she would finally have the little girl she'd always wanted? She was ready to love this child and take responsibility for it, and in so doing retake control of her life.

But when she thought of the child's father – a coward who had taken what he wanted and retreated. He'd told her they needed to cool things for a while. He'd been spooked by Izzy Keaveney's arrival at the cottage that night, had come to see her only twice after and on both occasions wanted reassurance that Izzy knew nothing of their affair. Cruel too – to make a fool of his wife in the way he had – and pinch-faced and belligerent as Dolores was, Colette knew she did not deserve an ounce of the pain they'd inflicted upon her. And the show she'd made of herself, sick with desire, dragging her tired body down to that man's front door time after time, to complain about the central heating. She could not stay under Donal's roof, she knew that. She could go to her mother's house, stay there, and while her mother would despair over Colette's situation, she would never kick her out on the street.

And finally she had written, with little enthusiasm or conviction, 'Go to England and get an abortion. Tell no one. You know other women who have done this. All possible scenarios require money.'

She heard a sound and looked up. The kitchen window was open and the noise was coming from outside. It was like a siren sounding from a very great distance away. But then the noise turned into notes and those notes turned into words, low and sweet. *'Baa baa black sheep, have you any wool?'* She shot up from the chair. It was a child – she could hear a child singing. She placed her hands on the table to steady herself. The sound disappeared and then a few seconds later it seemed to renew itself, to return louder and more insistent like it was summoning her. *'Yes sir, yes sir, three bags full.'* She stepped towards the window and peered out. Standing by the wall was Jessica Mullen. The child was wearing a little sleep suit made up of a patchwork of colours, like the motley coat of a jester. She held a stuffed toy that she seemed to be serenading. The breeze was tossing wisps of her pageboy haircut back and forth. Colette placed her hand upon her breast and waited for the beating of her heart to slow.

She went to the door, grabbed her scarf off the hook, and twirled it around her neck. She stepped outside and the child looked up at her.

'Jessica Mullen, what in the name of God are you doing all the way up here?'

Jessica returned her attention to the toy and began singing again. Colette could see now that it was a black horse with a red bridle. She walked over to the child.

'That's not a sheep, you silly billy – it's a horse.'

'Sheep,' Jessica said, shaking the toy by its hind leg.

She bent closer to her. 'Will I take you home to your mammy and daddy?'

Jessica nodded and offered her hand to Colette. The road was stony and the child was wearing no shoes, her feet just covered by the leggings of the sleep suit. She thought about carrying Jessica, but she seemed content to amble along, and so they made their way down the drive slowly, Colette holding the child's tiny hand between her thumb and forefinger. 'Your mammy'll be wondering where you got to. You shouldn't be running out of the house like that,' she said. At the end of the road they turned the corner into the neighbouring drive. There was a small incline leading up to the house and the child seemed to grow weary until she almost came to a complete stop. Colette gathered her up into her arms and began to walk more quickly. She could feel the child's warm breath against her neck.

And then Dolores sprang out the front door – really there was something comical about the way she appeared, like she'd been shot out of a cannon. She landed feline on her feet, and when she fixed her eyes on Colette and Jessica every inch of her body seemed to stiffen. Colette wrapped her arms more tightly around the child. Dolores bounded towards them.

'Dolores, you won't believe where I found—'

'What the fuck are you doing with my daughter?' Dolores stopped a few feet away from them, her hands trembling. 'Give her to me,' Dolores said, and Colette realised she'd been withholding the child in fear. She passed Jessica to her mother and Dolores took her carefully into her arms.

'Dolores, I found her up at the cottage. I have no idea how she got there but you must have left the front door open.'

Colette saw the way Dolores stared at her, the pure disbelief, like she couldn't understand a word she was saying.

'Just stop,' Dolores screamed. Her eyes were red from crying, her face wretched with exhaustion.

Colette opened her mouth to speak but nothing came out.

'Just stop,' Dolores said again. 'Don't come down to my house, and don't come anywhere near my children.'

Colette saw Donal step out the front door. He stuck his hands in his pockets and stood there watching them, like some casual observer.

'She's safe,' Colette said, and was surprised by how spiteful she sounded. She stepped back and turned on her heel. She tried to keep her head up, to walk at a steady, even pace as she headed down the drive, to not look back at the scene of the family reunited on the doorstep. And the next thing she was conscious of was the crunch of sand beneath her shoes as she moved off the road and the stone pathway became the beach.

Witch, witch, witch, she thought as she moved along the sand, the wind pulling loose strands of her hair. *Witch, witch, witch.* The mad woman in the cottage, the witch on the hill – she stole husbands and children. You placed a protective arm across the shoulder of whoever was in your company, drew them closer. She'd seen the way people avoided her on the main street of the town, crossed to the other side of the road, or lowered their gaze, smiling to themselves.

At the end of the strand was an enormous hunk of black rock that looked like it had broken free of the coastline. Sometimes she liked to climb right to the top of it and sit there and look out at the sea. In the summer months she'd bathe her feet in one of the pools that skirted its edges. Today, she reached out and placed her palm against its cold, wet surface. Surrounding her hand were patches of yellow and white lichen, neat spiralling patterns like crepe flowers. She turned and sat down on the rock and looked back in the direction she'd come from. The only other person on the beach was a stout little woman in a red headscarf walking a black Labrador almost the same size as her. But then another figure emerged from the Coast Road and despite the distance between them she knew it was Donal, would recognise the shape of him anywhere.

When he was closer, she could see he was wearing a black windbreaker, unzipped so the ends flapped around his waist as he marched towards her. A few feet away he slowed down. He placed his hands in his pockets. His demeanour changed, became sheepish almost. He took half steps in a sort of semicircle. He lowered his eyes then cast curious glances at her like she was something dangerous to be navigated.

'What do you think you're playing at?' he said at last.

She bent forward, placed her elbows on her knees. She looked into the little pool of water near her feet. She could hear him stepping closer.

'Are you listening to me?' he asked.

'I heard you, Donal.' She refused to look up at him, to meet his eye. 'I looked out my kitchen window and saw your three-year-old daughter standing there. I thought it was a good idea to bring her home. But your wife seems to think—'

'She thinks you're gone in the fucking head and I'm beginning to think the same. Can you not leave well enough alone? Coming down to my house asking stupid questions every other day. Do you think my wife's thick, that she doesn't know there's something going on with you sniffing around the whole time?'

'Believe me, Donal, I'm done trying to get your attention. And I'm fully aware that anything there once was between us is done.'

It was so brief, just a moment, a page turning and falling into place, but she saw that her words had hurt him.

'Good,' he said. 'Well, we're agreed on that. And I think it's about time you moved on.'

For weeks she'd been anticipating this, with every disdainful glance Dolores gave her, with every excuse he made not to see her. She'd become a nuisance to all involved. She'd served her purpose.

'The summer's coming,' he continued, 'we can rent that place out for twice the price. It doesn't make sense having you up there anymore. And it doesn't look good, you bringing fellas up there the whole time.'

'What are you talking about, Donal?'

'The whole town is talking about you – it's like a knocking shop. And Dolores saw that fella a couple of weeks ago. That fella from Dublin that you were riding.'

'John? John hasn't been to see me.'

'Oh, did you not know? Well, he's hand-delivering the letters now.'

'I didn't get any letter. And what was John—'

'Look, I'll be decent about it. You have until the end of the month and then you have to be out. That gives you a few weeks. And in the meantime I want no more of your fucking playacting. Stay away from me, stay away from the kids, and stay away from my wife. Do you hear?'

She pushed against the rock and rose to her full height. She folded her arms and took a few steps nearer to him. 'Look, I know I've acted strangely and I know that things are over between us, but there was a time, brief as it was, when we cared about each other.

Or I thought you cared about me at least. And now I'm begging you – if you have even an ounce of human feeling left in you . . . I need your help, Donal. I'm pregnant.'

She watched a look of pure shock etch itself into his features.

'Don't you fucking lie to me,' he said.

'Donal, as God is my witness—'

'Are you lying to me?'

'How do you want me to prove it to you? In a few months' time there'll be no disguising it.'

'And it's mine?' he said.

'It can't be anyone else's.'

'You're sure of that?'

'Oh, Donal—'

'How far along are you?'

'About six weeks, I think, maybe more. I've made an appointment to see the doctor next week.'

'You haven't seen a doctor yet?'

'No.'

'Then how can you be sure?'

'I've done two pregnancy tests. And I've had four children, Donal. My body knows what's going on.'

'That child could be anyone's. And it might not even survive inside you, you're as old as the fucking hills.'

He placed his face in his hands and let out a muffled roar.

'Look, Donal, you're right – I do need to move on. I can go to Dublin and stay with my mother.'

'And then what will you do?' He took a step towards her.

'I need to figure out what I want.'

'I know what you'll do,' he said, taking another step closer. 'You'll get on the next boat to England and you'll get rid of that child.'

She backed away from him. 'Donal, I don't know what I'm going to do but—'

'Are you mad? You can't keep it. You're too old. And what are you going to do with it? How will you raise it? You can never bring it back here. I swear to Christ if you even think about it, I'll break your fucking neck.'

He butted his head closer so that his face was just inches from hers.

She looked away from him. 'Donal, I need money. I have barely a penny to my name.'

He laughed. 'You're asking me for money?'

'It wouldn't need to be a lot. Just enough to get away. And whatever happens, I swear to you, once I'm gone, you'll never hear from me again.'

He moved towards her and she stepped back. She stumbled and fell against the rock. She could feel the dampness, the cold spreading across her back. He was in front of her, so close at that strange, unsteady angle, it was impossible for her to straighten herself, to step aside from him.

'If I give you a single penny,' he said, 'it'll be to get rid of that child.' He pointed at her stomach. 'Do you understand me?'

She looked down at the sand where bits of loose rock were scattered.

'Do you understand me?' he said again.

She nodded.

'Who have you told?' he asked.

'I haven't told a single solitary soul, Donal.'

He grabbed her throat. 'Who have you told?'

'Who can I tell about this?'

He released his grip on her and pointed his finger in her face.

'And you keep it that way. Because if I find out you've told anyone, I don't care where you are, Colette, I'll find you and I'll skin you alive. I'll rip the fucking head off your body. Do you hear me?'

Every inch of her was gripped by a cold trembling.

'And you can forget staying there until the end of the month – I want you out by next Sunday. OK?'

He turned and she watched his back, the great hulking sway of it as he moved away from her, his jacket a black sail filled with wind. She felt her knees buckle and placed her palms flat against the rock to keep herself in place. She took in great lungfuls of air, looking around to see if anyone had witnessed what had just happened. The sound of barking carried to her and she saw the black Labrador stretching its lead to reach Donal, the little woman's body tilted back to keep the dog restrained. But Donal didn't seem to notice. Steady and determined, his gait unchanged, he headed in the direction of his home, where she guessed his wife had stood at the window watching every moment of what had just played out between them.

CHAPTER 23

Izzy placed the blue plastic fish box on the bedroom floor, half full already with old tableware. She took down some bedclothes from the cupboard above the wardrobe and laid them carefully between the cups and plates. A car pulled up at the front of the house, and she heard the creak of the handbrake. She peered out the window and saw James hurry into the house. She listened to his panting as he climbed the stairs. When he stepped into the room he wore a strange look, at once shy and determined. He was carrying a white envelope. He lowered his eyes and she followed his gaze to the bed, where her suitcase lay open, packed with clothes and shoes and toiletries.

'There's a contract in here,' he said, holding up the envelope. 'It's for the purchase of the property on the main street.'

'Christ,' she said, 'you move quickly when it suits you.'

'It needs your signature. I'm going to leave this downstairs on the kitchen table, and if I come back tonight and these papers are unsigned, I'll know your decision.'

'When you come back tonight, I'll be gone, James.'

She sat on the end of the bed with her back to him and listened as he retreated down the stairs. She waited for the sound of the front door closing, the noise of his car heading down the drive, then lifted the box and carried it outside to the boot of her car. In the driver's seat she looked across the bay to where the cottage lay. On a clear day she could make out one corner of the house and knew when Colette had the fire lit because she could see smoke rising up from behind the hill. But today a veil of cloud hung between them. She decided to take her chance anyway.

As she pulled up at the cottage, her heart sank at the sight of Colette standing in the doorway. So often in the past weeks she'd wondered what Colette was doing at that moment, but if she'd not been standing in front of her now, she would have just left the box on the doorstep and driven away. Izzy felt shamed by the pure, solid sight of her.

'Is it yourself, Izzy Keaveney?' Colette asked.

'Hello, Colette,' she said, retrieving the box from the boot. Izzy turned and saw that Colette was staring down at the front door of the Mullens' house.

'Will you come in for a minute?' Colette said, retreating inside.

Izzy remained on the doorstep for a moment, holding the box on one hip. She saw that Colette had fixed a little wooden sign to the front of the house with 'Innisfree' written on it. She remembered the poem from her schooldays.

'I really should keep going, Colette, I have a few things to be getting on with.'

'Sure, you have time for a quick cup.'

Izzy stepped over the threshold and wiped her feet on the mat. Colette stood at the sink filling the kettle. A half-empty bottle of vodka stood on the counter beside her. Izzy carried the box to the table and placed it on a chair. One side of the table was covered in stacks of books and papers. The other end was free of clutter and she sat there and looked around her. How different it all appeared in daylight. The flagstone floor looked clean and well swept, the remains of a fire mouldered in the hearth. There was an order to things that surprised her.

'You should light that fire, Colette. There's not much heat in it today.'

'Do you take sugar?' Colette asked.

'Just milk, thanks.'

'Well, I hope I've put enough in that,' Colette said, handing Izzy a cup.

'That looks perfect.'

As Colette sat down in her chair the woollen roll-neck and scarves she was ruched in bunched up on her chest like plumage. She was still a handsome woman, with coal-black tresses and skin so white the bright blue of her eyes shrilled against it. But her body had become slack and thick with drink, her face riven by the lines of a much older woman.

'You'll have to forgive me, I've started early,' she said, taking a sip from her glass. 'I would have offered you one, but I don't suppose you're the kind for drinking in the afternoon.'

'A cup of tea is just grand,' Izzy said.

Colette took up her pouch of tobacco. Izzy watched Colette's hands tremble as she swaddled the little nub of tobacco with the paper.

Izzy rubbed the tips of her fingers against her palms. 'I was doing a bit of a clear-out and I thought you might need a few things – nothing much, just some old crockery and blankets and things to make the place a bit more homely.'

Colette tossed the pouch onto the table. She struck a match. For just a second the papery skin of her face lit up. She took a drag. 'Well, I hope my squalid conditions have made you feel better about yourself.' Colette's cigarette had not lit properly and she flicked at the tip with the flame of her lighter.

Izzy shifted in her chair and sat up, placing her palms together and pinning them between her knees. She cast a look around the room. 'It's very peaceful up here. You must get a lot of work done.'

'Oh. It's peaceful, all right. *For peace comes dropping slow.*' She performed the line with a deep, weighted tenor. 'But why are you really here, Izzy?'

'Well, I've decided to go away for a while.'

'Have you indeed.'

'I'm going to go and stay with my sister for a couple of weeks. If truth be told, things haven't been good between James and me for some time and I've finally decided to do something about it. I should have done something a long time ago but—'

'Well, there's your first mistake.'

'What?'

'Leaving the house – when you leave the house you relinquish control, you have no rights. And so you go off to your sister's house and return in a few weeks – what's going to be different about your situation then?'

'Things couldn't carry on the way they were.'

'What are you talking about? Things don't get better than the way you have them. You have a home and money and children. So what if your husband's a bit of a bully, they all are in their own way.

Do you want for anything? No. You have a house full of stupid statues and figurines that are worth more money than some people see in a lifetime.'

'I want my independence.'

'Independence? Independence? This is what independence looks like, Izzy.'

'You went about it all wrong.'

'So you think that if I was good, honest, virtuous, and true like yourself none of this would ever have happened to me?'

'No, I'm not talking about that, you should have seen a solicitor.'

Colette laughed.

'And you should give up that old drink while you're at it.' Izzy pointed at the glass and quickly withdrew her hand. 'Anyway, I didn't come up here to give you advice.'

'No, you came to give me your cast-offs.' A smile pulled at the edges of Colette's mouth. 'So why are you telling me all of this? Have I inspired you?'

'Well, I suppose I haven't treated you as well as I should.'

'By ignoring my phone calls?'

Izzy sat right on the edge of her seat now, her hands sliding back and forth across her knees. She looked out the window at the sea. The late-afternoon light had pooled at the horizon under a brow of dark cloud.

'Well, to be honest, Shaun arrived at James's office one morning in the new year and told him about our trips to the beach and Enniskillen. I don't know how he knew, but he knew. And on top of that he told James the whole town thought me and Father Dempsey were having an affair. As you can imagine, we had the most unmerciful row over everything. We've hardly spoken since. I was given express instructions to cease all contact with you, which

I should have ignored of course, kept coming to the classes but . . . well, I didn't have much fight left in me.'

Colette held her cigarette over the ashtray. She paused for a moment before tapping the ash off. 'I thought Shaun had something to do with it, all right.'

'Oh, as I said to James – any problems we had, we had before you and Shaun came along.'

'But by the sounds of it you'd become closer to Father Dempsey than the village elders deemed appropriate,' Colette said, raising her eyebrows.

Izzy sighed, opening her eyes wide and shaking her head. 'Nothing happened. Do you really think I'd have an affair with the parish priest? Jesus, I'd need to drink your whole bottle of vodka before it would even occur to me. No. We became good friends, that's all, and James became jealous. He thought he was interfering.'

'Well, priests are good at that, aren't they? For all they know about marriage they have no end of advice on the subject,' Colette said.

'He wasn't like that. He wasn't sanctimonious or dogmatic or full of shite about the Church. You could just talk to him.'

'But surely you have friends. Could you not talk to them?'

'And tell them what? Tell them you're lonely? Tell them you're unhappy? Who wants to know, Colette? Who has so little going on in their own life they need to hear that? People would only be talking about you. You know what this town is like – you can't even be friends with a priest but they think you're sleeping with him.'

'Well now, I'm not saying you were having mad passionate sex with the man. Although good for you if you were. But one minute you were spending every waking hour with him and the next thing he was gone.'

'Well, I know as much about that as you do. He never said a word to me before he went.'

'You're not trying to tell me James Keaveney had nothing to do with Father Dempsey's removal from his post?' Colette said. 'Do you know where he's gone?'

'Oh, some other parish,' Izzy said, with a throw of her head.

'You needn't pretend to me like he meant nothing to you. I can see you cared about him.'

Izzy felt her shoulders soften. She allowed her arms to fall loosely by her sides. 'It was just nice to have someone to talk to,' she said.

'Oh, Izzy, don't be a fool. We are stupid, aren't we? Stupid, stupid women. We'll go with anyone who'll listen to us.' Colette tried to stand up but fell back heavily in the chair. She looked defeated for a moment but made another effort and managed to haul herself to her feet. 'Will you have a drink now?' she asked.

'No, Colette. I won't. I should get going.'

Colette went to the counter and sloshed more vodka into her glass. She walked back to the chair and dropped down into it, spilling half the drink over her jumper.

She held the glass out in front of her. '*Arise and go now*, Izzy Keaveney. Forget about him. Go home to your husband. I absolve you in the name of the Father and the Son and the Holy Spirit,' she said, making the sign of the cross with the glass, the vodka lapping up against the sides of it. 'Go home and be forgiven, Izzy,' she said, her voice reducing as the glass drew closer to her mouth. 'It's very easy to become a ghost in your own life.'

Izzy got up and walked to Colette. She stood over her and laid her hand on her shoulder. 'And will you do something for me, Colette – will you mind yourself?'

She could only see the top of Colette's head from where she

stood but she watched her give a shallow nod. Then she placed her palm against Colette's cheek and allowed her to rest the weight of her head there. She felt Colette's warm tears meet her hand.

'Ah now, Colette,' she said, rubbing her back. 'There's no need for that. You'll see everything's going to work out all right for you.'

'I'm six weeks gone,' Colette said.

'What's that?'

'I said, I'm six weeks gone.'

Izzy stiffened. She stepped back from Colette and ran her eye up and down the length of her. 'What are you talking about?' she asked.

'Do you think I'm joking? I'm nearly two months pregnant,' Colette said.

'Are you sure?'

'I've missed my period, I've done two tests – I haven't been to the doctor's yet, but I'm sure,' Colette said.

Izzy caught her hand, pinched it between her thumb and middle finger; the impulse to strike Colette was so strong. 'You stupid fucking woman,' she said under her breath, dropping back down into her seat.

'I know, I know, I know,' Colette said. Her whole body appeared to shake. 'I'm the stupidest fucking woman who's ever lived.'

'How did you let this happen?' she asked.

'I don't know,' Colette said, 'maybe I thought I was past it.'

'And it's his?' Izzy nodded her head in the direction of the Mullens' house.

'Of course it's fucking his,' Colette shouted.

Izzy looked at the vodka bottle on the counter. 'But what are you going to do?' she asked.

'I'm going to go and stay with my mother for a while.'

'Right, that seems like a sensible enough idea.'

'But I need your help . . . Again . . . I'm sorry. I need to borrow a bit of money.'

'To get you to Dublin?'

'No.' Colette shook her head. 'It needs to get me a bit farther than that. I'd need a few hundred pounds maybe.'

Izzy looked down at the table.

'I can't have this child,' Colette continued. 'I've thought about it, believe me. But there's no place for me in the world right now, let alone a baby.'

'You still have a husband.'

'Oh, Izzy, Shaun won't even let me see the children I have, do you really think he's going to take me back and help me rear another man's child?'

'He wouldn't be the first man who's done that. And can your mother not help you?'

'How do I ask my mother for the money to have an abortion?'

'And yet you have no problem asking me.'

'Do you think if there was any other possible way that I'd be asking you? And please don't make me go down to that man and beg from him again.'

'Who? Shaun?'

'No. Donal.'

'You've told him?'

'I know – it was stupid. I knew he'd no more care for it than if it was something washed up on the beach. But he was trying to get me out of the cottage. He wanted rid of me altogether. I was fool enough to think that if I told him he might take pity on me.'

'And what did he say?'

'He told me to get rid of the child, that if I brought it back to the town, he'd kill me.'

'Colette, Donal Mullen can't make you get rid of your child. And you can't go running off to England like a teenager.'

'That's it, Izzy. I'm not a teenager. I'm forty-four years old.'

Izzy rose from her seat. She lifted her handbag from where it rested on the top of the box of objects. She opened the bag and took three crisp £20 notes from her purse. 'Colette – pack up your things and get in your car. There's enough money there to get you to Dublin. Go and see your mother. Go and have your child. I promise you for as long as I live I'll never breathe a word of this to anyone. No one ever has to know who the father is if you don't want them to.'

Izzy placed the notes on the table and watched Colette's eyes drift towards them. She walked to the door and let herself out.

Sitting in her car, she looked back at the cottage. A barrel stood under the eaves, to collect whatever rainwater overflowed from the gutters, she guessed. She recalled the conversation they'd had, when James joked that Colette had been reduced to washing from a barrel.

'Well, you know what those artistic types are like,' she'd said, playing along.

'Yes,' he'd said. *That's what poets do.*' And not for the first time they'd laughed over the misfortunes of Colette Crowley.

*

That evening when James Keaveney stepped through the front door of his home, he registered a change in the atmosphere. For months he'd come back to find the place empty, or with half the lights on and his wife and son sequestered in some corner of the house. Tonight, there was movement and activity, brightness and warmth. He walked down the hallway and stopped at the kitchen door.

'There you are,' his wife said, passing with a bundle of place-mats, throwing a smile in his direction. 'Niall,' she shouted.

James patted down his pockets, looking for his wallet or his keys or something he'd lost – he didn't know. Realising he was still wearing his coat, he went to hang it under the stairs.

'I got a few lamb chops from Breslin's this afternoon,' his wife said, and he followed the sound of her voice back into the kitchen, looked over to where his son was now seated at the table, swinging his legs back and forth and eyeing him suspiciously.

'Oh, great,' he said, and he could hear the forced enthusiasm in his voice. He took his seat at the head of the table.

A plate of food was placed in front of him – boiled potatoes neat as balls of soap, glistening green broccoli, lamb chops still sizzling from the pan.

'Now,' his wife said, taking her place at the table and laying a dishcloth across her lap.

And then she proceeded to talk, to confound him with chatter. She spoke of the people she had encountered while running her errands, the price of petrol, the news story about politicians accepting bribes.

'Eat your dinner,' she said. 'It'll get cold.'

He had not touched his food.

'Oh God, it's shocking,' he said, taking up his fork, but he did not know what he was responding to.

'Are you listening to me?' she asked.

'What?'

'I said to Niall that we might have a weekend in Galway over his Easter holidays. What do you think about that?'

'Oh, that's a good idea,' he said, as the potato burned the roof of his mouth and the food spilled out onto the plate.

'Here you go,' his wife said, handing him the dishcloth.

He wiped his chin and saw that his son was looking at their faces in turn, examining them. He felt something on the back of his hand and looked down to see his wife's fingertips placed gently there.

'It would do us good to get away,' she said.

And then he remembered what it was he had been looking for. He lifted his head and saw, at the end of the table, the contract, one half sticking out of the envelope with his wife's signature clearly visible.

He watched Izzy clearing away dishes, the studied, clean movements she made. She knew she was being watched, her eyes alert and fearful, like a single dropped fork could bring the house crashing down.

All that night James moved around his home slowly, carefully, like any sudden movement or misjudged step might disturb the deceit he found himself participating in. It was not until several hours later, when he pressed the button on the remote control and watched the image on the television disappear, and climbed the stairs to his bedroom, that he allowed himself to believe the turn of events his life had taken was in any way real. Sitting in front of her dressing table was Izzy, every object that had been moved to the spare room now returned to its rightful place. She was wearing a white sleeveless nightdress, rubbing lotion on her arms. She looked up at him with a vague smile. He sat on the end of the bed and caught her eye in the mirror. He felt his shoulders loosen and stared down at the floor. He pulled off his shoes, tossed them aside. He heard his wife's soft footsteps, felt the mattress dip beside him.

*

In her bed that night Colette Crowley lay on her side, her knees drawn to her chest, moaning softly. She had had a lot to drink. Phrases she'd written that day lumbered in her stomach. Sometimes, a soft flutter would pass through her, like the gentle beat of a bird's wings, and she'd allow one of these phrases to grow larger, more insistent, to quell her panic at the thought of the child growing inside her. But like a fog finding its way through some crevice in her mind, the knowledge that nearby there was someone who wished to do her harm would rise up and enshroud everything. In the morning she'd need to begin the process of packing up her life. But at some point the gabble in her head quietened and all became silence and blackness and she fell into a deeper sleep than she had experienced for months.

*

In her bed a few hours later, Dolores Mullen turned and woke. Six months pregnant, and neat as she was, the slightest movement roused her. She settled on her back and stared at the ceiling, trying to render her mind blank. She looked to the side and saw that her husband was not in bed with her and was overcome by a feeling of emptiness. But when she closed her eyes again, she heard him entering the room. He was panting. His footfall was soft and she realised he had taken off his boots. So often he dropped down on the bed and made a great performance of pulling off his boots and discarding them on the floor, huffing and puffing as he went. Tonight he had shown her this small consideration. She opened her eyes and saw him fumbling with the buttons on his shirt, becoming agitated, pursing his lips, trying not to sound his vexation.

When he climbed into the bed and pulled the covers up over him, she could tell by the stillness of him that he was just lying there, stiff as an antenna, listening out for something. The child moved inside her. She felt a tightening in her chest.

'What's wrong?' she asked.

He did not answer. And then even the moist rasp of his breathing evaporated. He was holding his breath. The silence was complete, and into that silence a low thrum entered and rose up around them. It was like an engine heard from a distance. Or a roar coming from a mouth with a hand clamped over it. The noise was not loud, but it was everywhere, as if they were inside it.

'Donal – what's that?'

'Shut up and go to sleep,' he said.

'Donal – you need to go out and check what that is.'

She sat up, moved the bedclothes aside. She felt his hand grip her arm, his fingers digging into her flesh.

'Stay where you are,' he snarled.

He swung his legs out of the bed and slowly began to gather his clothes off the floor. Dolores felt a cold sweat prickle her back, the long T-shirt she wore clinging to her in patches. 'Hurry up, will you, before the children wake,' she said. But still he did not quicken his pace, buttoning his shirt with care and tightening his belt. And before he left the room he cast an eye at the window. The curtains were closed but when she looked over at them there seemed to be light leaking from the narrow slit where they almost met. She climbed out of the bed and walked towards the light and when she pulled one curtain aside the brightness stung her eyes. She squinted up at the cottage. The right side of it was ablaze, flames flowing down from the windowsill and black smoke rising up, absorbed by the night sky. Grey smoke blew from the kitchen window. She was hypnotised for a moment by the unreality of it, the purity of the flames and the way, like water, they appeared to lap and lick at the air so that the night seemed marbled with fire.

'Donal!' she screamed. 'Donal – call the fire brigade.' She ran down the hall and saw him standing before the living room window, bathed in light, staring up at the cottage with his hands on his hips. 'Donal – what the fuck are you playing at? Call the fire brigade.' But he did not move. She ran to the phone and was dialling the numbers when Donal grabbed the phone and pulled it from her.

'Let me go up and check first,' he said.

'What are you talking about? The place'll be a shell by the time they get there. Is she up there? Do you think she's up there? Jesus Christ, what are we going to do?'

'Don't be getting fucking hysterical. I'll go up and check.'

'You'll not get next or near the place. You'll be burned alive.'

And when he opened the front door a waft of heat entered the hallway but even still she was shivering and her teeth were chattering and her mouth was emitting some sound, some garbled nonsense that was just pure fear, just her body's response to the terror she felt – and then she realised she was praying.

She called after her husband, who was already some distance away, sidling down through the front garden. He stopped at the foot of the hill and tilted his head back to look up at the cottage. She lifted the receiver again but let it hang loosely in her hand. Her husband turned and looked at her and then began to stride back towards the house. When he reached the front door, his face was beaded with sweat.

'Now you can call them,' he said.

*

Izzy Keaveney could not sleep that night. As morning approached she got out of bed and as she passed along the landing she stopped at the window and saw the strange light over the headland – the smoke rising up through it. She stood staring at it for some time until she felt her legs weaken and gripped the windowsill. She began to descend the stairs, holding tightly to the banister, as though with each step she was slowly lowering herself into the tide. In the kitchen she sat at the table and waited for the kettle to boil. In her mind she saw the sign on the front of the cottage that read 'Innisfree'. *For always night and day*, she thought. *For always night and day.* And a flash of terror sparked and shrivelled inside her.

She dressed quietly while James turned in his sleep. She got in her car and drove. It was barely light when she crossed the bridge into the town. Passing the little park that fronted the seashore, she noticed a flush of crocuses, purple and white, had shot up at the foot of the old oak tree. In the low tide, the boats cowered at the pier. Outside the Reel Inn, the two petrol pumps stood sentry over the deserted town. Pulling off the Shore Road and onto the Coast Road, the bay appeared in front of her, the morning light breaking through at the horizon. Low cloud decked the sky, so richly textured she felt she could reach out her hand and touch it. She slowed as she neared the beach, parked at the turn. At the entrance to the Mullens' property she saw two Garda cars parked nose-to-nose. The entrance to the cottage was blocked with police tape, and all that was left at the top of the drive was a charred ruin.

CHAPTER 24

Niall stared at the clothes his mother had laid out on his bed – a grey cardigan with fat buttons wrapped in brown leather, black trousers, and a white shirt. A pair of black lace-up shoes lay at the foot of the bed. He had asked his mother the day before if he should wear a tie and she'd told him not to be stupid. He'd found her in her room, just sitting on the end of her bed, staring into space. He'd caught her eye in the mirror on her dressing table, but at first she didn't move or speak, like she was pretending not to have seen him.

'But will Carl be wearing a tie?' he'd asked.

'Oh, probably,' she'd said. 'But it's not your mother who's dead, so don't be looking for notice.'

His face had gone very hot then. But no matter how hard he tried, once his face had that hot, stinging feeling, he could never stop himself from crying.

His mother had been like this for the past week, saying mean things all the time to him, and his father, and Orla. Orla had come home from school for the weekend and sulked the entire time because their mother wouldn't let her go out and meet her friends. 'I just want yous where I can see you at the moment, is that too much to ask?' she'd said. And every night, when she thought he was asleep, his mother came into his room and sat on his bed and brushed his hair from his forehead. But he didn't let her know he was awake in case she left.

Niall took off his pyjama top and bottoms, kicking aside his underpants, and slid on the fresh grey pair his mother had laid out for him. He put on his shirt and buttoned it in front of the mirror, and was still convinced he'd look better with a tie.

'Niall!' he heard his mother shout from downstairs. 'Right, come on, we're leaving in two minutes.'

He picked up the book on his bedside locker. He checked the page he'd stopped at. He'd reread a few of these poems every night since Colette had died. He remembered that when he'd shown it to his mother, she'd looked at it doubtfully, turning it over in her hands like she'd never seen a book before. 'Jesus, look at the size of that,' she'd said. 'You'll never get through all of those. Are they for children?' But they weren't children's poems, or at least not all of them were – and Niall had read every single one.

He put the bookmark back and pressed the book closed, feeling the thickness of it between his hands. He heard loud footsteps on the landing and the door flew open.

'Niall, what in the name of God are you doing?' his mother asked. She stared at the book in his hands and became very still. A concerned look came over her.

'You were great pals, the pair of you, weren't you?' she said.

He nodded. 'She was always nice to me.'

'She was that way with everyone, pet. That was the kind of her.'

His mother was wearing a long black skirt and a short black blazer and a white blouse with a high neck and a brooch at her throat. The brooch was gold with a piece of black glass at its centre that caught the light.

'Stop gawping at me, and get into the car,' she said.

In the church, when the coffin entered, six tall men carried it on their shoulders. Mr Crowley and Ronan were at the front and Barry at the back, and he didn't recognise the other men, but they all had black hair like Colette. The coffin must have been very heavy because it pressed down on their shoulders so the material of their black suits bunched up. Carl's daddy looked different. He'd always looked older than the other fathers of children in his class, but now he looked ancient, every line and crease in his face visible like he'd been dusted in chalk. And then Carl came into view, following behind, wearing a black suit with a white shirt and black tie, the same as the men who were carrying the coffin. But the sleeves of Carl's shirt were too long and the collar so big that you couldn't see his neck. He thought of the fight they'd had in the schoolyard. There was the same look of shock on Carl's face now. His cheeks were damp with tears and there were two red circles around his eyes. Carl was walking beside Mrs Diver, but when they got to the top of the church, she left Carl with his father and his brothers and sat a few seats behind. The rows filled up with more people – really, he'd never seen the church so full, not even at Christmas – and he lost sight of Carl.

While the new priest said the mass, Niall looked at the pamphlet printed for the service. There was a black-and-white photo of Colette on the front. In the photo she wasn't smiling, which was strange, because she was always smiling when you saw her. She looked happy though, wide-eyed, staring directly at the camera, her hair trailing back and away from her face like it was blowing in the wind. And her skin looked very bright like her face had absorbed all the light around her. And two of her poems were printed on the middle pages of the pamphlet. One was called 'Testament' and it was kind of like a prayer – the language was very plain and at the end of each verse there was a repeated line like when they did the responsorial psalm. But the other poem was different, it didn't rhyme and there were no verses, just a long list of lines down the page, and if it hadn't been called 'Mothering', Niall would never have guessed what the poem was about, because they were frightening, the things she promised to do to protect her children, and they were promises you could never keep.

When the priest spoke about Colette, he started by saying, 'I never had the good fortune to meet Colette Crowley but . . .' and then he went on to talk about her for what felt like a very long time, saying things that other people had told him, and Niall's mother began to sigh like she did when they waited at the doctor's or the dentist. But when the priest finished, he said, 'And now Barry Crowley will read a poem for us.' But Barry just bowed his head and sat there. Ronan turned to him and said something into his ear and Barry shouted 'No' with such force that his long hair leapt on his head, and the noise of his shout echoed through the church. Niall heard his mother tut. On Barry's other side his father turned to him and placed a hand on his shoulder but his whole body jolted and his father pulled away like he'd been shocked. Barry passed a piece of paper to Ronan, who approached the altar. He moved quickly, stood tall, an apology in his smile. He spoke about the poem he was about to read, and what it had meant to his mother. It was like he was trying to make them all feel better after the boring things the priest had said about Colette. And when he started to read the poem, Niall turned the page of the pamphlet and saw that it was printed there. 'Dirge Without Music' by somebody called Edna St. Vincent Millay. He wasn't sure what a dirge was but it sounded depressing, and the last verse began, '*Down, down, down*', and that was how the poem made him feel, like he was being pulled under by the words. And there were a couple of lines that kept repeating and at the end they were repeated together: '*But I do not approve. And I am not resigned.*' But when Ronan reached these words, he wasn't smiling anymore. He wasn't looking out at the faces of the people in the church as he had been. He just stood there for a while, as if he was unable to move, unable to stop himself from staring down at the page. But every face in the church was lifted to him. And when Niall looked up at his mother, he could see her pulse beating in the curve of her throat, like her heart was caught there.

The end of the mass came and the priest said, 'And now the Ardglas Choral Society will sing for us.' The song was in Irish and Niall couldn't understand every word, but there was something about the sea, and the way it made him feel was like a warm current running through him, and even though it was sad there was something hopeful about it. Everyone stood very still, listening through the first verse, until the men at the front of the church moved to lift the coffin. When Carl passed by him again, filing out of the church, Niall tried to catch his eye but Carl just stared ahead the whole time.

Walking behind the hearse, Niall watched Carl's head move in and out of view at the front of the crowd. He was determined to walk up to Carl and say something before the end of the funeral.

Losing your mother was the worst thing that could happen, and if Niall wanted to make himself cry, he just had to imagine his mother dying. He thought that perhaps Carl might be nicer now and that things could be different between them, or at least more like they were before. But as soon as they reached the graveyard, the procession spread out around the mouth of the grave and he lost sight of Carl. His mother was still holding one of the pamphlets from the church and he slipped it from her hand.

The priest started to say something but Niall couldn't make out any of it because he was too far away. He tried to catch a glimpse of Carl when some of the people blocking his view moved apart, but then there was a lot of movement because someone was coming through the crowd. People were making a great effort to spread apart from each other, and into the space they made stepped Donal Mullen.

'Jesus Christ,' his mother whispered, and when he glanced at her, he saw the muscles in her cheeks ripple as she clenched her jaw. And even though she didn't move, his father put his arm out in front of her, like she was about to bolt away.

And people continued to edge farther from Mr Mullen and the space around him grew so it was like he was surrounded, like *he* was the centre of the scene and not the people standing at the grave who Niall could now see through the gap in the crowd – Carl, then his brothers, then his father, all lined up in order of size, staring down into the mouth of the grave in their matching suits, like paper cutouts joined at the elbow.

The pamphlet dropped from Niall's hand and blew across the grass, stopping near Mr Mullen's feet.

Niall took one step forward and he felt his father's hand fall heavy on his shoulder.

'Stay where you are, Niall,' his father said.

But he wanted to take Colette's poems home so he could read them in bed that night, and his gaze kept drifting back to the pamphlet. And when he looked up, Mr Mullen was staring over his shoulder at them, his eyes dark and shining, like the black glass in his mother's brooch.

His mother dug her knuckle into his shoulder and he felt her breath on the side of his face. 'Stop staring,' she whispered. 'And for the love of God stop pulling at your hair.' Niall took down his hand and there were a few strands between his thumb and forefinger.

The priest raised his arm and made a blessing in the air as the coffin was lowered into the ground. Each of the Crowley brothers dropped a single white rose into the grave.

'Take me home,' his mother said.

'Will we not go to the hotel for the meal? Shaun invited us,' his father said.

'I will not be anywhere there's a chance of running into that man again.'

'Ah, come on – he's not going to show up at the afters. He wouldn't have the nerve.'

'He's here, isn't he?'

And with that his mother headed off in the direction of the gates, his father following behind. Niall retrieved the pamphlet from the grass, the pages so wet now, the image of Colette was almost washed away. Looking up, he saw the mouth of the grave covered by planks of wood draped in green felt, the wreaths piled on in one great colourful mound.

*

Dolores lay on the sofa, her rosary wound tightly round her fist. With each whispered prayer she eased a bead between thumb and knuckle. The repetition of these words, the trance they placed her in, was the only release she could find. She was capable of sleeping and eating when the child inside her demanded it. She was able to take care of her children, to smile when required and tell them everything was going to be OK. But the moment she was alone a panic flooded through her, so pervasive, the only thing she could do was lie down before it.

'Hail Mary, full of grace, the Lord is with thee, blessed art though amongst women . . .'

The sweep of tyres on the drive, the noise of a car door slamming shut. The rustle of keys followed by her husband's footsteps moving softly, carefully through the house.

'Jesus Christ,' he said, 'when you pull up outside every curtain in the place is closed. How do you think that looks? It's not us who's having the funeral.' He marched to the window and dashed the curtains apart.

'Don't,' she shouted.

He turned, fixed her with a look. 'What's wrong with you?'

'We need to talk.'

'Where are the kids?'

'I left them down with Mammy.'

His eyes rested on the rosary beads in her hand. 'Ah Jesus, Dolores.' He came and sat beside her, leaving space between their bodies. He leaned forward, placing his elbows on his knees, his hands clasped. 'It would've suited you better to be at the funeral than sitting around here saying the rosary.'

'What was it like?'

'How do you mean?'

'The graveyard – how was it?'

'Oh, it was packed, the whole—'

'No,' she said. 'No, no, no. Stop. Please. I don't want to know.'

His head turned slowly. She could feel his eyes examining her. 'You need to start pulling yourself together.' His voice was soft, controlled. 'We need to look like we have nothing to hide, and you lying here with the curtains pulled in the middle of the day will make people think—'

'I know what people are thinking, Donal.'

'And you know what can happen when rumours get out of hand, all it will take is for us to be questioned again and you may forget it – that's it. I've lost one job already this week and there won't be much more work coming in until this all blows over. We can't afford this with another child on the way.'

'Donal?'

'But people have short memories when it suits them – all we have to do is ride this out.'

'Donal?' She watched him grow very still. 'Did you set that fire?'

After fourteen years of marriage it was still extraordinary to her how he continued to find new ways of being silent.

'Donal? I need to hear you say it.'

'The less you know, the better.'

'Donal, I've already lied to the Guards for you. It's too late to protect me now.'

'I know,' he said. 'This looks bad for both of us. But it doesn't matter as long as we stick to the same story – I was in the pub, a few will have seen me there – and when I came home, we watched a bit of telly and went to bed. If they start asking more questions, we can tell them half the men in the town were going up there for a good time. It wouldn't be far from the truth. But for now we'll just keep saying how much she was drinking, that she was smoking up in the cottage, that she was behaving erratically.'

'Jesus Christ,' she said, 'you've really thought this through.'

'This all needs to look like some kind of accident if we're going to get the insurance money, but there's a chance it's covered for criminal damage as well, I'd need to look at the policy.'

'The insurance!' she shouted. 'The insurance!' She landed two blows with her closed fists square on his head before he had time to put his arms up. She felt the beads crunch against his skull. 'The fucking insurance.' She continued to pummel him as he cowered and shouted. 'We could lose everything, Donal, and you're worried about the insurance?'

When she stopped, he looked up at her, his arms still shielding his head. 'She wouldn't have suffered,' he said. 'She was fast asleep in her bed, drunk . . . The smoke. A fire like that. You'd take in a few lungfuls and you'd be knocked out before the flames would even touch you.'

'Well, that's another lie, Donal, because you know where they found her body. They peeled her off the kitchen floor because she crawled on her hands and knees to try and escape that fire.' And she proceeded to hit him again but the energy required was consumed by the racking sobs passing through her. She collapsed against him, her face pressed into his side, and she could feel him adjust his body to get a better handle on her, to corral the great heaving mess of her. She felt the warmth in his hands as they moved across her, down her thigh, the touch of his palm against hers as he slipped the rosary from her fingers.

CHAPTER 25

The house came into view around the curve of a short drive. It lay in the shadow of the church. When Izzy had called the night before, he'd said, 'Just aim for the steeple and you can't miss me.' And there he was now cutting at the ivy on the front of the house with a pair of shears. He was in civvies – black slacks, a red jumper over a white shirt, a pair of black rubber-soled shoes. How like any other middle-aged man he looked, his grey hair licked up in waves on the crown of his balding head. He paid no attention to the noise of the car, just carried on cutting.

She had surprised him by phoning, certainly, and surprised him further by telling him she would be down to see him the following afternoon. She'd been expecting some level of hostility, but in fact his tone was so affectless as to offer no indication of his feelings.

She pulled the handbrake and stopped the engine, watched him take a moment to appraise his work. He appeared to be out of breath, his shoulders rising and falling. He bent down to lean the shears against the wall and then rose without quite meeting her eye, his mouth hanging open in a way that at least resembled a smile.

'Isn't it a grand place they gave you?' she said, getting out of the car.

It was a much more handsome property than the parochial house in Ardglas. There was a cut-stone exterior and it was elegantly proportioned, and the grounds were mature, the branches of the tall trees like a vaulted ceiling over the drive. Neat little hedgerows squatted under the ground-floor windows.

'Oh, I'm well looked after,' he said, approaching her.

She cast an eye back down the drive. 'But you must have your work cut out for you with these grounds.'

'Oh, I have a fellow who comes and does a bit of work for me one day a week. The rest of the time I just do a bit of maintenance, you know, to keep myself out of trouble.' He was fussing with his gardening gloves.

'Come here to me,' she said, and peeled apart the Velcro at one wrist, then the other. She slid the gloves off and handed them to him, trying not to catch his eye. She turned to the car and opened the back door. 'Eclairs,' she said, taking out a white box. 'You're fond of those, I seem to remember.'

'You'll come in,' he said, taking the box from her. She followed him through the front door. He stopped halfway down the hall and nodded in the direction of an open doorway. 'Sit yourself in there and I'll make the tea.'

The house stank of damp. When she stepped into the drawing room, she had to stop herself from going around and throwing every window open. She took a seat on a high-backed sofa that sank so uncomfortably low it was like sitting on the floor. Feeling foolish, she moved to an armchair that faced the door and gave her a view of the entire room. They were such strange places, these priests' homes, the décor always a couple of decades behind. This room was all textured wallpaper and shag-pile carpet. There were coverlets draped over the backs of chairs, sleeves dressed the arms. The house was decorated with the fuss of an old woman, yet was still so identifiably inhabited by a man. Not a single flower anywhere or an ornament that might make the place look homely. And what items there were – a chessboard, a black-and-white photo of his parents she recognised from his living room in Ardglas – were so isolated as to look temporary, stagey. Even the tall bookshelf that took up one entire wall was only half filled. And lamps. Everywhere there were lamps, but none of them were turned on and the room was in near darkness. She didn't know where to start with all the lamps.

The door edged open as Brian butted his way into the room with the tea tray.

She laughed. 'Well, that is a sight to behold,' she said. 'Never in my life have I seen a priest make his own tea.'

'Well, I have no housekeeper on the weekends,' he said, as he struggled to place the rattling tray on the low coffee table.

'Is she as much of a bitch as your old one?' Izzy asked.

'Now, Izzy,' he smiled, 'it doesn't behove you to be making fun of poor Stasia Toomey.'

'Poor Stasia, my eye. She's a battle-axe if ever there was one blessed, marked, or made.'

'She served me very well during my brief station as parish priest of Ardglas.'

'I bumped into her in Doherty's the other day and she says to me, "I suppose you've been down to Claremorris to see him –

you were great friends, the pair of yous."' Izzy used a simpering voice and fluttered her eyelashes like a schoolgirl. 'And then I said, "Claremorris? The pope couldn't get me to go to Claremorris." That took the wind out of her sails.'

He sat down heavily in an armchair across from her, expelled an exhausted breath. She looked at the eclairs, thrown on a plate with absolutely no finesse whatsoever.

'It wouldn't have been too hard to find out where I was,' he said. 'If you'd wanted to know.'

'I knew where you were,' she said. 'It was no great secret.'

The look he gave her then was so unguarded, she hadn't the strength to meet it. She busied herself with pouring the tea.

'The new priest seems to be getting on well, Father Garvin,' she said. 'But I can't say I'm all that fond of him. More of the same, you know? Too sweet to be wholesome. It would do them all good to be a bit more like you, to spend a bit of time out in the real world. None of them have a clue – advising people on how to live their lives, when they go straight from under their mothers' skirts to the seminary.'

He coughed, laid down his cup on the table with a clatter.

'You're determined to punish me, aren't you?' she said, and she reached down at her feet for her handbag but she hadn't seen an ashtray anywhere. 'Have you given up?' she said.

'What?'

'Smoking – have you stopped?'

'Two weeks,' he said.

'Well done.' She let her handbag drop back onto the floor. 'That's a big achievement.'

'But you can smoke if you want.' He laid his hands on the arm-rests and made to get up. 'I'll get you an ashtray.'

'No, I won't,' she said, taking up her cup and saucer again. 'I won't. I wouldn't do that to you. It's hard enough.'

'I suppose I'll have to get used to it. I tried chewing the gum—'

'Oh, it's a dirty, disgusting habit that, you'd be better off smoking.'

'And then I decided to just persevere.'

'It's the only way to do it. Every week I say to myself I'm giving them up. But sure, now's not the time.' She took a sip from her cup. 'Anyway, how are they treating you down here?'

'Oh, you know yourself, there are good, kind, generous people everywhere – here's no exception.'

'Don't give me that shit – there are bad, evil, cruel, ignorant bastards everywhere as well. That wasn't what I asked you.'

'I have been treated with the utmost kindness and courtesy by every single person I have encountered,' he said. 'Does that satisfy you?'

'You can be as angry as you like,' she said, 'but I didn't know a thing about it. I showed up at your house one day and you were gone and that was the first I knew.'

'It was a surprise to me too.'

'And if it's worth anything to you, I'm sorry. I'm sorry for all of it.'

'It's not worth much as it happens, because I know that none of it was your fault. I didn't need you to apologise. What I needed . . . what I expected, was just some message. But there wasn't a word from you. And I was angry. It was a big upheaval in my life, you know, moving down here, when I'd just settled in Ardglas, and made friends – or thought I had. And one of the old tricks we're taught is to pray for people when we feel hurt by them and so I prayed for you and I prayed for your husband—'

'Oh, don't waste your prayers on him, he's a dead loss.'

'It didn't seem to be working. But when you have a job like mine, people are coming to you every day – telling you things, terrible things. People really have terrible, difficult, hard lives. And when you hear them, you realise you've never really had a bad day. And that seemed to help me to forget or to reduce my anger at least, but I was foolish to think that was the same as having forgiven you. And when you phoned last night, I realised I'd failed in that.'

'If you knew the row we had over you.' Her throat tightened so the last word came out choked. She shook her head, tried to blink away the tears.

'I'd say that, all right. But I'd also say any problems you and James have, you had before I came along.'

'And that's the truth,' she said. 'But that's not what I'm trying to say. I'm not trying to blame you. I'm trying to say that . . . well, I almost left him. I was almost out the door. Bags packed. I'd seen a solicitor. I'd even told James. We'd had the talk.'

'And what changed your mind?'

She stared down into her cup. 'Colette,' she said.

He sat up and hunched over, placing his palms together between his knees. 'That was a terrible thing,' he said, his voice directed at the floor.

'You've heard?'

'The whole country's heard. I've said more prayers for that woman in the past few weeks.'

'And Christ, she needed every one of them. If you'd seen the way she ended up. She had nothing. Alone in that cottage. Out of her mind with drink. Pregnant.'

He raised his head and looked at her.

'That's what she told me,' Izzy said. 'I visited her on the day before she died, and she sat in front of me, and told me she was nearly two months pregnant and Donal Mullen was the father.'

She watched something change in his expression, some unfolding of a thought.

'And she asked me for money. To get away. She'd told him about the child and he'd threatened her. And do you know what I did?' She smiled. 'I gave her sixty pounds.' She spoke the amount slowly. 'That was noble of me, wasn't it? How far would that get you? And honestly, if you'd seen her, how wretched she was – any decent person would have bundled her into the car and taken her home with them.'

'And have you gone to the Guards?'

She shook her head. 'See, I knew for a while that they'd been carrying on. I'd met her down in the bar of the Harbour View one night and she was drunk as a skunk. I practically had to drag her out of the place. And when I dropped her off at the cottage, he was standing there at the door waiting for her. I mean, he scarpered as soon as he saw me – but that's how familiar they were with each other, that he could just crawl out of his bed at night and saunter up there. And my God – if ever there was a pair designed to cause trouble for each other. He'd throw his leg over anything, that fella, and she'd taken to the drink so badly I wouldn't say she even knew who was coming through the door some nights.'

'But I don't understand. Why haven't you told all of this to the Guards? Does James know?'

'Of course he knows – but you can imagine what he thinks about the whole thing, that as soon as it becomes public knowledge the wife of a TD is involved all of the focus will be on us. As you well know, that's James's biggest fear – scandal.'

'So he's stopping you from coming forward?'

'He's not stopping me from doing anything. He wouldn't dare at the moment. We've only just patched things up. But he's not exactly full of encouragement either. He says that if they need to speak to us, they'll be in touch.'

'Well, that's nonsense, Izzy. Why would they start an investigation if they have no reason to?'

'But I have no real proof.'

'And that's as it may be but if you tell them what you know they might find proof. They'll question Donal again. They'll search his house. What's really stopping you?'

It was as though someone had their hand on her back and was pressing her to the ground. She wrapped her arms around herself and folded in two. 'I'm so frightened,' she said. 'I'm terrified out of my wits. I haven't slept a wink. If you'd seen the way that man looked at me at the funeral.'

'Donal?'

She nodded. 'He knows that I know. And him and Dolores have been questioned. Anyway, they haven't charged him with anything.'

'Not yet. But they'll have their suspicions about him already. They'll know from the post-mortem that she was pregnant – that won't be news to them.'

'But what if . . . what if I make a statement and it comes to nothing and all the while I have to live in the same town as him and his wife and his children, and his holier-than-thou parents? Or what if there's a trial and I have to get up in front of people and testify against him and he gets off? What happens then? I'll forever know that he killed Colette and he'll forever know that I know, and every day I wake there's a chance I'm going to run into him.'

'But you don't have a choice, Izzy. I know you've come looking for me to tell you the right thing to do. Did you really think I was going to tell you to go home and keep your mouth shut?'

'I came to you looking for some kind of certainty.'

'But what more certainty can I offer you than telling you going to the Guards is one hundred per cent the correct way to proceed – it's what God would want, it's what I want, it's what anyone in their right mind would advise you to do.'

'No. I don't mean that kind of certainty. I mean proof. Do you know anything?'

'What do you mean do I know anything? I left the town weeks ago.'

'But before that – if anyone would hear something it would be you.'

'If I'm guessing correctly, you're asking me if I heard something in the confessional, and you know that anything I'm told during confession is completely—'

'OK, OK, I don't need you to say anything, I don't need you to give me details, but I suppose what I need is some certainty that I'm not going mad, that I haven't made all of this up in my head.' She looked at him. 'Maybe I'm not the only person who knew they were having an affair? Maybe Dolores knew as well?'

He met her gaze and gave a long, slow nod.

She sat forward in the chair and lifted her handbag from the floor. The action felt so sudden and decisive, but for a while she just sat there allowing her eyes to light on various objects in the room, running the leather strap of the handbag through her fingers. She looked down at her watch and then covered the face with her hand.

'I'll go,' she said. 'If I leave now, I'll be just in time to collect Niall from school.'

'You'll be OK, Izzy,' he said.

She rose from her seat and let out a long exhalation. 'Have you nothing more for me than that? Some bit of catechism, or a psalm or a quote or something that'll inspire me and send me on my way full of gusto.' She threw out her hand, fingers splayed, like she was delivering this speech on a stage. She looked at him from the corner of her eye, and while he did not look entirely convinced by the performance, there was something in his half-smile, some residue of fondness that reminded her of the way he used to look at her.

'I'll pray for you,' he said, and they both smiled.

'Oh, you're full of old shit, you lot,' she said.

He followed her out to her car and as she was unlocking the door, he said, 'I missed you, is what I was trying to say, earlier, when I was going on at you like a demon.'

She stopped and looked across the lawn, to where two beds had been cleared, the weeds and uprooted shrubs still strewn across the grass. 'I hope you're not planting anything this early,' she said. 'We haven't even had the last frosts yet.'

He bowed his head.

'Oh no,' she said, 'it could be May before you could even chance putting something in the ground.'

A rush of wind heaved through the trees. The branches swayed and creaked, and she had the sense of being sheltered there with him. She sat in the car and waited until he had gone back into the house before she started the engine.

CHAPTER 26

Dolores was dredged to the surface of a fitful sleep. She blinked at the sunlight beaming through the slit in the curtains. *Madeleine, Jessica, Eric* – Madeleine was at school, Jessica at nursery, and Eric asleep in his cot. It was her habit now, throughout the day and when she woke in the night, to account for each of her children in this way. Not until she'd fixed them in her mind could she take another breath.

She sat up and swung her legs out of the bed, slid her feet into her slippers. A sliver of the cottage appeared through the curtains, just a flash of scorched brick, and she turned her head away. She rose from the bed, smoothed the covers. Donal's jeans were still thrown across the end of the bed. He'd put on a shirt and tie that morning and had driven her car to visit a solicitor in Sligo, where he'd be less likely to see anyone he'd know. He thought it looked better, more respectable, to show up in the family car rather than his white work van, and he was all about respectability these days, her husband. He had her out the door to mass on a Sunday even though she was hardly fit to stand. He was friendly with everyone he met, all firm handshakes and nervous laughter. He was even being polite to her parents. She'd never seen him so ingratiating.

It was only at home that he was low and fearful – angry and silent. He barked at the kids, snarled at her, and then became soft, anxious, his need for her pitiable. But two weeks had passed since the fire and not another question had been asked of them. Even his trip to the solicitor was just to be on the safe side, he'd said – to ask a few questions about his situation. And while things would never be the same, it seemed possible they might one day at least resemble the life they'd had before.

She folded Donal's jeans, turned out his pockets, as was her habit – to go over every stitch of clothing he owned for a stray strand of hair or a whiff of perfume. And sometimes this evidence was there, but never once had she found anything more substantial; no pair of knickers stuffed away or a receipt for dinner. But she guessed Donal wasn't really the kind for taking his lovers out for romantic meals. In the wake of the fire her searches had become more thorough. She'd unlocked the shed, picked through his toolboxes; had to slather her hands in butter after to get rid of the oil and grease. She had prowled the house in his absence, combed every inch of it. The only thing of interest she'd found was a box of condoms hidden under the bathroom sink that he'd bought in the North and never had the good sense to use. What more proof she needed she didn't know, and she couldn't say exactly what she was looking for. Something she could confront him with, or something she could keep to herself until the time when she might need it.

She listened at the door of Eric's room, heard his soft, vaporous breathing, and continued down the hall to the sitting room, surveying her work as she passed, pleased to see the house as neat as a new pin. Between bouts of sleep, she did what she always did when she was at the end of her pregnancy and prepared the nest for the new arrival. She was aware of being especially meticulous on this occasion, cleaning behind furniture three or four times, when she'd barely let the dust settle again. And Donal kept telling her to stop fussing – she had him agitated. Her husband's fingernails were chewed to the quick. Because he put on a good show, of being full of swagger, his hands on his hips the whole time, like he was surveying the world and all that was in it – like he owned it. But all he was doing was bolstering himself. Because no one knew him like she did, and it was the first thing she had noticed about him when they'd started courting as teenagers, those chewed fingernails on those otherwise beautiful, strong hands. He could carry a ball down the pitch and kick it over the bar – he could score the winning goal. But his hands were shaking and he had to occupy them to steady them.

She had loved that, watching him play Gaelic, the way the other girls looked at him, like he was a prize worth winning – and he was hers. The first time they'd had sex was after he'd won the county final. She had never really known what desire was until then, had not felt what it was like to walk around all day filled with a secret heat that made you heavy and listless, light and determined all at once. She'd decided then, that was what being alive felt like. In her life Dolores had grown used to not getting what she wanted, but she remembered praying for Donal Mullen to be hers, and that had happened. And she sometimes wondered if she'd been punished for that – for wanting someone, needing them so badly she'd never questioned what their true value was. She hadn't even cared that their families had pushed them together – she had asked God for something and it had been delivered to her and Donal would grow to love her over time, she was certain of that, naïve enough to believe children bonded people in that way. She wished she could be naïve again, just for a second.

She looked out the window and remembered that her car wasn't there, saw Donal's van parked in its place. Every day since the fire she had thought about putting her children in her car and driving to her parents' house. In those first days her mother and father and sisters had hovered around her, watchful of Donal. She knew her parents would take them in and protect them – all she had to do was ask. But that wasn't a life, living under your parents' roof with three children and a newborn baby. Nor was it a life to remain with a man who was cruel and withholding, where their entire existence was maintained by lies. She'd tried to imagine going to confession and telling a priest what she'd done. Had she the courage for that, at least?

And then it occurred to her that Donal's work van was the one place she hadn't searched. She grabbed the keys from the hallstand and walked out to the car, squeezed into the driver's seat, and pushed it back a few inches to make room for her belly. She checked the sun visors and his driver's licence fell in her lap. She rummaged through every compartment and pocket, looked through cassette cases with no idea what she hoped to find in them. She opened the glove compartment again, this time taking out the manuals and flicking through them. A grey envelope fell out and landed in the footwell. She struggled to reach over for it, the gear stick poking into her belly. 'Sorry, pet,' she said. Written on the envelope in a florid cursive was 'Colette'. She removed the letter from inside.

The Harbour View Hotel, Ardglas, 1 March 1995

Colette,

You'll see from the address that we are not so far apart as the crow flies or at least I'm guessing we are in close proximity to each other. Part of this journey is to determine that you still exist, that you ever existed, that you were not something conjured by my mind. I sometimes imagine that my letters are carried off on an errant wind in the direction of Donegal and delivered to the Atlantic.

I have driven for four and a half hours to speak with you and if you are reading this then I have failed in that mission. When one doesn't hear from another person for months it is easy to imagine that your message isn't getting through in the most literal sense. What if Cliodna gave me the wrong address, what if you have moved somewhere else? Who is to say if any of the forty-five letters I have written have ever reached you? But tonight I fell into company with a man in the hotel bar (said he was the local butcher – fat fellow, bad colour, cheeks marbled with broken capillaries) and I showed him the address. He gave me directions to 'The Cottage' and told me 'the Crowley woman' was renting it, and I think it depressed me even more to know that I was just being ignored.

Forty-five letters – I can only apologise. Could you burn them for me? I am embarrassed by the cliché I have become and I promise you this will be the last letter I write. I will hand-deliver it in the hope of seeing you but if that doesn't happen then I will be in the bar of the hotel until 5 p.m., when it will be time for me to get back on the road again.

You would think after forty-five missives everything that needs to be said would have been said, but if this is the last contact I will have with you, then there are a few things I'd like to say. If you look at the back of this letter you will find my new address and phone number. I'm living in an apartment near campus, not far from the one we briefly shared. I think I can finally say without any doubt that my marriage is over, and while our affair certainly precipitated that breakdown, there is not a second that I blame you for that failure.

And if you'll allow me one final indulgence, there is something I have been thinking over. You said that I ran at the first sign of trouble, but it was you who asked me to leave when I showed the first sign of weakness. Also, you said that I was a man who needed a woman, and that you could have been anyone – that you were simply fulfilling a role. I have given a great amount of thought to that statement, because it troubled me all this time that there was something in the way I had behaved towards you that made you think you were anything less than the most important and singular and beloved thing in my life. Yes, I was useless, and slovenly, bad with money – I am working on those things – but there is no doubt in my mind that you are the truest love I have ever experienced and had I the chance to go back and correct my behaviour, if there was anything I could have done to change the outcome of things, I would do so in a second. But I am beginning to think that it was in fact I who could have been anyone, that you were looking for an escape route, a life raft, something to be jettisoned once you had reached dry land.

I don't care. Give me five minutes and I promise I'll never bother you again.

Love always,

John

Dolores folded the letter and looked up at the jagged outline of the cottage, its ruins written against the cold grey sky. This man thought Colette had reached a place of safety. She could almost taste the bitterness he felt at her need to be free of him. And she knew how that bitterness could poison a life, could make you lousy with exhaustion. She knew what it was to not be wanted.

But Colette had had a husband, a man who wrote her love letters, and a lover. And Dolores recalled the day when she saw 'John' put the letter through Colette's door and her husband had jumped out of his seat and run to get a look at him. He was determined to keep Colette within his sights. But not a week later he had pursued her down the beach, and when he'd returned to the house, he'd said, 'She'll be out by Sunday.' And she'd wanted to say, 'Lover's tiff?' But when she'd looked at him, he was so angry – it was like a heat rising off his body.

She wouldn't have suffered. She could hear his words repeating in her head. *Fast asleep in her bed . . . A fire like that. The smoke. You'd take in a few lungfuls and you'd be knocked out before the flames would even touch you.* And after all the bargaining she'd done with God to be rid of Colette, now she knew she'd never be free of her, that every time she closed her eyes she'd see Colette's body being lifted from the smoking shell of the cottage.

Dolores put the letter back in the envelope and placed it in the pocket of her cardigan.

CHAPTER 27

Izzy dragged the hoover around the good sitting room. She pulled the plug from the wall and the trill of the doorbell filled the sudden silence. She jumped, knocked against a side table. The figurine perched there did a backwards dive onto the hearth.

'Oh fuck,' she said, staring down at the remnants of what had once been *Just Out of Reach* – a willowy girl with her left leg pointed behind her and her right hand reaching for the sky, her body one long, graceful curve. Now her pink skirt and white blouse were sundered. But her head was perfectly preserved, shiny and round as a marble.

She looked out the window and saw a car she didn't recognise parked in James's spot. That would piss him off, she thought. She checked her watch. They were almost half an hour early, and that would piss him off even more. 'Fuck, fuck, fuck,' she said, stepping closer to the window. Pat Farrelly stood on the doorstep in full

Garda uniform, next to a man in a checked blazer with a head of glistening black curls.

When she'd phoned the Garda station the day before she'd asked to speak to Sergeant Farrelly. She'd known Pat for years, played bridge with him most Tuesday nights, was friendly with his wife, Marjorie.

'I have information relating to the death of Colette Crowley,' she'd said and it felt unnatural to be speaking to Pat in this way. The only time she'd met Pat in a Garda station was when he'd signed her passport forms. Hearing her say Colette's name, Sergeant Farrelly muttered, 'Oh dear, oh dear.' Like when they played bridge and he had a bad hand. Never once looking up from his cards, he'd say, 'Oh dear, oh dear.'

'This is serious, Pat. You'd better come out to the house and talk to me.'

He explained that the earliest they could get a detective down from Letterkenny would be the following day. And she implored him to conduct the interview at her home. She would like James to be present also, and she didn't want the two of them to be seen going into the Garda station. She was sure he'd understand that.

'If you knew how difficult it was for me to make this call, Pat,' she'd said.

She'd told James as soon as he'd arrived home from work, that the Guards would be coming to the house the next day to speak with her. She was so full of determination that it came out as a taunt. He'd bucked his head and puffed out his lips and sat in front of the television for the rest of the night saying nothing. Later in bed, staring up at the ceiling, she'd said, 'Look – be there if you want or hide in your office, I don't care what you do. But I think it's important we show a united front. You're the one who's always going on about doing things the right way.'

He'd rolled over, presenting his back to her. 'Oh,' he'd said, 'don't you *know* I'll be there.'

The bell rang more insistently. She hurried to answer the door.

'Gentlemen, how are you? Come in,' she said. 'You're very good to come out to me. But you're early. I haven't had a chance to throw a shape on myself at all.' She placed her hand to her chest, demurring, even though she knew she looked respectable enough in the black slacks and white tunic she was wearing.

'Oh, will you stop,' Pat Farrelly said, in that clipped way of his. 'You don't need to be dressing up for the pair of us. Sure we're just here for a chat.'

She was introduced to a Detective Blakemore, shook his hand. She ushered the men into the sitting room.

'That's an unusual surname,' she said. 'What part of the country is that from?' But the detective did not answer. She seated the men on the sofa and went to fetch a dustpan. She got down on her knees, scooped up the debris, and presented it to them. 'Here,' she said, 'have you ever seen two hundred pounds in a dustpan before?' She turned her wrist, shifting the remains around in the pan like a prospector, then sank down on her heels and laid it aside on the hearth.

'I'm sorry,' she said.

'That's all right,' Pat Farrelly said. 'Take your time.'

But the other man did not appear to be as sympathetic. Her resolve had deserted her, and he was looking at her doubtfully, like she might never get up off the floor. She heard a car coming up the drive – James, early as usual. She rose stiffly, pushing herself up off one knee, and sat on the sofa opposite the two men. She felt like giving up already, telling them there had been some kind of mistake. And then James appeared in the doorway. She knew he'd be annoyed that they'd arrived before him and he hadn't quite had the time to adjust his expression. But she was glad to see he had a blazer on over his shirt and tie rather than the ratty old anorak he usually wore. He shook hands with the detective.

'Will you make the tea, James. I haven't had a minute all morning.'

'Aye,' James said, but he just stood there with his hands behind his back, shifting his weight from one foot to the other. Not until she cast an angry glance at him and mouthed 'go on' did he depart the room.

'Do you want your husband to be present, before we start, Mrs Keaveney?' the detective asked.

She didn't trust the man with his small, watchful eyes. Two deep lines furrowed his forehead so it was forever scored with suspicion. His eyebrows were grey and wiry but his head of tight curls was jet black. *He dyes his hair*, she thought, and that made her trust him even less.

'I'm grand,' she said, and focused her attention instead on Pat Farrelly. He was a big man, broad in the shoulders, and the thick, heavy material of his uniform made him appear even more sub-stantial. She had spent so much time imagining this moment, but of all the things, the pure, irreducible fact of Pat Farrelly sitting on her sofa in his stiff navy cap – this was the thing that made it most real to her.

'So, Izzy,' Pat said. 'You said you had some information for us.'

The detective turned over the cover of the notepad he was holding.

'Well,' she said, 'I'm afraid I do, and I'm afraid that I've been sitting on it for a while. I should have said something straight away but I suppose I was in shock. Because I knew as soon as it happened.'

There was a tap at the door, rattling – it edged open a few inches. Izzy walked over and opened the door for James, took the tray from him. 'Didn't I say it to you, James?' she said, laying the tray on the coffee table. 'The morning after the fire – didn't I say to you that something terrible had happened?'

'Oh Jesus,' he said. 'She was in a bad way. I couldn't settle her at all.'

'Because I knew something had happened. Even before I really knew, I *knew* – do you know what I mean?'

The two men stared back at her.

'I couldn't sleep that night,' she said, 'I was awake at all hours and at some point I got up to use the bathroom and when I looked out the window—'

'Was there a particular reason you were awake?' the detective asked.

'Sure I hardly sleep a wink at the best of times.'

'And do you remember what time that was, Mrs Keaveney?'

'It must have been near morning because there was a bit of light in the sky. I don't have a clear view of the cottage from here, you can just make out the gable. But I thought it was strange – all that black smoke. And I just knew.'

'But *how* did you know, Izzy?' Sergeant Farrelly asked her.

'Well, when I saw the smoke I—'

'No, Mrs Keaveney,' the detective said. 'How did a woman living two miles across the bay look out her window and see a bit of smoke and know the fire had been set intentionally?'

'Oh. That's another story altogether,' she said. 'On the day of the fire, I visited her at the cottage and she told me that she was pregnant with Donal Mullen's child and that he'd threatened her.'

The detective stared down at the blank page in front of him and then glanced up at Pat Farrelly, who sat there, silent. *Oh dear, oh dear*, Izzy heard him saying in her head. The detective drummed his pen a couple of times against the pad. And despite the stunned aspect of the two men, Izzy was uncertain she had said anything at all. To have agonised for two weeks over speaking this information, and to have been able to deliver the sum total of it in one sentence seemed impossible.

She poured tea for the detective and handed the cup and saucer to him. He took a sip and, as though something had been righted by the sheer ordinariness of the ritual, he continued his questioning in a matter-of-fact tone. 'And what was the reason for your visit to Mrs Crowley's home that day?' he asked.

'Well, I had a few bits and pieces to give her, sort of hand-me-downs to help her decorate the cottage a bit.'

'So you and Mrs Crowley were close?'

She felt James adjusting his position beside her and something of the slow, deliberate way he moved reminded her to proceed with caution. 'Well, not really,' she said. 'I couldn't say that, but we had certainly become closer over the past six months. I'd started to attend the creative writing classes she was doing up at the Community Centre.'

'And Mrs Crowley confided in you about her relationship with Mr Mullen?'

'No, you see, what happened was I saw her in the bar of the Harbour View one night, back in January. The thirty-first it was. I was having dinner with my friend Margaret Brennan, and just as we were walking out the door of the hotel, didn't I see Colette sitting up at the bar.'

'Was she alone?' Pat Farrelly asked.

'She was, yes.' She noticed this was the first time the detective had written down anything she'd said.

'And what time of night was this?' the detective asked.

'I can't remember exactly but it was near closing time 'cause they were throwing people out. Anyway, I offered to give her a lift home—'

'Because she'd been drinking?'

'Well yes, but also because she was telling me she was going to walk home herself, and it was a bad night—'

'And did Mrs Crowley seem intoxicated when you were speaking to her?'

She'd known they'd ask this, that they could use the fact of Colette's drinking to discredit her – but there was no way around it, there were a dozen other people in the pub that night who could testify to how drunk she was. 'She was ossified,' Izzy said. 'And when I got her into the car, I drove her home, and as we were driving up the road to the cottage, I saw Donal Mullen standing at her front door.'

'And you're certain it was him?' the detective asked.

'I'm one hundred per cent certain. He had on a sort of coat with the hood up – but he looked directly at me, and I saw his face as clearly as I can see yours now. Then he ran off down the hill and went in the door of his own house – sure, who else could it have been?'

'And did Mrs Crowley discuss their relationship with you?'

'She was drunk. She was barely able to talk. She collapsed into the bed.'

'Well, not that night, but the next time you saw her – did she talk about it then?'

'The next time I saw her was the day of the fire, when she told me she was pregnant.'

'And can you talk us through exactly what Mrs Crowley told you on that day.'

She sat up straight, placed her palms on her thighs.

'Take your time, take your time,' Sergeant Farrelly said.

She took a deep breath. 'She said that she was maybe two months pregnant. She hadn't been to the doctor but she'd done two tests and they'd both come back positive. She'd told Donal he was the father and he was trying to get her to go to England for an abortion. He told her if she ever brought the child back to the town, he'd kill her.'

'That's exactly what she said?'

'As God is my witness.'

'And had she been drinking on that day?'

She felt James's hand on her shoulder. 'She'd been drinking, yes, but she didn't seem drunk. She was alert and articulate and I believed every word she told me. The woman was terrified out of her mind. She prostrated herself before me and begged me to help her and I'll regret it till the day I die that I didn't put her in the car and drive her home with me.'

'And do you mind me asking why you didn't come forward with this information sooner?' the detective asked. 'It's been over two weeks since Mrs Crowley's death.'

'I know exactly how long it's been,' Izzy said. 'Every day I got up I thought about phoning yous. And every day I was angrier with myself. But I'm sick of it. I'm tired of being scared of that man. I'm sick of worrying about where the kids are every minute of the day or that I'm going to run into him somewhere. He has a bad eye in his head, that fella. I've always said it, haven't I, James?'

'You have,' he said.

'Has Donal Mullen threatened you in some way?' the detective asked.

'No,' she snapped. 'But he saw me that night. And when we were at the graveyard . . .'

'Did he try to intimidate you, Izzy?' Sergeant Farrelly asked.

James took her hand. 'Well, you might have heard that he had the nerve to show up at the burial,' she said, 'and when he was there, he spent most of his time staring at me. Someone I've barely said two words to in my life, looking at me like he wished I was the one going in the ground. And I'm not imagining it, am I, James?'

'No, you're not,' he said, squeezing her fingers.

'And just to be clear,' the detective said, 'that was the only time you've come into contact with Mr Mullen since Mrs Crowley's death?'

'Yes,' she said. 'To be honest I haven't come into contact with many in the past few weeks. I've hardly left the house. And every time I did I was sorry. Anywhere I went someone would corner me and all they'd want to talk about was Colette, and the terrible end she came to, and how she'd taken to the drink. And then when people heard Donal had been questioned, they were all, *What was she doing living up there on her own with her family only a few miles away, drinking by herself in every pub in the town?* Like if she'd just behaved herself and stayed at home, she'd still be alive. And you there,' she pointed at the detective, 'with your little notepad, writing down every time she got drunk, like that's the crime, like that's the worst sin imaginable – a woman drinking on her own in a pub.'

The detective laid down his notepad and put the cap on his pen. 'Right, well, I think we have all we need for now, but you can rest assured that everything you've told us will be treated with the utmost seriousness. We're going to need you to come into the barracks tomorrow to sign a statement – can you do that for us?'

'But what will you do?' she asked.

'Excuse me?'

'You said you're taking this seriously,' Izzy said, 'but what are you actually going to do?'

He hesitated. 'Well, we'll look into . . . there are procedures in place when witnesses come forward with information, to deal with accusations of this kind.'

'What procedures? Will he be questioned again? Will the house be searched? Will Dolores be questioned again? You have to talk to her. She knows. The wife always knows. There is no way he was going up to that cottage every night and Dolores had no idea what was going on.'

'If we investigate further and it proves necessary to question Mrs Mullen again then we will certainly do that.'

'No. You're not listening to me,' she said. 'You have to speak to her.'

'Izzy,' Pat Farrelly said, 'you can leave it with us now. We'll do everything that needs to be done.'

Izzy nodded and cast her eyes down at the hearth where the figurine lay shattered in the dustpan.

'Will I see you at bridge on Tuesday, I will?' Pat Farrelly asked.

'Oh, probably,' she said, unable to bring herself to look at him.

And then there was some babble of farewells in the hallway, and the front door closed and she listened to the noise of the engine as it disappeared down the drive.

James returned to his place beside her. She folded her arms and sank into the sofa. He slid his arm around her back and she felt herself soften.

'You did all right,' he said, and held her tighter to him.

'I did my best, I suppose – it's up to them now.'

'What happened there?' he asked.

'What?'

'In the dustpan?'

'Oh,' she said, 'my lovely girl, the tall, slim one reaching for the sky. I destroyed her. Shattered her. I was arsing around with the hoover and I jumped at the noise of the doorbell and smashed her into bits.'

'Oh well, not to worry.'

'Oh well indeed.'

'You'd have some job gluing that back together.'

This made her laugh and then very quickly that laughter dissolved into tears. She placed her head against James's chest and wept.

CHAPTER 28

Dolores placed her weekend case on the bed and lined it with a baby blanket covered in little green turtles. She didn't want the first thing her child felt to be one of those scratchy blankets the nurses gave you. And for herself she placed a nice soft towel and a decent bar of soap so she could keep away from the caustic stuff they used at the hospital. Nappies, baby grows, twenty pairs of knickers went in on top of that. Her fourth child, she could have left this to the last minute and still done it with her eyes closed, but this child was impatient.

She placed her hand on her stomach. 'You may wait a while yet,' she said. 'I'm not quite ready for you. I'm trying to make everything nice.'

Dolores pulled out the top drawer of her dresser and at the back she found a translucent plastic statue of the Blessed Virgin filled with Holy Water, "Knock Shrine" written at her feet. She threw this into the bag and pulled the zip.

The phone rang. She carried the weekend case down the hall and placed it under the stairs, ready for when the time came to go to the hospital.

She answered, 'Hello. Dolores speaking.'

'Dolores, how are you? Are you keeping well, you are?'

She knew it was Sergeant Farrelly from his voice. He was from down the country somewhere and spoke in a soft, lilting accent and had a way of asking questions and answering them for you. He was an affable, approachable sort of man but today there was a hard edge to his tone.

'I'm not too bad,' she said. 'Almost ready to pop, but there's nothing I can do about that at this stage. Is there something I can help you with?'

'Is Donal there, he is?'

'He's off somewhere on a job,' she said. 'I don't know where but he'll be back soon.'

'This concerns you as well. We're going to need both of you to come into the station to answer a few more questions – nine o'clock in the morning. Is that all right for you, it is?'

She curled the cord of the telephone round her finger, pulled it tight. 'Has something happened?' she said.

'There's been a few developments in the investigation so you'll come down to the station in the morning, you will?'

'Investigation?'

'You'll come in the morning. Nine o'clock?'

She felt like she was sinking down slowly through soft, cold earth.

'Dolores, love, are you there?'

'We'll see you then,' Dolores said, and hung up.

She walked to the stairs and eased herself down onto the

bottom steps. The child inside her pressed its foot up against her ribs. *Madeleine, Jessica, Eric* – school, nursery, with her parents. She had asked her mother to take Eric that morning so she could get on with a few things. And at any second her husband would return, and her children would need to be collected, and fed, and washed, and these routines would carry her over into the next day, and the next. And if she didn't move now, she would miss her chance.

She grabbed the banister and hauled herself to her feet. She lifted the receiver, dialled the station, and asked to be put through to Sergeant Farrelly.

'Sergeant Farrelly spe—'

'What if I came in to talk to you?' she asked.

'Is that you, Dolores, it is? You'll come in at nine o'clock tomorrow morning, love, like we discussed.'

'No. What if I came to talk to you now? Alone.'

Sergeant Farrelly cleared his throat. 'Dolores, if you come in and talk to us now, I promise that anything you say will be treated with the strictest confidence.'

'But what will happen to me?' she asked. She could hear her voice breaking, how each word seemed to splinter, to come apart as it fell from her mouth.

'Dolores, you're not in any trouble. If you get in your car and drive down to us now, we'll look after you. I can call your mother and father and have them meet you at the station. Do you want me to do that for you, love?'

She placed her back against the wall and closed her eyes.

'Dolores, I'll treat you like you're one of my own.'

She heard the noise of an engine coming up the drive, saw Donal's van through the frosted panels on the door.

'Dolores?'

'There's Donal back now,' she said. 'Call my father. I'll be down in half an hour.'

She heard Sergeant Farrelly say something as she hung up.

She crossed the hallway, placed herself on the sofa. She wrapped her arms around her stomach, so swollen she could see the ripple of life moving beneath her top. She looked up at him as he walked in.

'We had a call when you were out,' she said.

He stopped and stood at the centre of the room. 'Who?'

'Sergeant Farrelly,' she said. 'He wants us to come into the station in the morning to answer a few more questions.'

'Fuck,' he said, dropping down on the opposite end of the sofa. He placed his elbows on his knees, made a steeple with his fingers.

'He said there's an investigation, which means they must know something.'

'Fuck, fuck, fuck,' he said, jouncing his elbows with his knees.

'Donal?'

He was staring at the floor in front of him, his palms placed together now and pressed to his lips.

'Donal – she was pregnant, wasn't she?'

He turned his head slowly to look at her and the face she was presented with was almost unrecognisable. His features were raw with terror, his eyes bloodshot with the sting of tears.

'That was why you . . . why you wanted her out of the cottage,' she said.

He was pushing back his cuticles with his thumb. He drew sharp, seething breaths through his clenched teeth. 'She threatened me,' he said. 'She wanted money, and she said that if I didn't give it to her, she'd tell everyone the child was mine. But that child could have been anyone's. And that's what we'll say, if they ask, we'll tell them about that fella you saw going up there. He was a lover of hers. A fellow from Dublin. He was obsessed with her, stalking her, writing her love letters the whole time. You could describe him if they asked you to, couldn't you?'

She was silent. She watched him turn his eyes on her then, and as though registering her doubt, her fear, he said, 'I did this for us. I was scared for you, for the kids. She was acting so mad I didn't know what she might do. I panicked. She was blackmailing us. Did you want her to have that child, to go parading it around, to have that kind of hold on us for the rest of our lives?' He was shaking, snivelling noises squirming out of him. 'She didn't suffer,' he said.

She rose slowly and the child moved inside her and she had to brace herself against the unsteadiness that washed over her.

'You're right about one thing,' she said. 'You keep saying it. We need to show a united front. I need to pull myself together, start showing my face.'

'That's it,' he said, and the look he offered her was blissful with relief.

'I can't stay hiding in the house. I'll drive into the town and collect Jessica from nursery, then I'll drive to my mammy's and collect Eric afterwards.'

'Why don't I take the van and collect Eric,' he said.

'Sure, that doesn't make sense, making two trips. And anyway, I phoned Mammy earlier and told her I'd be down around three – they'll be expecting me.'

He nodded, absently. 'But you won't be long?'

'I'll be back as soon I can,' she said. 'Can you get me Jessica's wee coat? The pink one. I forgot to put it on her this morning and it's going to rain.'

'Where is it?'

She paused. 'It's hanging by the back door.'

Donal walked in the direction of the kitchen and she took the car keys from the drawer in the hall, opened the cupboard under the stairs, and lifted out her weekend case.

'I can't find it,' Donal shouted.

'Try in their bedroom,' she called.

She moved quickly out the door and put the bag in the boot of the car, closing the lid gently.

When Donal came out of the house, she was standing at the driver's side watching him approach, the tiny pink coat bunched in his fist. She took it from him and sat in the driver's seat. He tapped on the window and she rolled it down a few inches.

'Dolores,' he said. He was bent over, his hands placed on his knees so his face was level with hers. He was out of breath suddenly. 'I'm sorry,' he said.

Her eyes scanned his face. 'What for, Donal? What are you sorry for?'

And then it was as though he had to search the farthest reaches of his mind to come up with an answer to that, and failed. She rolled up the window.

He stepped aside and she was confronted by the sight of the cottage, looming over her on the hill. Like a featureless face – the roof, the windows, the door – anything that had once identified it, erased. She started the engine. As the last of the daylight bled away, the blackened ruin of the cottage faded into the sky. In the rearview mirror, she couldn't stop herself from taking one final look at her home, where Donal stood on the doorstep, watching.

CHAPTER 29

Izzy approached the display table near the back wall of the café. She reached for the books in her handbag, but it didn't look like any had sold since the last time she'd checked. She looked around for a member of staff and saw a young waitress taping a poster to the wall. Izzy thought about mentioning the conditions of the lease. The premises had to be handed back in the state it was found in, allowing for reasonable wear and tear. But she didn't have the heart to say anything. The place had lain empty for most of the summer and she was just glad to have a bit of money coming in for it at last.

Towards the end of July she'd received a phone call from Ronan Crowley. The week before her death, Colette had sent a few new poems to her publisher. *Solace: Poems 1994–1995* – a slim volume, there was to be a small number printed, more to commemorate his mother's life than anything else, Ronan had explained. But he'd asked if she'd be willing to help him organise some kind of launch, if she could rally the other members of the creative writing group. She'd suggested holding the event at the café. And so one evening in the last week of August a small crowd had raised a glass to Colette's life and work. Shaun and Ann, and Colette's three sons, had lined up at one side of the room, like they were waiting for a procession to pass by and pay their respects. The creative writing group had gathered around the drinks table. And as Izzy had expected, Eithne complained about the heat, Fionnuala complained more generally, Thomas bored them with anecdotes about Colette's life, and Helen cried. The whole thing had felt so paltry.

For the briefest of moments, Izzy had considered inviting Dolores Mullen. She'd seen Dolores several times over the summer, pushing her newborn baby around in a pram. She was seldom alone, usually accompanied by one of her sisters or her mother. And she'd wanted to go up to her and tell her that she understood, that no one blamed her for a thing that had happened. But she wasn't sure that was true, and she reassured herself with the knowledge that Dolores had her children, the support of her family – she would be OK. And Dolores had enough to contend with. In the not-too-distant future a hearing would take place where Donal would be sentenced, and the only possible outcome for a man who'd killed a pregnant woman was life imprisonment. She would raise her children alone, and her husband would spend the next thirty years in jail, where she had helped put him. And Izzy struggled with that idea, of what 'life' meant, when in thirty years' time Donal could be back in the town enjoying his retirement.

Izzy's attempts to engage with Carl and Barry during the evening had met with reticence, like they were suspicious of her sudden significance to their lives. And she didn't blame them. But Ronan was a grown man, solid and serious like his father. He'd asked her if she'd mind holding on to a box of the books. The café had agreed to keep a small table where the books could be purchased and he asked Izzy to keep an eye on it from time to time. And every week since, Izzy had visited the café, tending to it like an altar.

But today the table looked a mess, she thought, and she'd told the staff several times that the books should not be fanned out in this way but piled one on top of the other so that people could actually see the cover. Izzy gathered them together and placed them in two neat piles.

Passing the waitress on the way out the door, she said, 'You'll mind those walls – we spent a fortune having the place done up.'

Outside, the street was lined with signs for the divorce referendum, every telephone pole and lamppost swathed in them. 'Hello Divorce . . . Bye Bye Daddy!' one of them read and she thought that a good laugh. Her children hardly saw their father. James spent most of his time in Dublin supporting his party's campaign to ensure divorce was legalised. And every time she watched the news or turned on the radio there was some discussion of the subject, but in day-to-day life people skirted around the issue, giving little indication of what their real feelings were. And she had thought a great deal about what all of this would have meant for Colette. She knew how Colette would have voted, or thought she did. An educated woman like her – she could have headed back to Dublin, gotten a job teaching, and remarried if she'd wanted to. But for a middle-aged woman who'd left school at sixteen and known little else but married life in Ardglas, where the scope of her life was so small – what material difference would any of this really make for her?

She lowered her head and kept it down. A few drops of rain

began to fall. She hurried along the main street towards the Harbour View, and was about to cross to where her car was parked on the Shore Road. She looked left and she looked right and then she looked left again because something had caught her eye – a young fellow in a St Joseph's uniform barrelling down the street. He had a head of thick dark hair that hung down over his eyes. She waited until he came into focus.

'Barry Crowley!' Izzy said, as the boy got closer, but he ignored her and walked straight past.

'Come back here, Barry Crowley, ya scut. I know you heard me.'

He stopped but did not turn around to face her.

'Don't think you can go pushing past me in the middle of the day and I won't stop you.'

'Oh, piss off, you!' he said.

'Where are you going?'

'None of your business.'

'Barry? Why in God's name aren't you at school at this time of day?'

'I told you – it's none of your fucking business.'

'Well, see if I don't make it my business, Barry. What have you done this time?'

A light rain filled the air like a cold mist gathering round them.

'Come on, Barry – out with it,' she said.

'They've sent me home.'

'Why?' But she couldn't make out his response. 'What?' she asked.

'I called Mrs Frawley an old wagon,' he shouted.

'And they sent you home for that?'

He bucked his head.

'I'd say there's a bit more to it than that, Barry. I'd say you have their heart broke out there. And why if you've been sent home are you not heading in that direction?'

She knew that he was probably headed for the lane beside the chip shop where the boys went to smoke at lunchtime.

'I can't go home,' he said.

'Why not?'

'I need a lift.'

'Are you too scared to go out to the factory and ask your father for one?'

'Master O'Connor said he's going to expel me,' he said.

'Well, Barry,' she said. 'I think we need to go and have a chat with Master O'Connor about that. Come on.'

She strode away from him along the footpath, Barry's voice calling after her and growing faint. She stopped and turned. 'Come on now, Barry. You may as well follow me because if you don't, I'll do it on my own,' she said, and continued on her way, past the newsagent's and past the Ulster Bank.

'But what are you going to do?' Barry asked.

She could hear him shuffling along behind her.

'What are you going to say?' he pleaded. 'He's not going to listen to you.'

'We'll see about that.'

They were meeting other students from the school now coming in the opposite direction, heading into the town for lunch. One lad stuck his head out of the group he was filing along with and shouted, 'Where the fuck are you going, Crowley, I thought you were turfed out?'

Barry was tripping along beside her. 'Ah please, calm down. Don't do that. I'll go and talk to my father. He'll talk to Master O'Connor. Please.'

'Sure, it won't do any harm for me to have a chat to him in the meantime.'

They'd reached the main road leading into the town. Huge fish lorries swept past them, their tyres raising a thin spray from the wet ground.

'But what are you going to say to him?' Barry asked.

'Well, Barry, we need to get this straight – do you want to be at school?'

He was silent for a moment. 'Yeah,' he said.

''Cause you probably think you don't need it – that you'll always be OK, that your father will look after you, that he'll sort you out with a job. But you'll not be much use to anyone without some qualification. And if you want to spend the rest of your life stuck in this town, you're going the right way about it. So are you sure that you want to be at school, Barry, because you don't sound very sure?'

'Yes,' he said.

'OK, well, can you sound a bit more convincing when we talk to Master O'Connor?'

'I said I want to be here.'

As they walked up the school steps, groups of students began whispering and turning their heads to get a look at them.

'And you may start practising your apology now,' she said, 'because you might have to do some grovelling and you'll have to at least look like you mean it. Do you hear me?'

'I hear you.'

'Well, what are you going to say to him?'

She pushed through the heavy glass doors.

'I'll tell him that I'm sorry and that I'll apologise to Mrs Frawley and that I'll keep my head down and I won't cause any more trouble if he'll just give me one more chance.'

'No. Don't start mentioning anything about chances or ultimatums – you'll be in trouble again next week and you don't want him using that against you. Say you're sorry and you've been having a hard time, and turn on the bloody waterworks if you need to, Barry.'

The corridor was lined with students idling by their lockers.

'Where's his office?'

'Up the stairs and at the end of the hall.'

She stomped up the stairs and followed the corridor to a door with "Principal" marked on it. She knocked, and when there was no response, she walked straight in, with Barry trailing behind. The room was small and windowless, with breeze-block walls painted white. Master O'Connor looked up from his desk and did not have time to disguise the look of annoyance on his face before he recognised Izzy. He had a sandwich in one hand and with the other he dabbed at the corners of his mouth with a paper napkin. He placed the sandwich back in its Tupperware.

'Mrs Keaveney,' he said, still chewing. 'What can I do for you?'

'I found this fellow wandering the streets,' she said. 'I thought you might appreciate his safe return.'

He kept looking past her at Barry. 'Last time I checked, Izzy, you didn't have any children at this school.'

She chose to ignore this.

'And Mr Crowley,' he said. 'I didn't think I was going to see you again today.'

Izzy took a seat. Barry stood beside her looking at the floor and grasping the straps of his school bag.

Master O'Connor clasped his hands together on the desk in front of him. 'Did Barry tell you why he was sent home today, Izzy?'

'He did indeed, and it seems to me that insulting Mrs Frawley, although very rude, is a minor misdemeanour that can be easily forgiven. And Barry promises to not only give a full apology to Mrs Frawley but to yourself.'

She shook Barry's elbow.

'I'm sorry, Master O'Connor,' he said, with so little conviction that Izzy wanted to shake him again.

'That's as may be, Izzy, but what Barry might not have told you is about the numerous times he has disrupted classes and other pupils' education, the numerous times he has skipped class or not done his homework or not bothered showing up for school at all. You probably don't know about the insults he has launched at other teachers, besides Mrs Frawley, and has Barry mentioned the damage he did to the science classroom last year? I'm sorry, Mrs Keaveney. We have done every single thing we can for Barry and I'm afraid we've come to the end of what is possible to achieve with him here at this school.'

'Barry has had a difficult year and you're telling me that you're not even going to try and help this boy—'

'These problems began with Barry a long time ago.'

'And you're just going to give up on him?'

'We've done a lot to try and help Barry.'

He was so tired-looking, she thought, that waxy skin and such deep lines scoring his forehead. His fingers were yellow from smoking. The headmaster of a school, she thought he could make more of an effort, sitting there in his short-sleeved shirt – no wonder the kids had so little respect for him. 'Stand outside, Barry,' Izzy said, and Barry shuffled off into the corridor. 'And shut that door behind you!' She listened out for the click of the door closing. 'Now, listen here to me—'

'No. You listen to me, Mrs Keaveney—'

'Are you not even going to speak to the boy's father before you suspend him?'

'I'm afraid we're looking at expulsion at this point, Mrs Keaveney. But I shouldn't be talking to you about this and if you don't mind me saying it has very little to do with you.'

'But when do you plan on telling his father? Have you even phoned him?'

'His father has been phoned and he has been invited to come in and have a full discussion about this.'

'But you haven't made contact with him yet?'

'We've left a message with his secretary.'

'And why is that? Because Shaun Crowley is a very busy man. And in the absence of his mother that boy has no one else to stand up for him.'

'We are all very sorry for what Barry has gone through.'

'You have no idea what he's gone through, and you know that if his mother was alive, she would be sitting here arguing with you and not me. And I think you're playing a very dangerous game, Master O'Connor, because you do not want people in this town thinking you took advantage of Colette's death to expel a boy who you clearly have an agenda against.'

'Now, Mrs Keaveney, I would be very careful about making an accusation like that.'

'And Shaun Crowley might be a busy man but I have a lot of time on my hands, and every day Barry is not sitting at his desk I will be sitting outside your office, Master O'Connor, and I'm a patient woman. And I will have James's full support in this.'

'Mrs Keaveney, this is none of your or your husband's business and I'm affronted by the gall—'

'Oh, affronted, are you? Well, not half as affronted as you're going to be if you don't sort this out. What do you do for a living?'

'What?' he asked.

'I'm asking you – what is your job?'

'I am an educator—'

Izzy laughed. 'You're a headmaster in a secondary school in a small town. And what is that?'

'Izzy, what are you talking about?'

'I'm asking you, what kind of position is that?'

'I'd thank you to leave now, Mrs Keaveney.'

'Well, I'd say being a teacher in a small town is kind of like being a priest or a Guard or one of those jobs – it's kind of a political appointment. Wouldn't you say? Or at least there's a kind of politics attached to it.'

The expression emptied from his face, like the wind leaving a sail.

Izzy continued, 'And when that's the case, someone with a bit of influence could make life very difficult for you. Phone calls can be made and letters can be sent – a little campaign could be mounted. And I'd say I'm not the only person in this town you've pissed off.'

Master O'Connor rose from his desk and placed his hands on his hips. He turned away from her and took a few steps towards the wall, and stared at it for some time like he was looking through a window. Then suddenly and decisively, he turned around and walked back, lifted his pen, and tapped it a few times against the surface of his desk.

'I will,' he said, 'arrange a meeting with Barry and Mr Crowley for first thing tomorrow morning.'

'And after that Barry will be back at his desk?' Izzy said.

'Based on how the meeting goes and the commitment Barry makes during that meeting to improve his behaviour—'

'And Barry will be back at his desk,' she said and rose from her seat. 'You make that phone call to Shaun now and I'll explain everything to Barry. Good day to you, Master O'Connor,' she said.

Barry was in the company of some other boys when she stepped out into the corridor, but when he spotted her, he peeled himself away from the group.

'Come on,' she said, 'I need to talk to you.' She slung her handbag over her shoulder and descended the stairs.

'What did he say?' Barry asked.

'Walk with me for a bit, Barry,' she said.

Outside the day had grown brighter and there was a haze of light spreading over the bay. Barry walked alongside her now and she stole glances at him. She saw that he was pale like Colette, but much more fair-skinned, with light freckles dusted all over his face.

'Haven't you the lovely freckles,' she said, because really they were of such neat and particular shapes and spaced so evenly on his skin.

'Aye, they're all right,' he said.

'I'd say you have all the young ones giddy out in that school. Do the girls be counting your freckles for you?'

He laughed.

'Do you have a girlfriend?' she asked.

'Not really . . . a kind of a one.'

'Well, a kind of a one is good enough for now, isn't it, because you wouldn't want to be too tied down at this stage. Cross here,' she said, and they made their way over the main road to the little park that fronted the shore. There was an ancient oak with a bench built around the perimeter of the base and more benches lined up in front of the playground. Mothers with prams had already taken up some of these benches but they found an empty seat. In the playground a few very young children were being pushed on swings or caught at the bottoms of slides.

'So what did he say?' Barry asked again.

'What time does lunch break end at the school?'

'One forty,' Barry said.

She checked her watch. 'Well, then you're back in class in twenty minutes.'

'Ah fuck,' Barry said.

She laughed. 'Oh, you're good craic, Barry.'

Barry sat forward and placed his elbows on his knees, all his concentration focused on the ground in front of him.

'Just be damn glad you're getting another chance.'

'I know,' he said, lifting the toe of his boot and bringing it down again on an empty chip wrapper.

'I wasn't that fond of school either, but then I wasn't much good at it. I've always thought that was the problem. I was treated like I was stupid.'

'They all have it in for me out there. Anything that goes wrong, I get blamed for it. I can't open my mouth but I'm shouted at. I can't do anything right.'

'That all sounds very unfair, Barry, but you're not going to sit there and convince me you're some angel. Keep your head down, and your mouth shut. No one's asking you to come top of the class, but what was the point in dragging a school bag out that road for five years if you don't at least pass your exams? And Master O'Connor will phone your father and you might have to have a meeting with him tomorrow morning, during which I want you to

303

promise me you'll be on your best behaviour. Agree with whatever he says, and do whatever you're told. And just get on with it.'

'It makes me angry, that's all.'

'Your mother told me you were born angry. And that she loved you for it.'

'What else did she say about me?'

'That you were a lot like her when she was a teenager – that she was so full of the unfairnesses of the world that she fell out with everyone. That she fought with her sister and her parents and her teachers. And that she was like that for the rest of her life, that whatever she felt, she felt it in a big way, whether it was sadness or anger or love, and that when she had children, she felt the love so fully she thought she was going to explode with it. It was so *extravagant*. That's what she said, and I remember that so clearly because I adored the way your mother spoke – she loved you *extravagantly*. And that she looked forward to seeing what you'd do with all the feelings that you held, because you had so many of them. Just like her.'

'She left us.'

'She came back.'

'And if she hadn't, she'd still be alive.'

'And you have every right to be angry. But I learned a lot from your mother. She taught me how to write poems, for one thing. Not that I'm any great shakes at that, but she also taught me how to see myself and my life more clearly. She was determined to be happy and to have no regrets and to live her life fully and I will forever admire her for that. But some people, they think if you've made mistakes or you've suffered, you should kowtow to life. Some people think there's such a thing as being too free, and your mother didn't believe that was possible. And I'll tell you one last thing, Barry – as you get older and things happen to you in life, you'll realise that what you thought was important meant nothing, and the only things you'll regret are the times when you were cruel or unkind or ungenerous towards another person, or when you allowed your judgements to get in the way of helping them. And your mother did not have one cruel or unkind thought or intention in her heart.'

Something changed in his face then. She could see the boy was trying not to cry.

'Oh, Barry,' she said. 'You may ignore most of what I said – there's a chance I've got it all wrong. I haven't made that great a go of things myself as it happens.'

'Can I go?'

'I'm not keeping you. And remember – head down, mouth shut.'

He stood and picked up his school bag from the ground and mumbled, 'Thank you'. She watched him moving away from her but she couldn't look at him for too long – it seared her heart. Instead she looked out at the sea, and thought about moving and walking to her car, but remained seated. In this position, at this point on the curve of the coast, it occurred to her that she was almost halfway between her own home on one side of the bay and the cottage on the other. For so long her life had stalled, hanging in the distance between those two places. Since walking into the Community Centre for the first workshop, she was changed. And in the past few weeks she had pored over Colette's new poems, felt that she had come to a deeper knowledge of who she was in the reading of them than in all the time she'd known her. Each poem was like a chastisement for any doubts she may have had about Colette's suffering. They were ferocious, and the anger distilled by them, the total control that required, frightened Izzy. But what frightened her more was how fully she felt she understood them. And yet, if she had read them correctly, so many of the poems were about the failure of words to describe pain in any meaningful way. And returning to them again and again had done nothing to assuage her guilt.

Months spent in this way, trying to find the language to describe who she was now, when nothing in her day-to-day life had altered in the slightest. She woke beside the same man, they joked and laughed about the same things, she felt so many of the same resentments towards him. And in a month's time she would step into a small wooden cubicle and a curtain would fall to behind her, and in that secret space cross YES or NO on a ballot paper. And whatever decision she made, she knew she would never leave her husband. Something told her now that they would grow old together, and sick together, and while they might remain strangers to each other, she needed him. She had exhausted herself with stories, spent her life and energy in always wanting things to be another way. The only thing that seemed to offer her comfort was the lesson she had taken from Colette – that acceptance was not the same as resignation.

She rose from the bench. She was ready to move forward, to try again. She was ready to make peace with herself.

AUTHOR'S NOTE

On 24 November 1995 the people of Ireland voted in a referendum to remove the constitutional prohibition on divorce. The amendment to the constitution was approved and signed into law on 17 June 1996. The law was passed by less than one percentage point.

A NOTE FROM THE COVER DESIGNER

The main thing I wanted to convey with the cover was the emotional weight that Colette, the main character, is facing when she returns to her former town.

I chose this powerful, turbulent Irish sea to be the main character of the cover and have it enveloping the typography, making the tiny characters and house seem so small and at its mercy.

I felt it was a nice visual metaphor for Colette's journey and resolution.

—Greg Heinimann

ACKNOWLEDGEMENTS

I would like to thank my first readers – Jessica Miller, Emma Flynn, Mikaella Clements, and Onjuli Datta – for the advice that got me started.

To my lockdown writing group – Adam Fearon, Anna Szaflarski, John Holten, Mitch Speed, and Jasmine Reimer – thank you for keeping this book going during difficult times.

To my early readers – Kate Wills, Rozalind Dineen, and Ben Eastham.

Kate Butler, Derek Larkin, Vanessa O'Loughlin, and Marie O'Halloran – thanks for giving so generously of your time to answer my questions.

To my trusted readers – Yeo Wei Wei, Campaspe Lloyd-Jacob, Joe Walsh, and Julie McGee.

To Gabriella Page-Fort and all the team at HarperVia, thank you for your kindness and patience throughout this process.

Special thanks to Anna Stein, Caroline Wood, and Alexis Kirschbaum.

ACKNOWLEDGEMENTS

Thank you to the Arts Council of Ireland for their ongoing support.

To my father, Joey Murrin, and to all my family, especially Eilish, Malachy, Edel, and Joseph.

And to my mother, Betty Murrin – thank you for everything.

Here ends Alan Murrin's
The Coast Road.

The first edition of this book was printed
and bound at Lakeside Book Company
in Harrisonburg, Virginia, in June 2024.

A NOTE ON THE TYPE

The text of this novel was set in Adobe Garamond, a typeface designed in 1989 by Robert Slimbach. It was based on two distinctive examples of the French Renaissance style: a Roman type by Claude Garamond (1499–1561) and an Italic type by Robert Granjon (1513–1590). The typeface was developed after Slimbach studied the fifteenth-century equipment at the Plantin-Moretus Museum in Antwerp, Belgium. Adobe Garamond faithfully captures the original Garamond's grace and clarity, and is used extensively in print for its elegance and readability.

HARPERVIA

An imprint dedicated to publishing international voices,
offering readers a chance to encounter other lives and other
points of view via the language of the imagination.